ALISON DARE

THE HEART OF THE MAIDEN

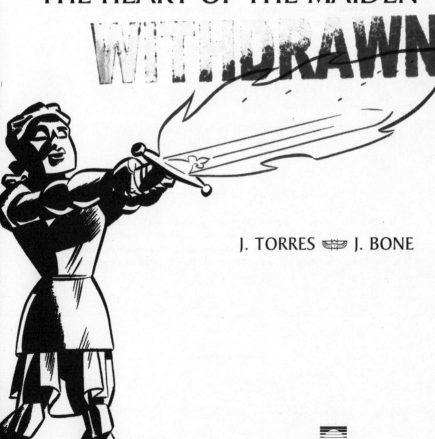

J. TORRES J. BONE

TUNDRA BOOKS

Published in Canada by Tundra Books,
75 Sherbourne Street, Toronto, Ontario m5a 2p9

Published in the United States by Tundra Books of Northern New York,
P.O. Box 1030, Plattsburgh, New York 12901

Library of Congress Control Number: 2009929063

Library and Archives Canada Cataloguing in Publication

Torres, J., 1969-
Alison Dare, the heart of the maiden / J. Torres ; J.
Bone, illustrator.

Previously published as v. 2 of Alison Dare, little Miss Adventures.
ISBN 978-0-88776-935-1

I. Bone, J. (Jason) II. Title.

PS8639.O78A653 2010   j741.5'971   C2009-905056-0

We acknowledge the financial support of the Government of Canada through the Book Publishing
Industry Development Program (BPIDP) and that of the Government of Ontario through the Ontario
Media Development Corporation's Ontario Book Initiative. We further acknowledge the support of
the Canada Council for the Arts and the Ontario Arts Council for our publishing program.

ONTARIO ARTS COUNCIL
CONSEIL DES ARTS DE L'ONTARIO

Design by Jennifer Lum
Cover illustration by J. Bone

Printed and bound in Canada

1 2 3 4 5 6 15 14 13 12 11 10

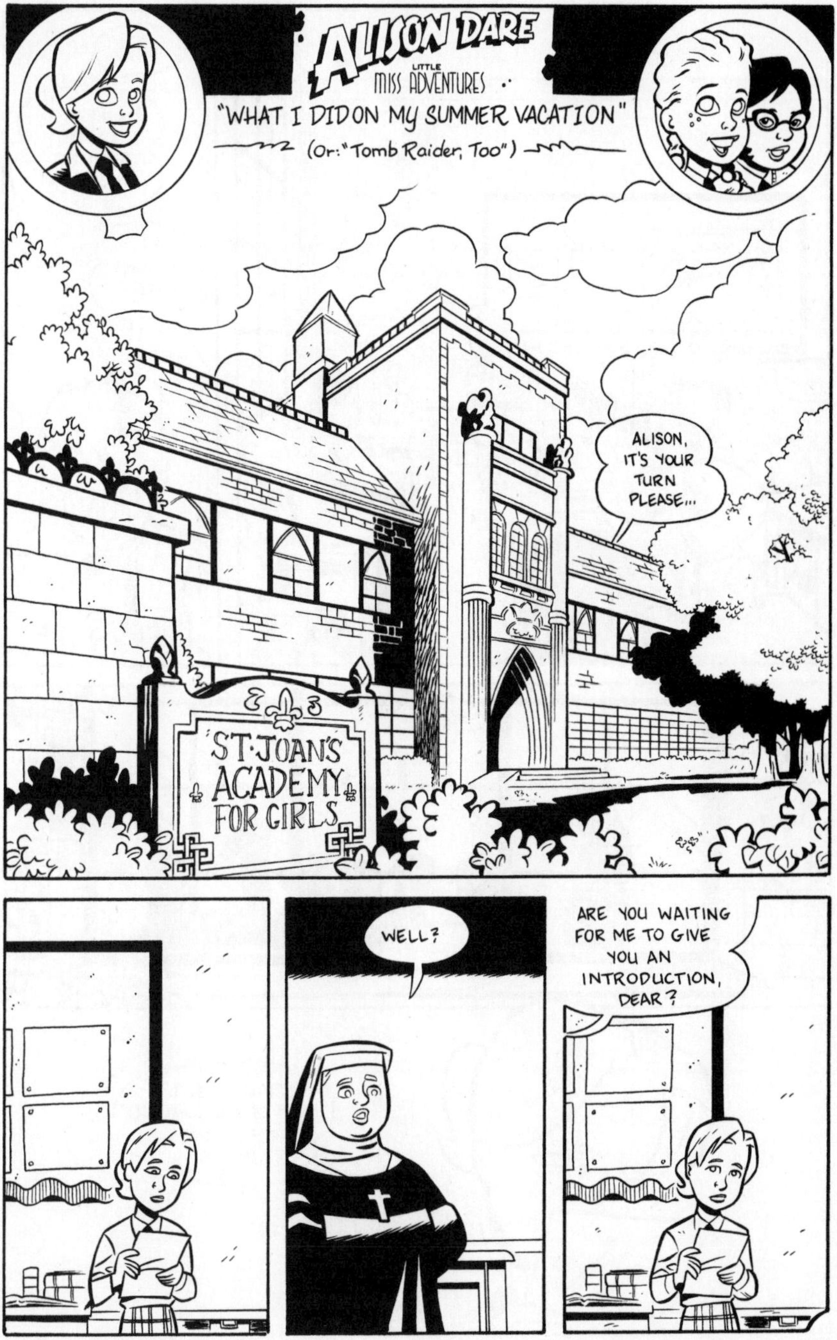
ALISON DARE
LITTLE MISS ADVENTURES
"WHAT I DID ON MY SUMMER VACATION"
(Or: "Tomb Raider, Too")
ALISON, IT'S YOUR TURN PLEASE...
ST. JOAN'S ACADEMY FOR GIRLS
WELL?
ARE YOU WAITING FOR ME TO GIVE YOU AN INTRODUCTION, DEAR?

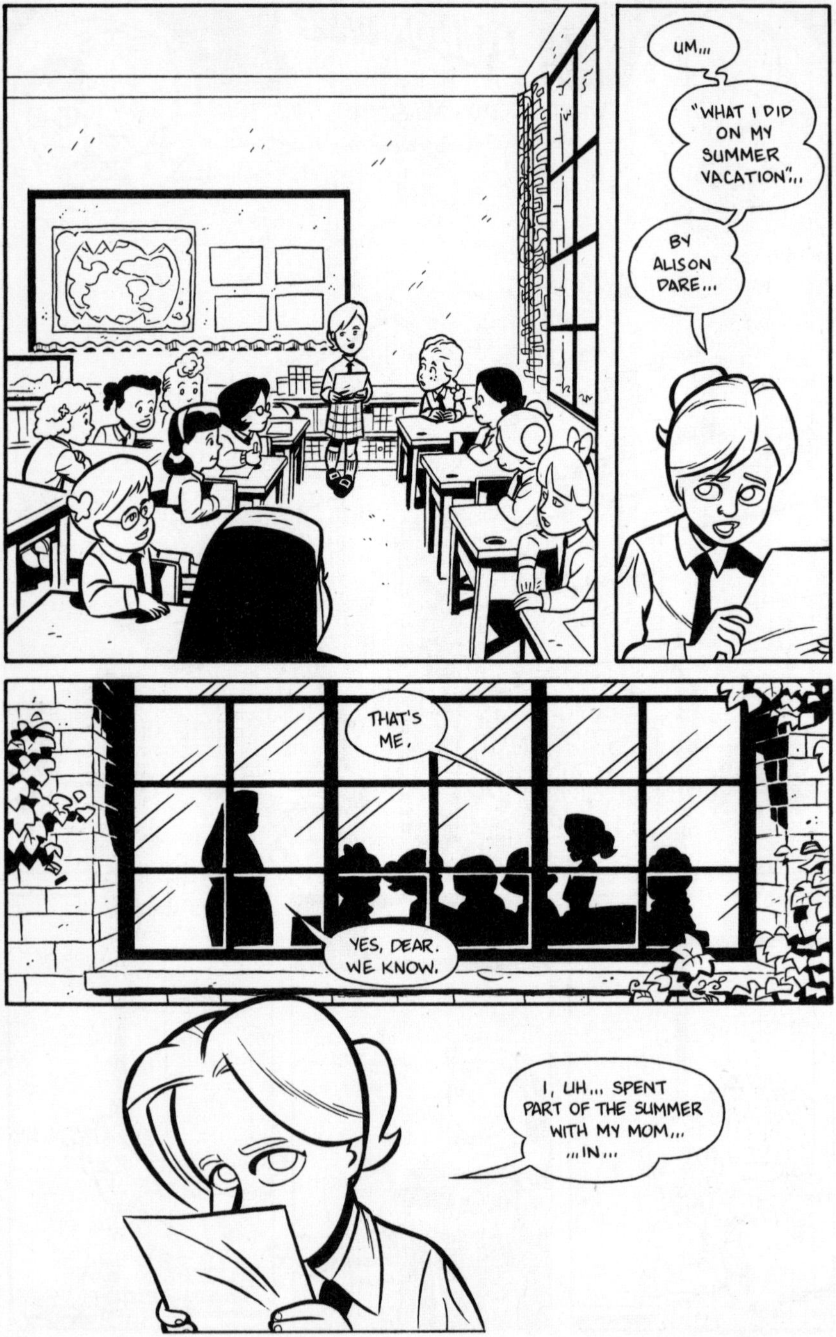
UM...
"WHAT I DID ON MY SUMMER VACATION"...
BY ALISON DARE...
THAT'S ME.
YES, DEAR. WE KNOW.
I, UH... SPENT PART OF THE SUMMER WITH MY MOM...
...IN...

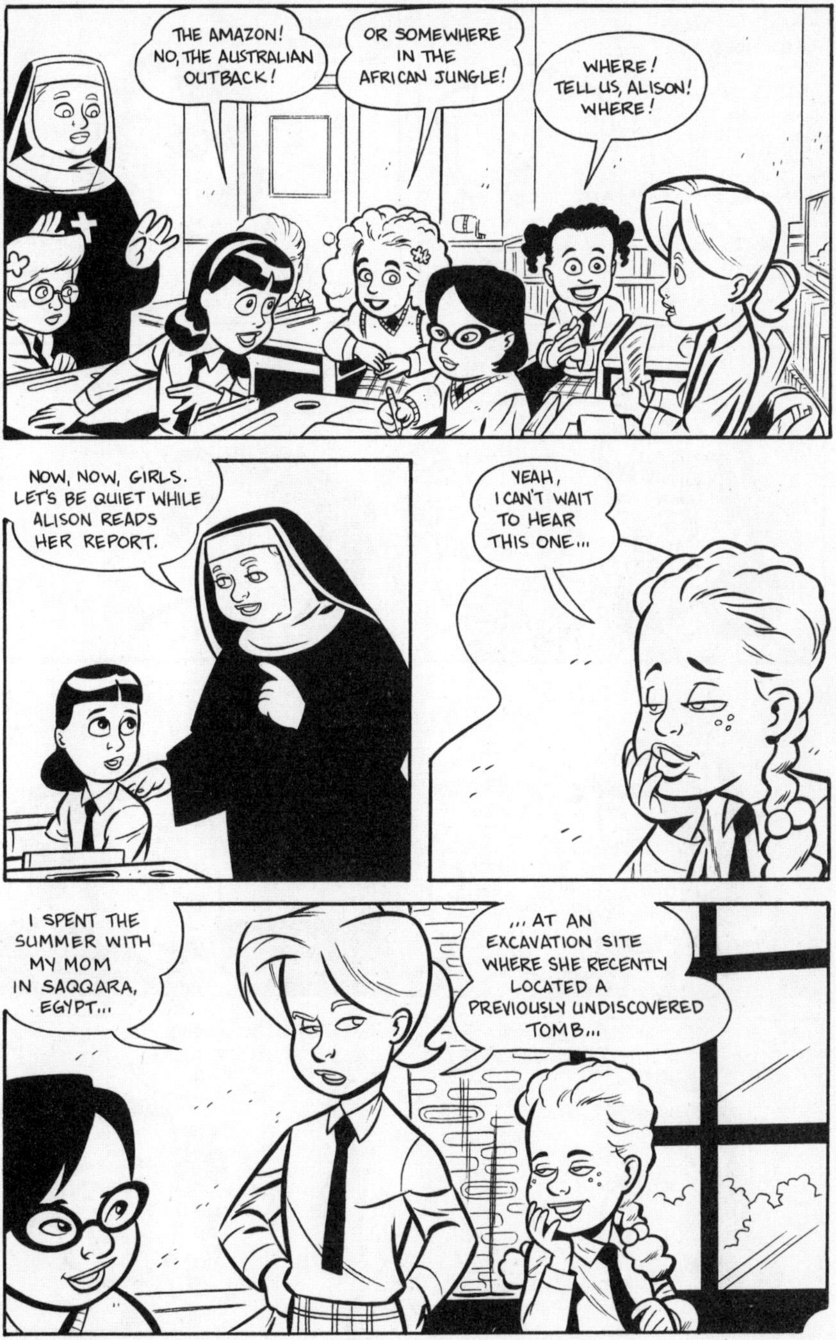
THE AMAZON! NO, THE AUSTRALIAN OUTBACK!
OR SOMEWHERE IN THE AFRICAN JUNGLE!
WHERE! TELL US, ALISON! WHERE!
NOW, NOW, GIRLS. LET'S BE QUIET WHILE ALISON READS HER REPORT.
YEAH, I CAN'T WAIT TO HEAR THIS ONE...
I SPENT THE SUMMER WITH MY MOM IN SAQQARA, EGYPT...
... AT AN EXCAVATION SITE WHERE SHE RECENTLY LOCATED A PREVIOUSLY UNDISCOVERED TOMB...

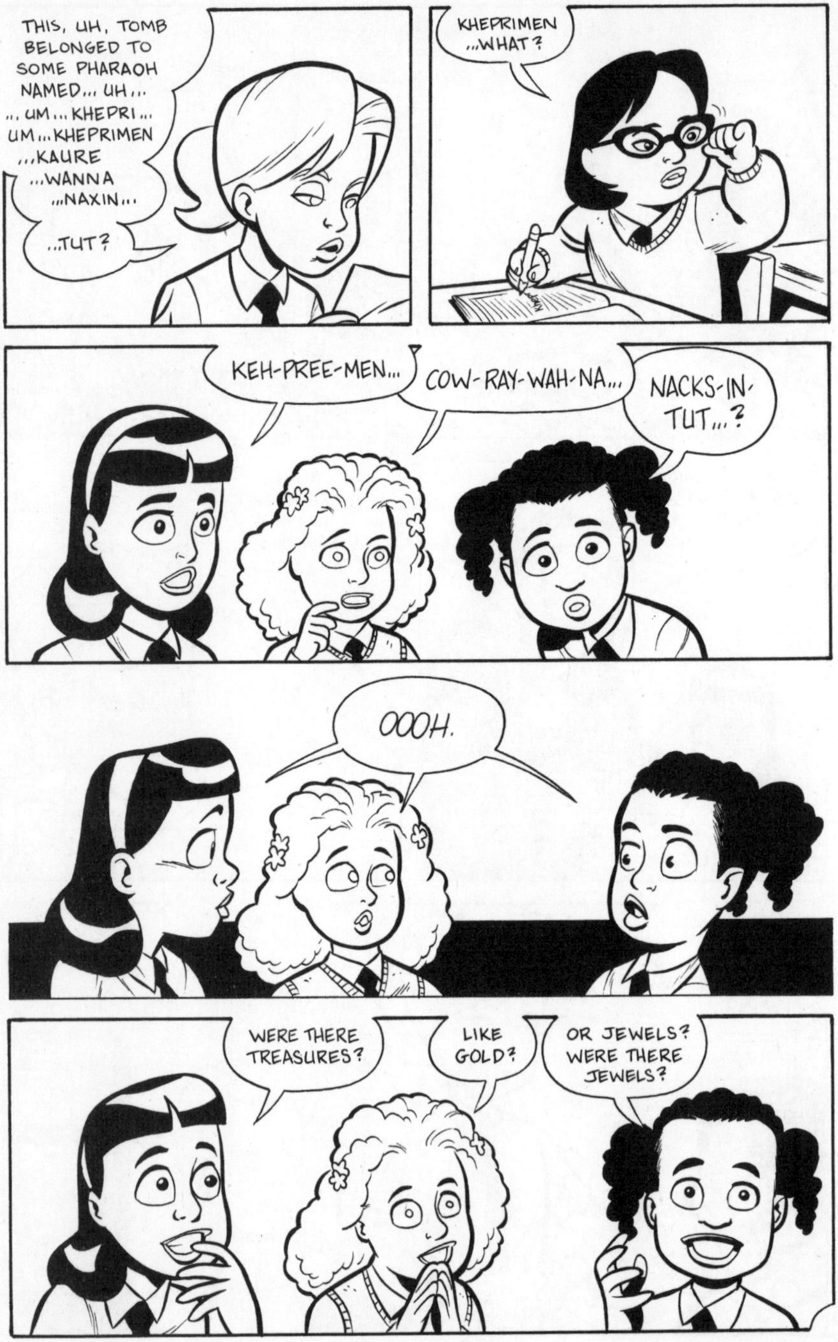
THIS, UH, TOMB BELONGED TO SOME PHARAOH NAMED... UH... ...UM... KHEPRI... UM... KHEPRIMEN ...KAURE ...WANNA ...NAXIN... ...TUT?
KHEPRIMEN ...WHAT?
KEH-PREE-MEN...
COW-RAY-WAH-NA...
NACKS-IN-TUT...?
OOOH.
WERE THERE TREASURES?
LIKE GOLD?
OR JEWELS? WERE THERE JEWELS?

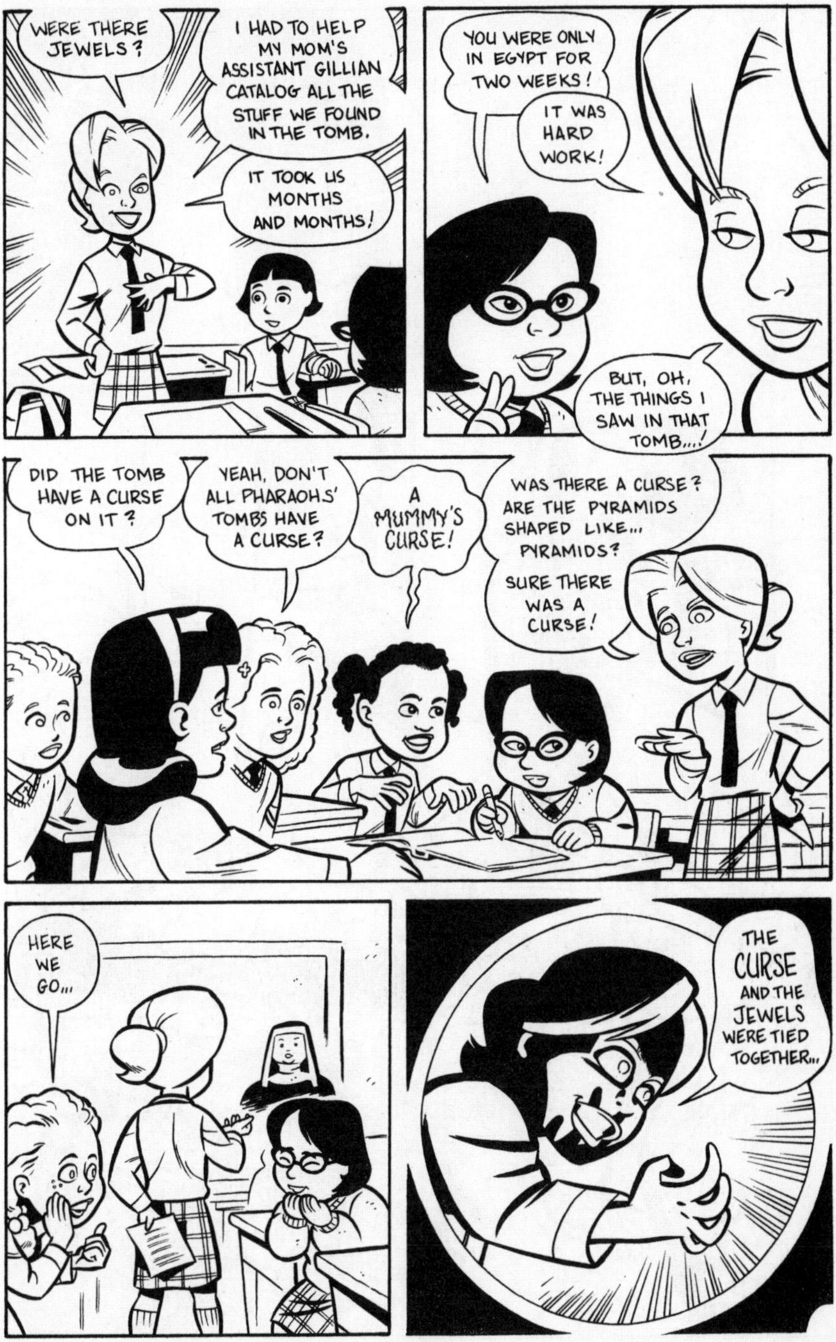
WERE THERE JEWELS?
I HAD TO HELP MY MOM'S ASSISTANT GILLIAN CATALOG ALL THE STUFF WE FOUND IN THE TOMB.
IT TOOK US MONTHS AND MONTHS!
YOU WERE ONLY IN EGYPT FOR TWO WEEKS!
IT WAS HARD WORK!
BUT, OH, THE THINGS I SAW IN THAT TOMB....!
DID THE TOMB HAVE A CURSE ON IT?
YEAH, DON'T ALL PHARAOHS' TOMBS HAVE A CURSE?
A MUMMY'S CURSE!
WAS THERE A CURSE? ARE THE PYRAMIDS SHAPED LIKE... PYRAMIDS?
SURE THERE WAS A CURSE!
HERE WE GO...
THE CURSE AND THE JEWELS WERE TIED TOGETHER...

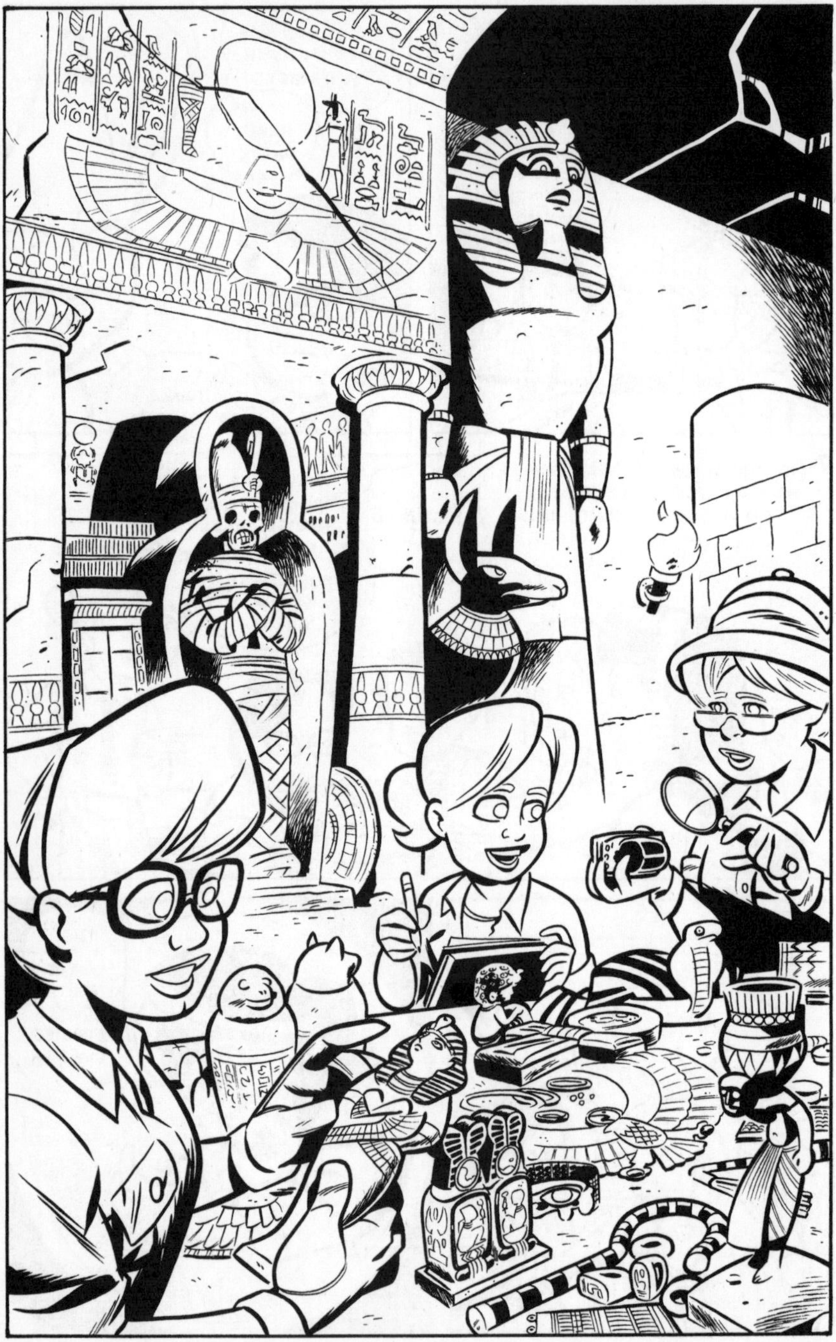

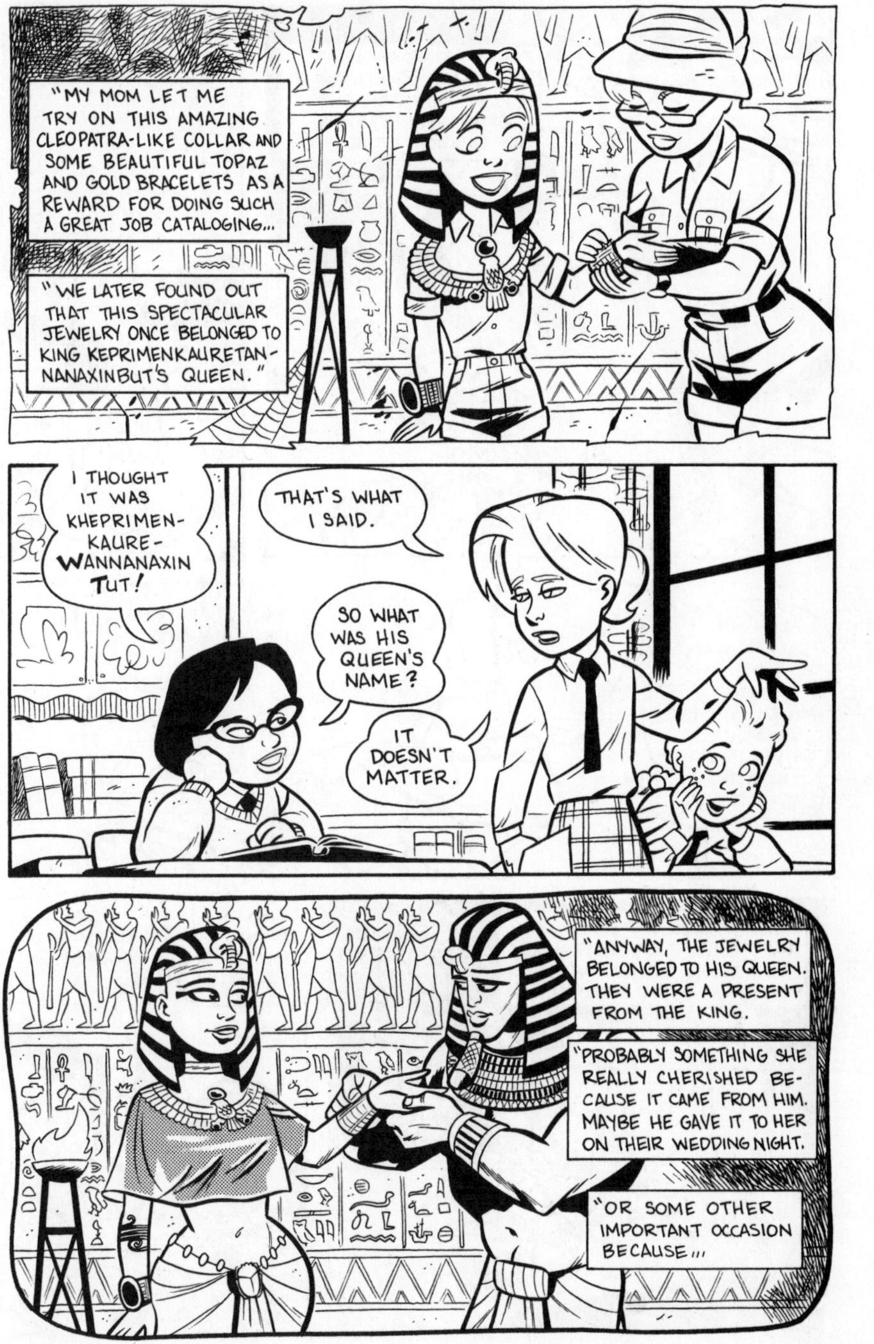
"MY MOM LET ME TRY ON THIS AMAZING CLEOPATRA-LIKE COLLAR AND SOME BEAUTIFUL TOPAZ AND GOLD BRACELETS AS A REWARD FOR DOING SUCH A GREAT JOB CATALOGING...
"WE LATER FOUND OUT THAT THIS SPECTACULAR JEWELRY ONCE BELONGED TO KING KEPRIMENKAURETAN-NANAXINBUT'S QUEEN."
I THOUGHT IT WAS KHEPRIMEN-KAURE-WANNANAXIN TUT!
THAT'S WHAT I SAID.
SO WHAT WAS HIS QUEEN'S NAME?
IT DOESN'T MATTER.
"ANYWAY, THE JEWELRY BELONGED TO HIS QUEEN. THEY WERE A PRESENT FROM THE KING.
"PROBABLY SOMETHING SHE REALLY CHERISHED BE-CAUSE IT CAME FROM HIM. MAYBE HE GAVE IT TO HER ON THEIR WEDDING NIGHT.
"OR SOME OTHER IMPORTANT OCCASION BECAUSE...

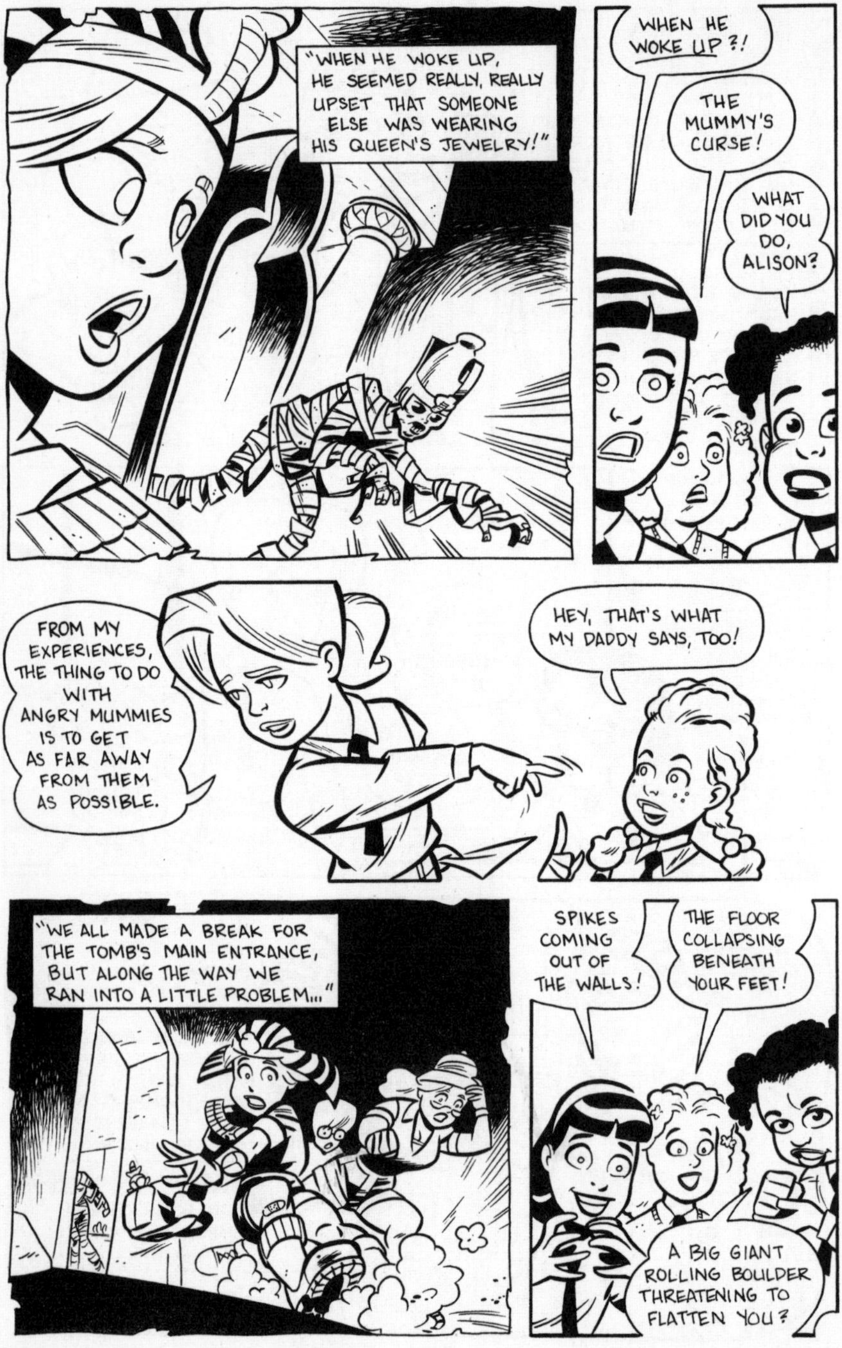
"WHEN HE WOKE UP, HE SEEMED REALLY, REALLY UPSET THAT SOMEONE ELSE WAS WEARING HIS QUEEN'S JEWELRY!"
WHEN HE WOKE UP?!
THE MUMMY'S CURSE!
WHAT DID YOU DO, ALISON?
FROM MY EXPERIENCES, THE THING TO DO WITH ANGRY MUMMIES IS TO GET AS FAR AWAY FROM THEM AS POSSIBLE.
HEY, THAT'S WHAT MY DADDY SAYS, TOO!
"WE ALL MADE A BREAK FOR THE TOMB'S MAIN ENTRANCE, BUT ALONG THE WAY WE RAN INTO A LITTLE PROBLEM..."
SPIKES COMING OUT OF THE WALLS!
THE FLOOR COLLAPSING BENEATH YOUR FEET!
A BIG GIANT ROLLING BOULDER THREATENING TO FLATTEN YOU?

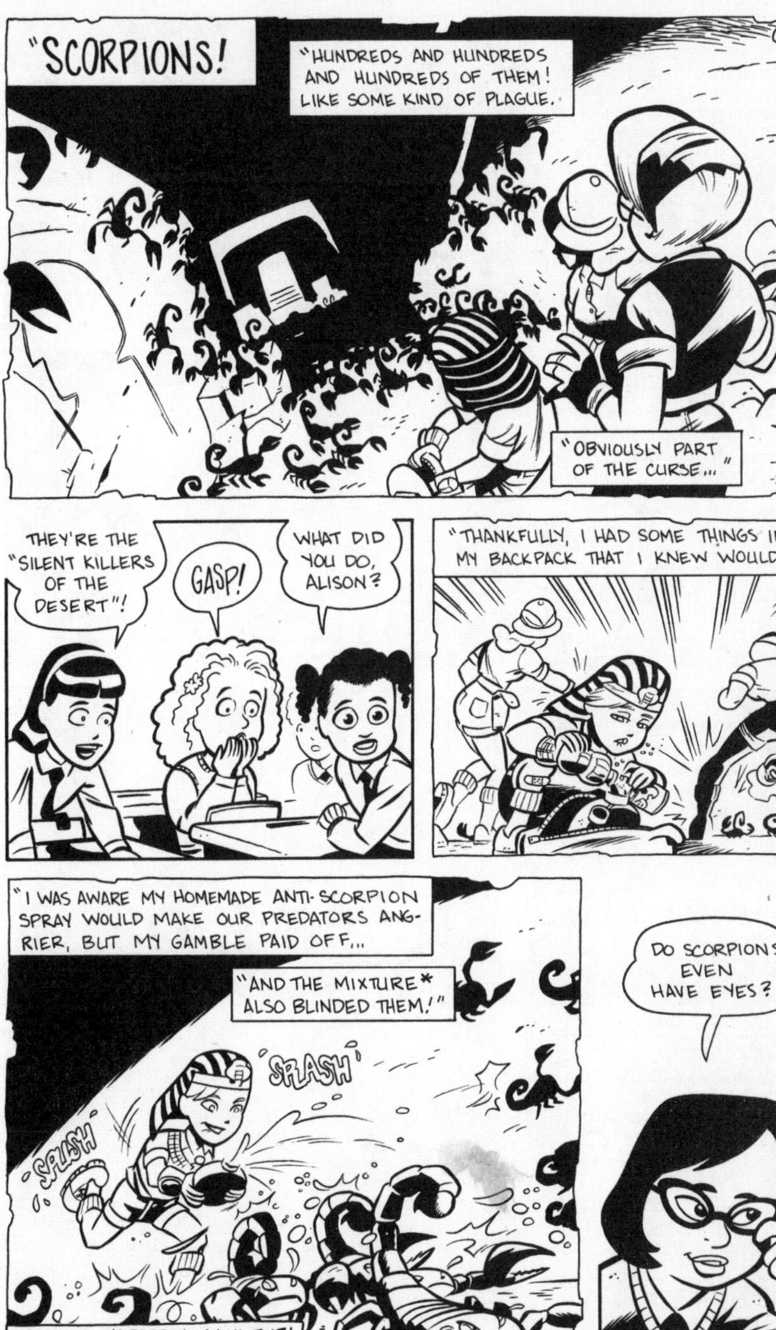
"SCORPIONS!
"HUNDREDS AND HUNDREDS AND HUNDREDS OF THEM! LIKE SOME KIND OF PLAGUE.
"OBVIOUSLY PART OF THE CURSE..."
THEY'RE THE "SILENT KILLERS OF THE DESERT"!
GASP!
WHAT DID YOU DO, ALISON?
"THANKFULLY, I HAD SOME THINGS IN MY BACKPACK THAT I KNEW WOULD HELP.
"I WAS AWARE MY HOMEMADE ANTI-SCORPION SPRAY WOULD MAKE OUR PREDATORS ANGRIER, BUT MY GAMBLE PAID OFF...
"AND THE MIXTURE* ALSO BLINDED THEM!"
SPLASH
SPLASH
*SODA POP + HAIRSPRAY = AY-YI-EYE!
DO SCORPIONS EVEN HAVE EYES?

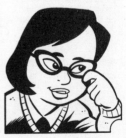

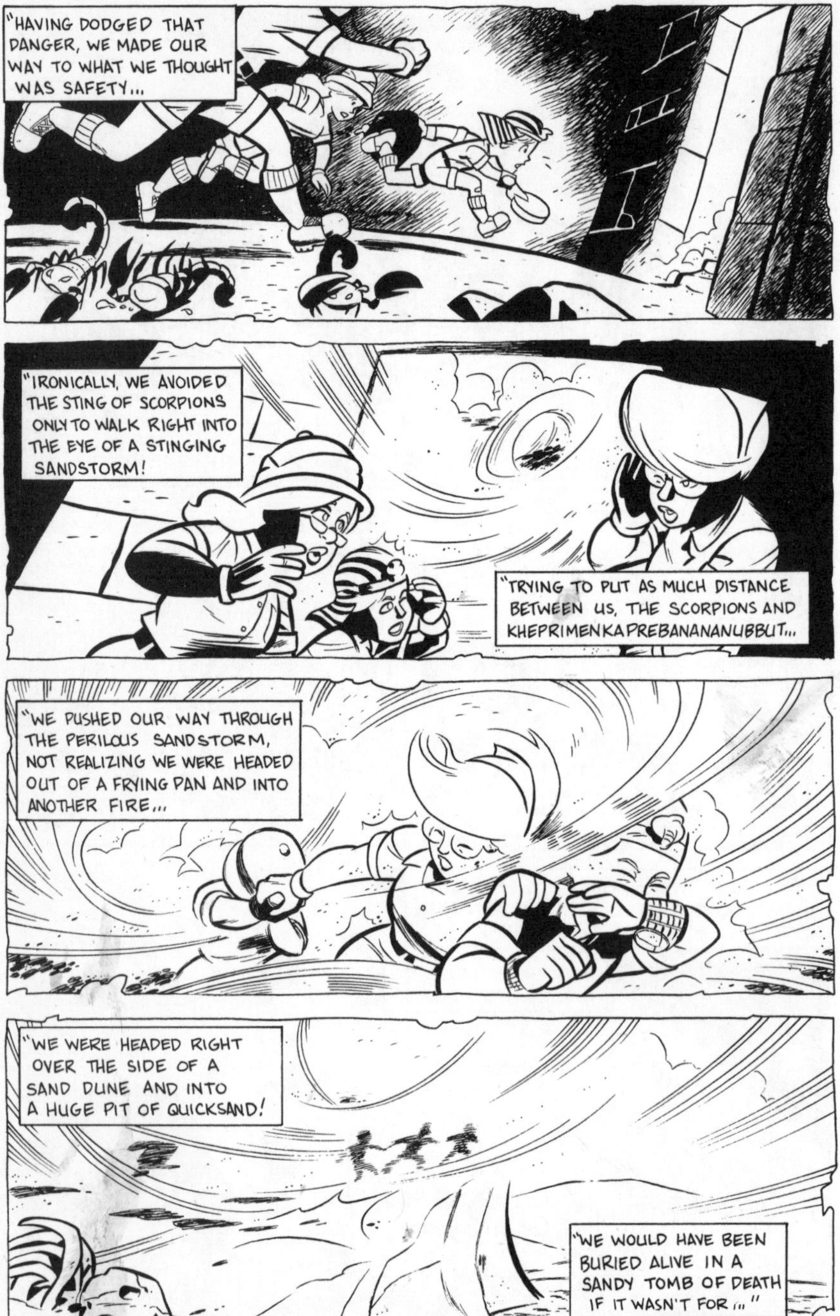
"HAVING DODGED THAT DANGER, WE MADE OUR WAY TO WHAT WE THOUGHT WAS SAFETY...
"IRONICALLY, WE AVOIDED THE STING OF SCORPIONS ONLY TO WALK RIGHT INTO THE EYE OF A STINGING SANDSTORM!
"TRYING TO PUT AS MUCH DISTANCE BETWEEN US, THE SCORPIONS AND KHEPRIMENKAPREBANANANUBBUT...
"WE PUSHED OUR WAY THROUGH THE PERILOUS SANDSTORM, NOT REALIZING WE WERE HEADED OUT OF A FRYING PAN AND INTO ANOTHER FIRE...
"WE WERE HEADED RIGHT OVER THE SIDE OF A SAND DUNE AND INTO A HUGE PIT OF QUICKSAND!
"WE WOULD HAVE BEEN BURIED ALIVE IN A SANDY TOMB OF DEATH IF IT WASN'T FOR..."

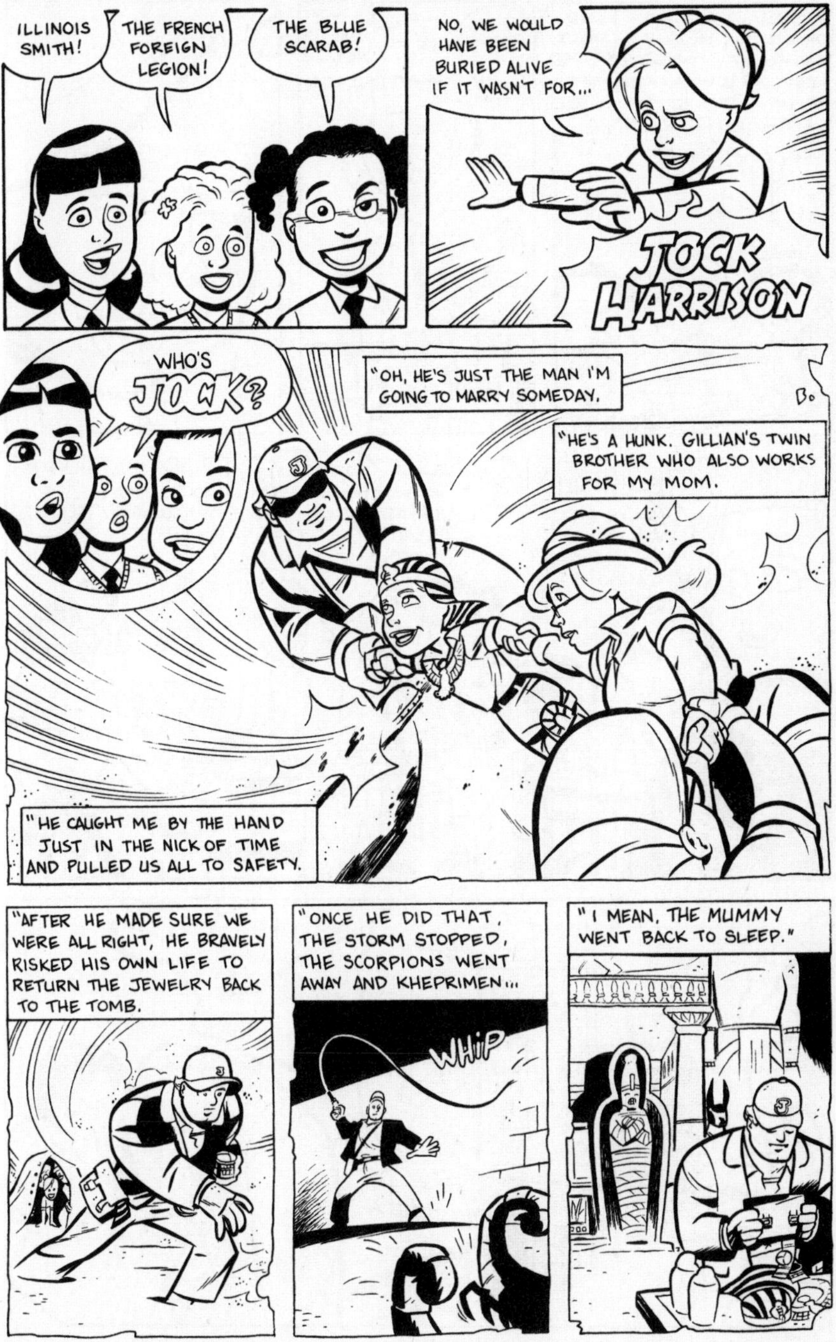
ILLINOIS SMITH!
THE FRENCH FOREIGN LEGION!
THE BLUE SCARAB!
NO, WE WOULD HAVE BEEN BURIED ALIVE IF IT WASN'T FOR...
JOCK HARRISON
WHO'S JOCK?
"OH, HE'S JUST THE MAN I'M GOING TO MARRY SOMEDAY.
"HE'S A HUNK. GILLIAN'S TWIN BROTHER WHO ALSO WORKS FOR MY MOM.
"HE CAUGHT ME BY THE HAND JUST IN THE NICK OF TIME AND PULLED US ALL TO SAFETY.
"AFTER HE MADE SURE WE WERE ALL RIGHT, HE BRAVELY RISKED HIS OWN LIFE TO RETURN THE JEWELRY BACK TO THE TOMB.
"ONCE HE DID THAT, THE STORM STOPPED, THE SCORPIONS WENT AWAY AND KHEPRIMEN...
WHIP
"I MEAN, THE MUMMY WENT BACK TO SLEEP."

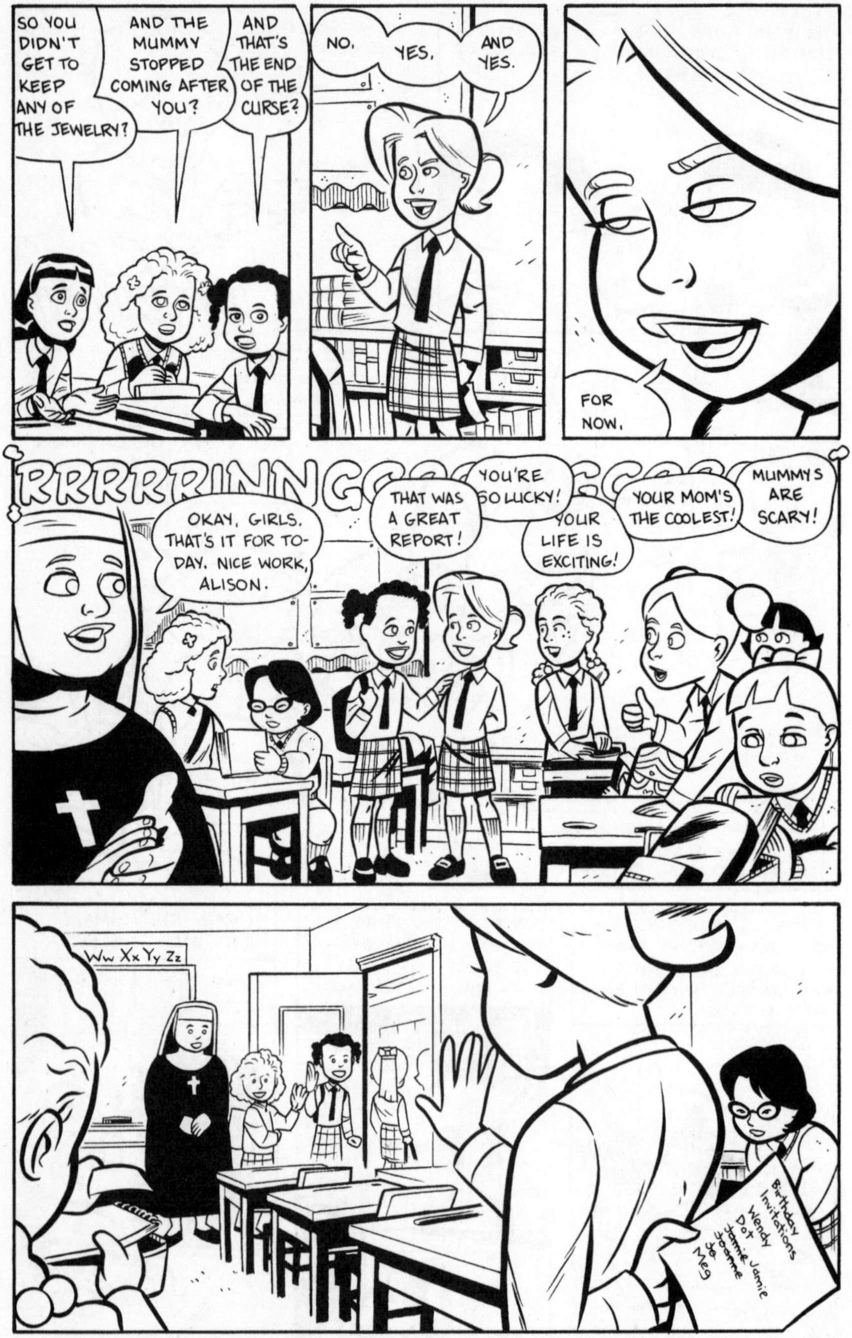
SO YOU DIDN'T GET TO KEEP ANY OF THE JEWELRY?
AND THE MUMMY STOPPED COMING AFTER YOU?
AND THAT'S THE END OF THE CURSE?
NO.
YES.
AND YES.
FOR NOW.
RRRRRINNG
OKAY, GIRLS. THAT'S IT FOR TO-DAY. NICE WORK, ALISON.
THAT WAS A GREAT REPORT!
YOU'RE SO LUCKY!
YOUR LIFE IS EXCITING!
YOUR MOM'S THE COOLEST!
MUMMYS ARE SCARY!
Ww Xx Yy Zz
Birthday Invitations
Wendy
Dot
~~Jamie~~ Jamie
~~Joanne~~
~~Jo~~
Meg

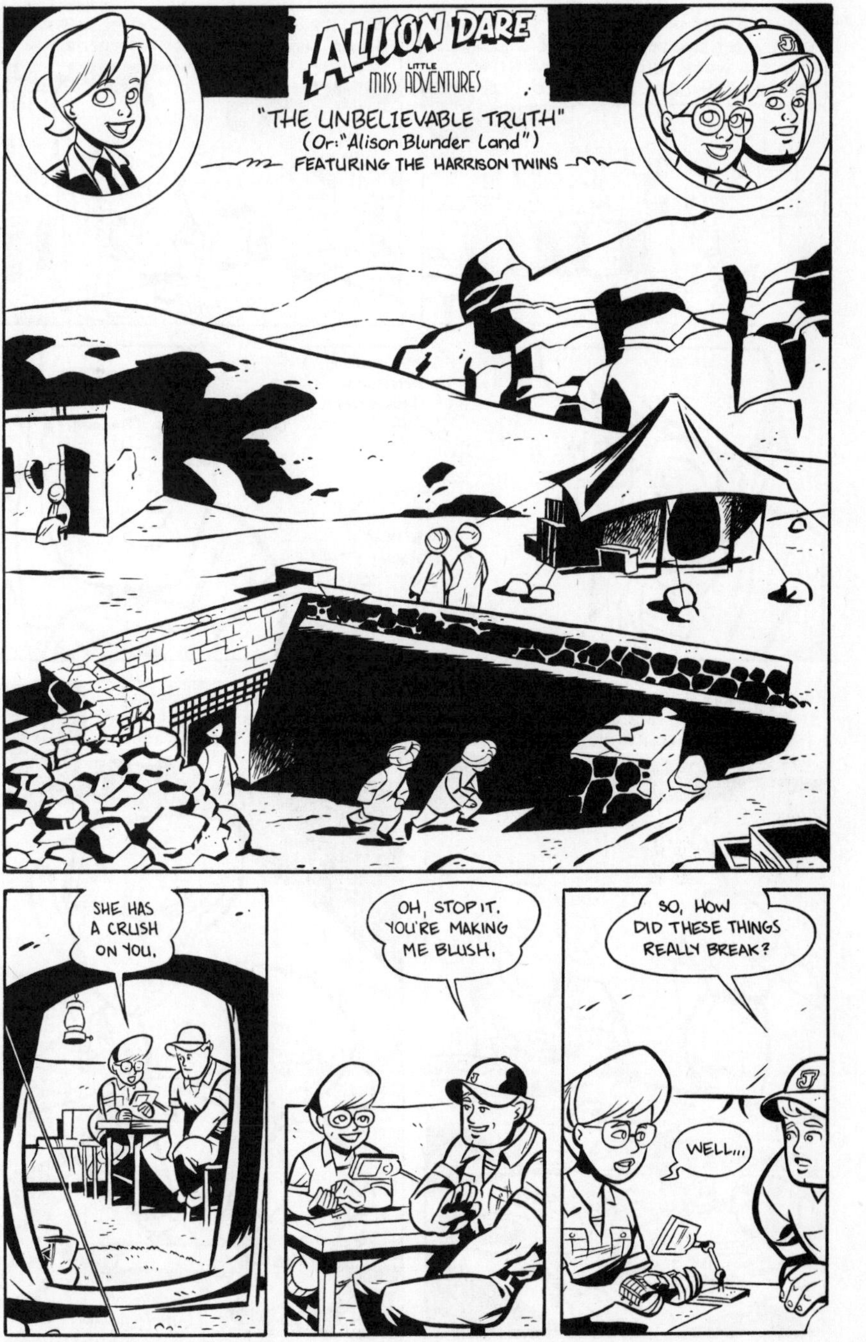
ALISON DARE
LITTLE MISS ADVENTURES
"THE UNBELIEVABLE TRUTH"
(Or: "Alison Blunder Land")
FEATURING THE HARRISON TWINS
SHE HAS A CRUSH ON YOU.
OH, STOP IT. YOU'RE MAKING ME BLUSH.
SO, HOW DID THESE THINGS REALLY BREAK?
WELL...

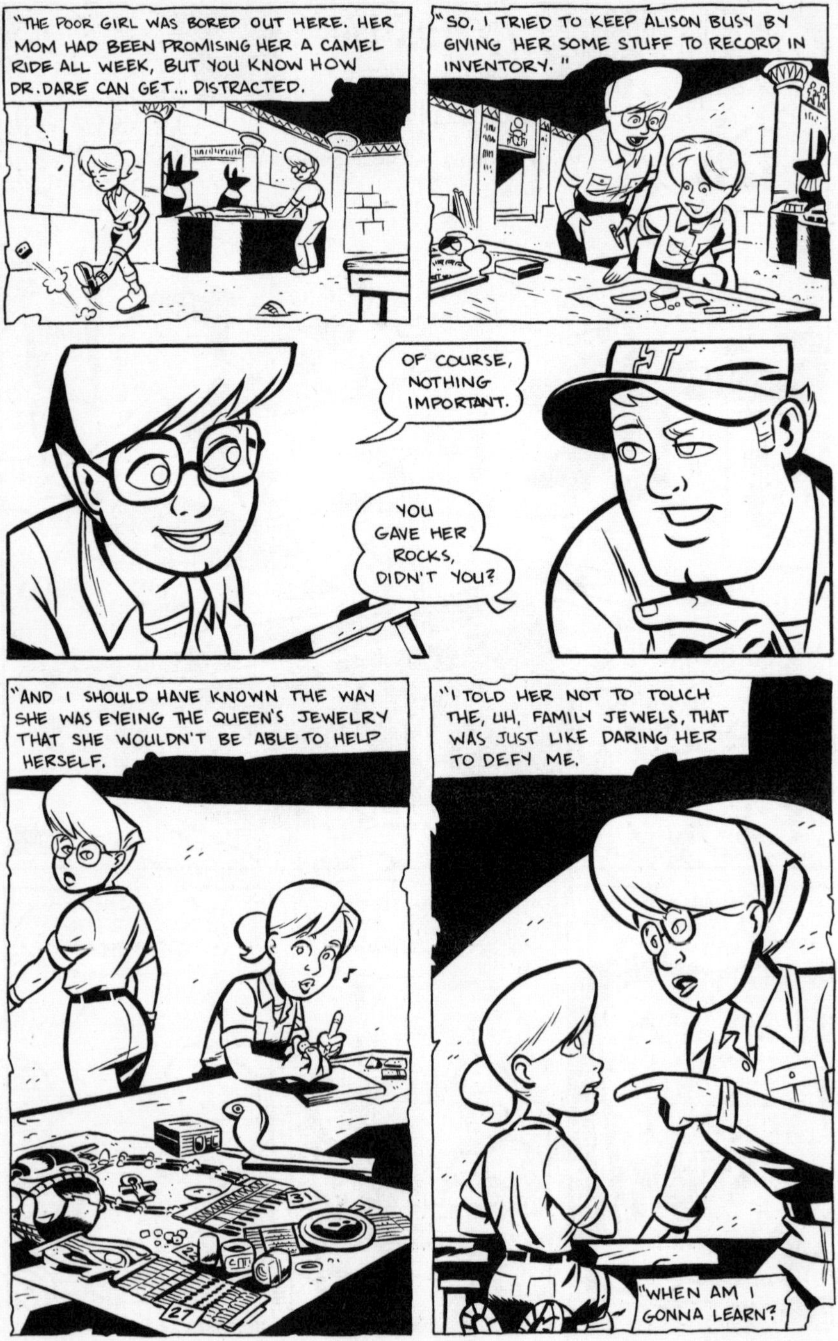
"THE POOR GIRL WAS BORED OUT HERE. HER MOM HAD BEEN PROMISING HER A CAMEL RIDE ALL WEEK, BUT YOU KNOW HOW DR. DARE CAN GET... DISTRACTED.
"SO, I TRIED TO KEEP ALISON BUSY BY GIVING HER SOME STUFF TO RECORD IN INVENTORY."
OF COURSE, NOTHING IMPORTANT.
YOU GAVE HER ROCKS, DIDN'T YOU?
"AND I SHOULD HAVE KNOWN THE WAY SHE WAS EYEING THE QUEEN'S JEWELRY THAT SHE WOULDN'T BE ABLE TO HELP HERSELF.
31
27
"I TOLD HER NOT TO TOUCH THE, UH, FAMILY JEWELS, THAT WAS JUST LIKE DARING HER TO DEFY ME.
"WHEN AM I GONNA LEARN?

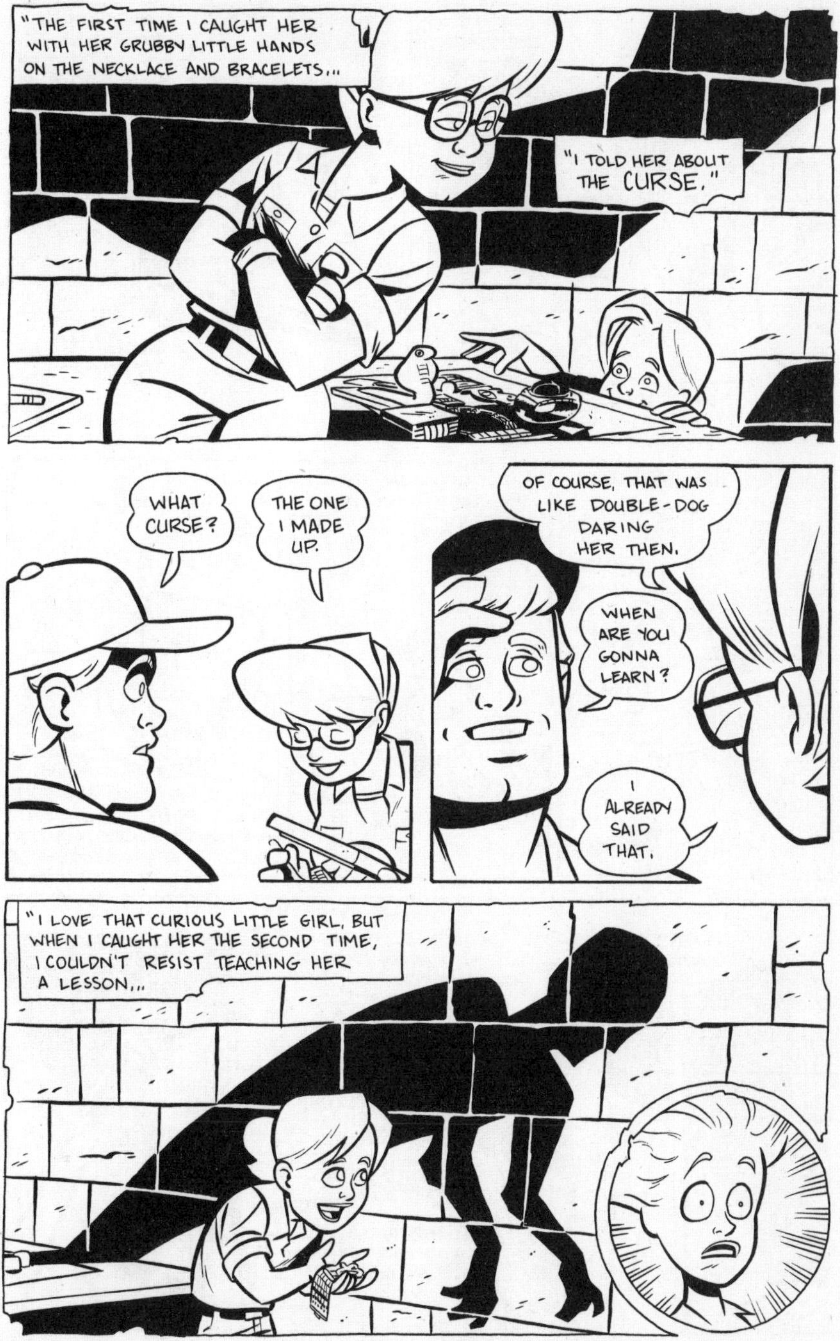
"THE FIRST TIME I CAUGHT HER WITH HER GRUBBY LITTLE HANDS ON THE NECKLACE AND BRACELETS...
"I TOLD HER ABOUT THE CURSE."
WHAT CURSE?
THE ONE I MADE UP.
OF COURSE, THAT WAS LIKE DOUBLE-DOG DARING HER THEN.
WHEN ARE YOU GONNA LEARN?
I ALREADY SAID THAT.
"I LOVE THAT CURIOUS LITTLE GIRL, BUT WHEN I CAUGHT HER THE SECOND TIME, I COULDN'T RESIST TEACHING HER A LESSON...

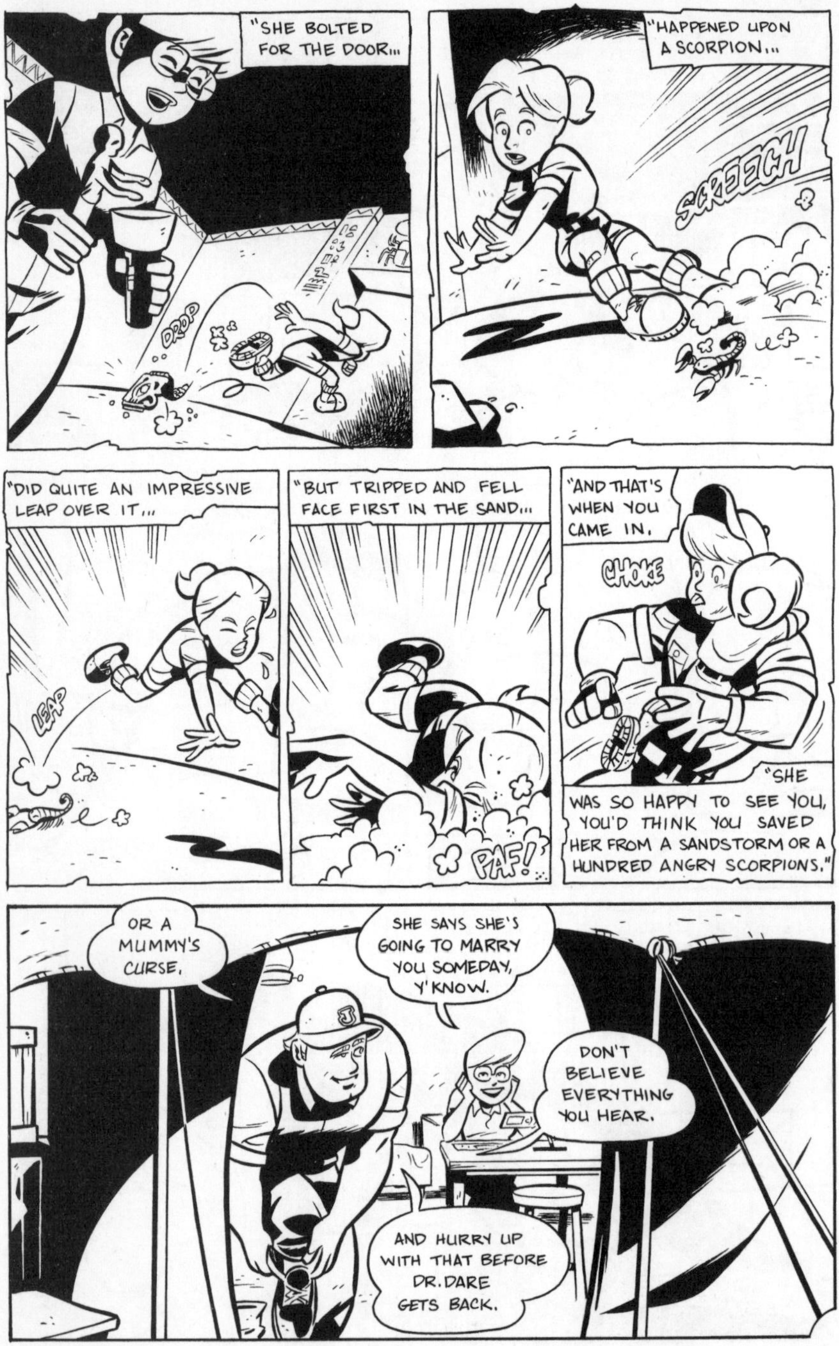
"SHE BOLTED FOR THE DOOR...
DROP
"HAPPENED UPON A SCORPION...
SCREECH
"DID QUITE AN IMPRESSIVE LEAP OVER IT...
LEAP
"BUT TRIPPED AND FELL FACE FIRST IN THE SAND...
PAF!
"AND THAT'S WHEN YOU CAME IN.
CHOKE
"SHE WAS SO HAPPY TO SEE YOU, YOU'D THINK YOU SAVED HER FROM A SANDSTORM OR A HUNDRED ANGRY SCORPIONS."
OR A MUMMY'S CURSE.
SHE SAYS SHE'S GOING TO MARRY YOU SOMEDAY, Y'KNOW.
DON'T BELIEVE EVERYTHING YOU HEAR.
AND HURRY UP WITH THAT BEFORE DR. DARE GETS BACK.

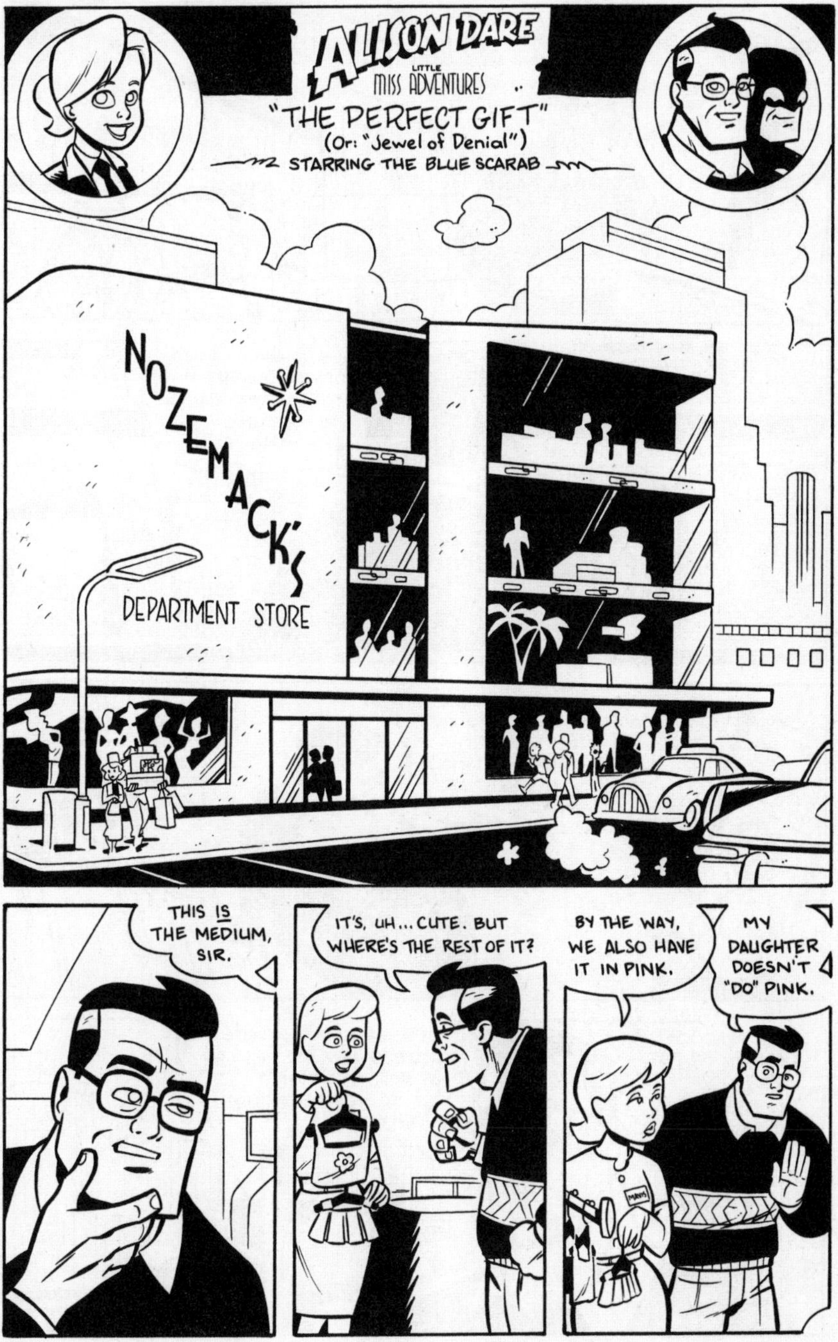
ALISON DARE
LITTLE MISS ADVENTURES
"THE PERFECT GIFT"
(Or: "Jewel of Denial")
STARRING THE BLUE SCARAB
NOZEMACK'S
DEPARTMENT STORE
THIS IS THE MEDIUM, SIR.
IT'S, UH... CUTE. BUT WHERE'S THE REST OF IT?
BY THE WAY, WE ALSO HAVE IT IN PINK.
MY DAUGHTER DOESN'T "DO" PINK.

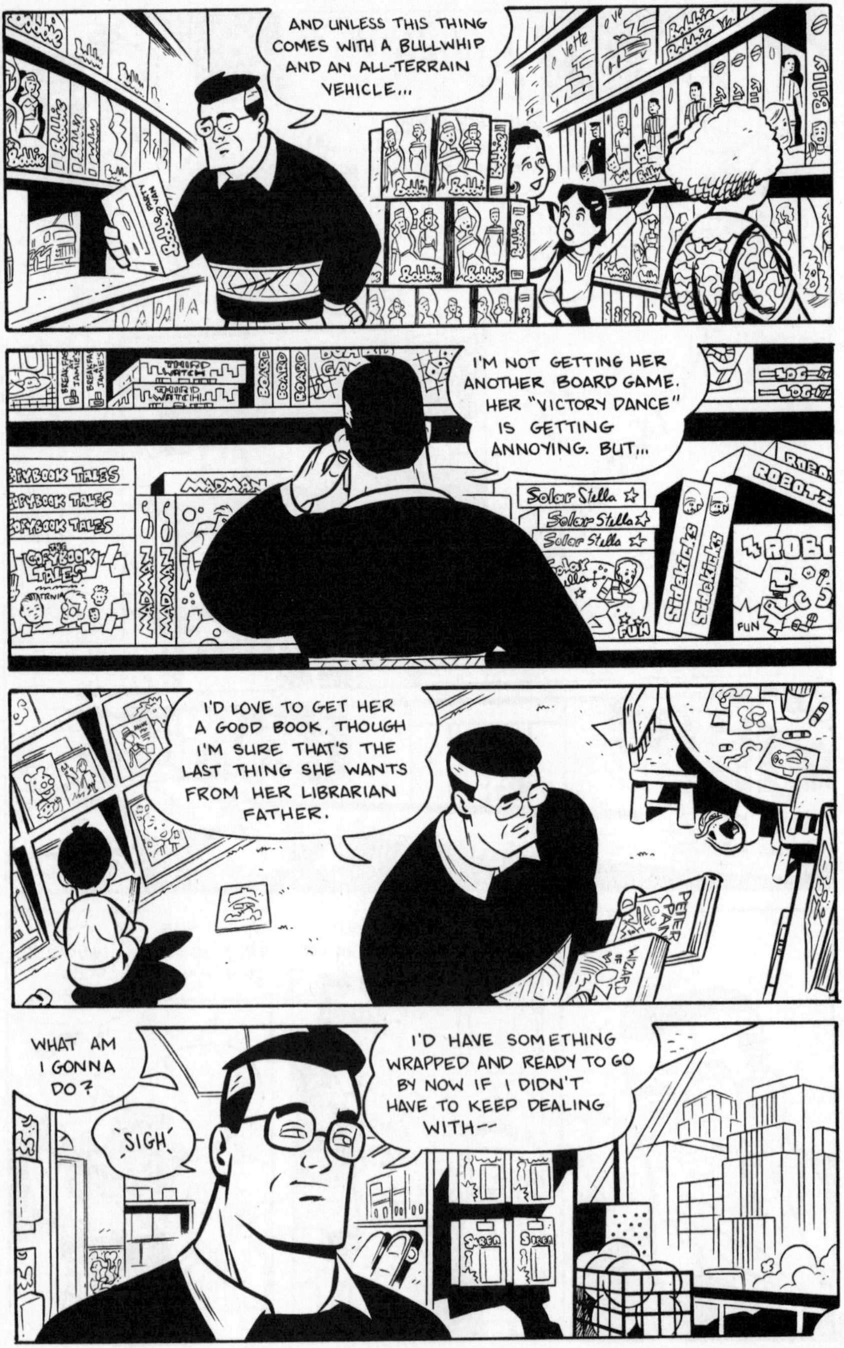
AND UNLESS THIS THING COMES WITH A BULLWHIP AND AN ALL-TERRAIN VEHICLE...
I'M NOT GETTING HER ANOTHER BOARD GAME. HER "VICTORY DANCE" IS GETTING ANNOYING. BUT...
I'D LOVE TO GET HER A GOOD BOOK, THOUGH I'M SURE THAT'S THE LAST THING SHE WANTS FROM HER LIBRARIAN FATHER.
WHAT AM I GONNA DO?
SIGH
I'D HAVE SOMETHING WRAPPED AND READY TO GO BY NOW IF I DIDN'T HAVE TO KEEP DEALING WITH--

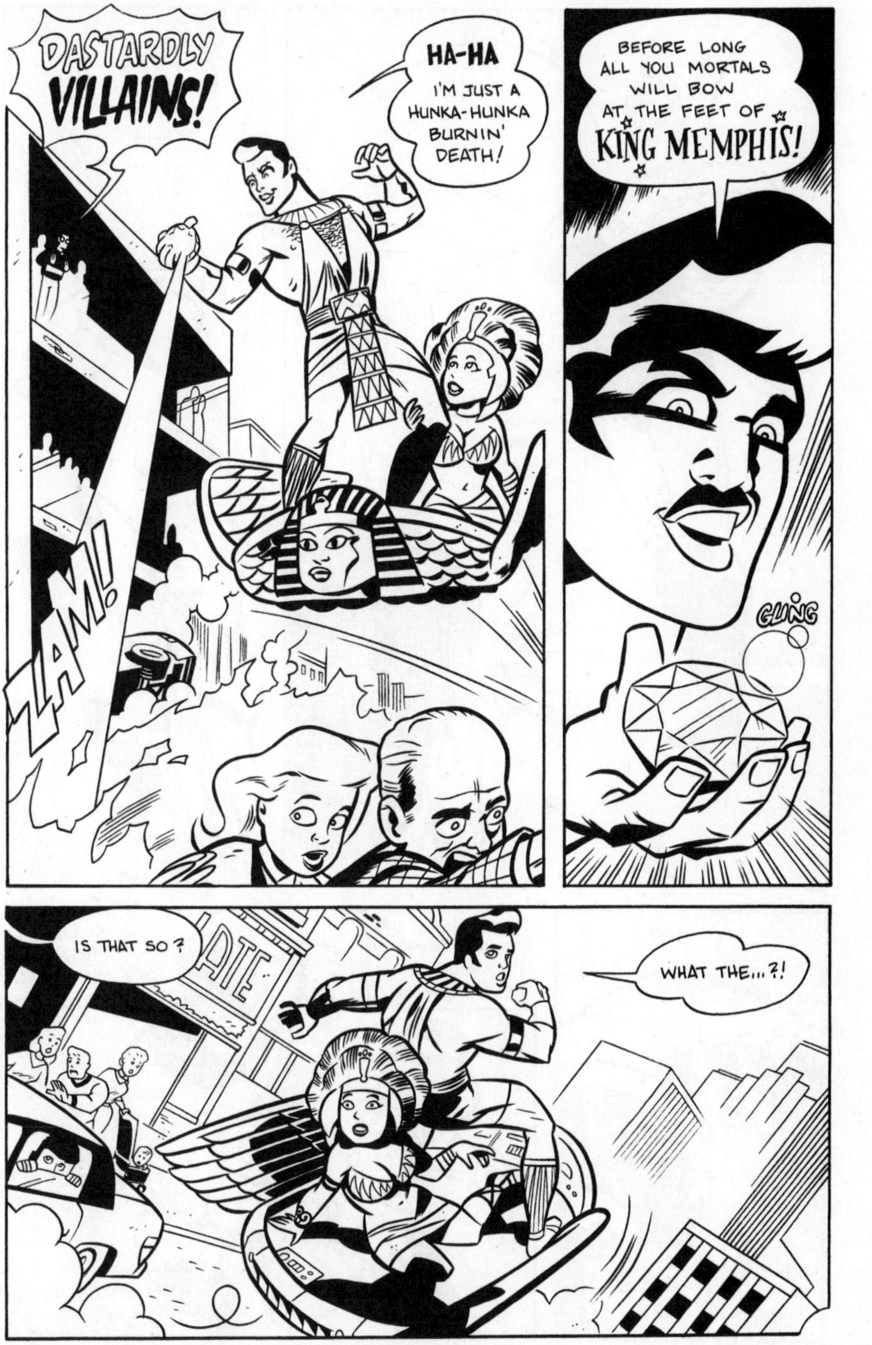
DASTARDLY VILLAINS!
HA-HA
I'M JUST A HUNKA-HUNKA BURNIN' DEATH!
ZAM!
BEFORE LONG ALL YOU MORTALS WILL BOW AT THE FEET OF KING MEMPHIS!
GLING
IS THAT SO?
WHAT THE...?!

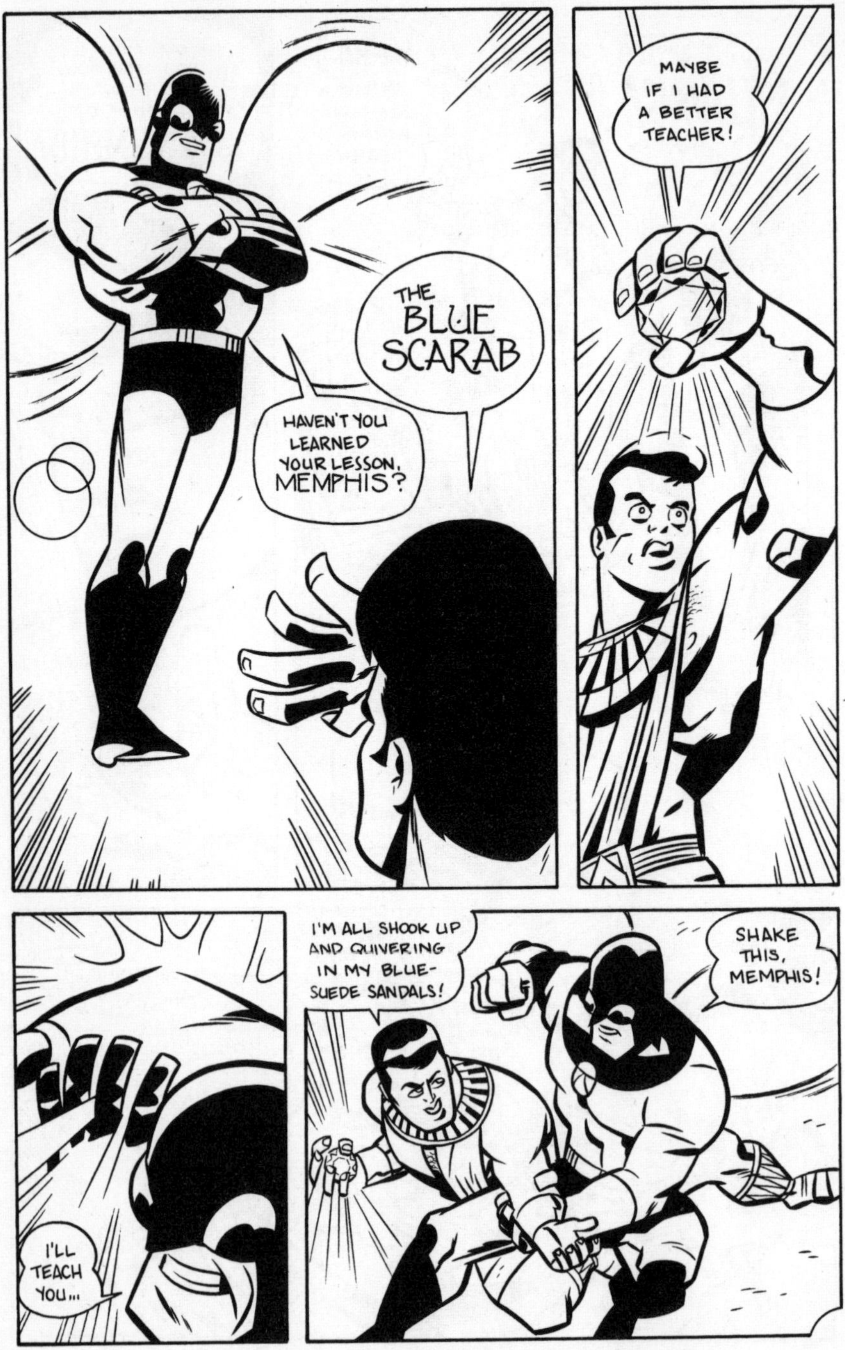
THE BLUE SCARAB
HAVEN'T YOU LEARNED YOUR LESSON, MEMPHIS?
MAYBE IF I HAD A BETTER TEACHER!
I'LL TEACH YOU...
I'M ALL SHOOK UP AND QUIVERING IN MY BLUE-SUEDE SANDALS!
SHAKE THIS, MEMPHIS!

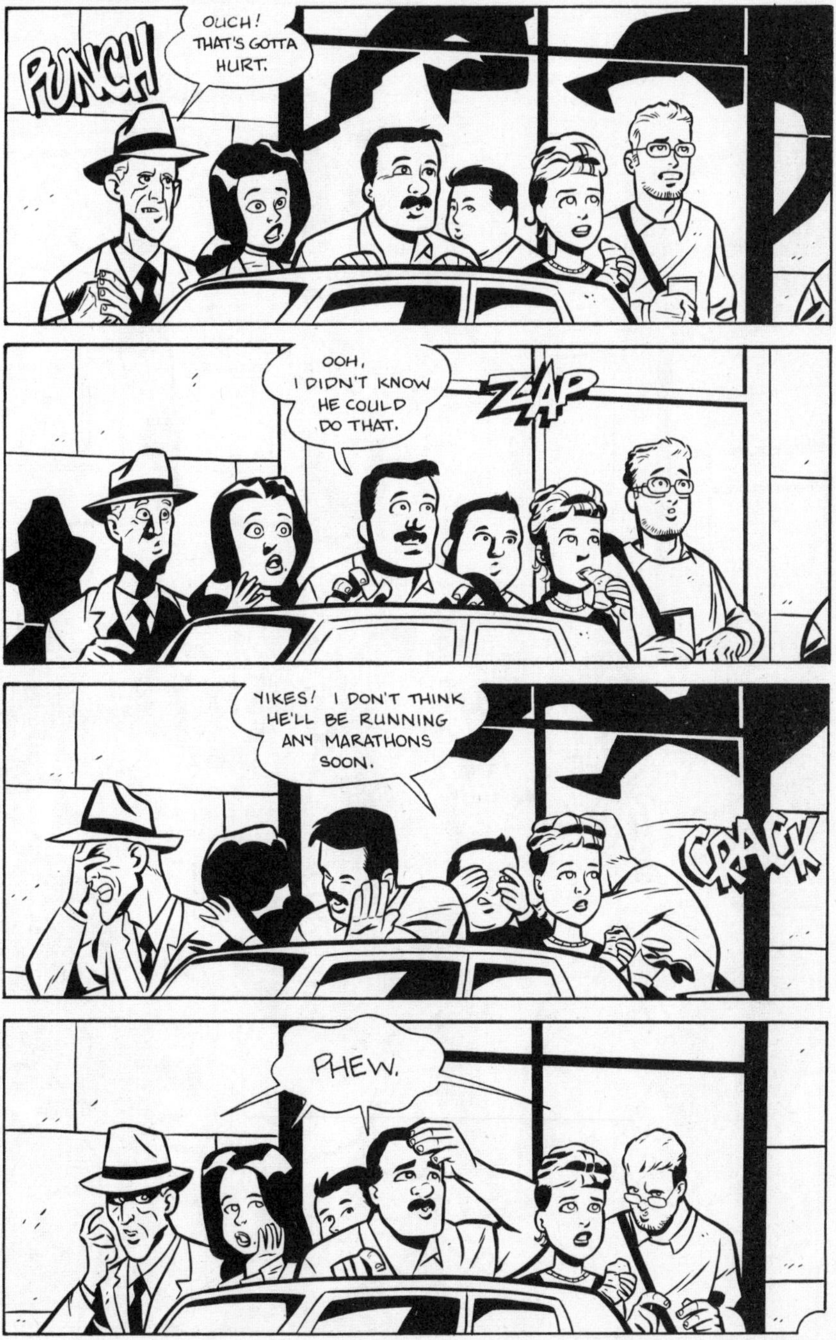
PUNCH
OUCH! THAT'S GOTTA HURT.
OOH, I DIDN'T KNOW HE COULD DO THAT.
ZAP
YIKES! I DON'T THINK HE'LL BE RUNNING ANY MARATHONS SOON.
CRACK
PHEW.

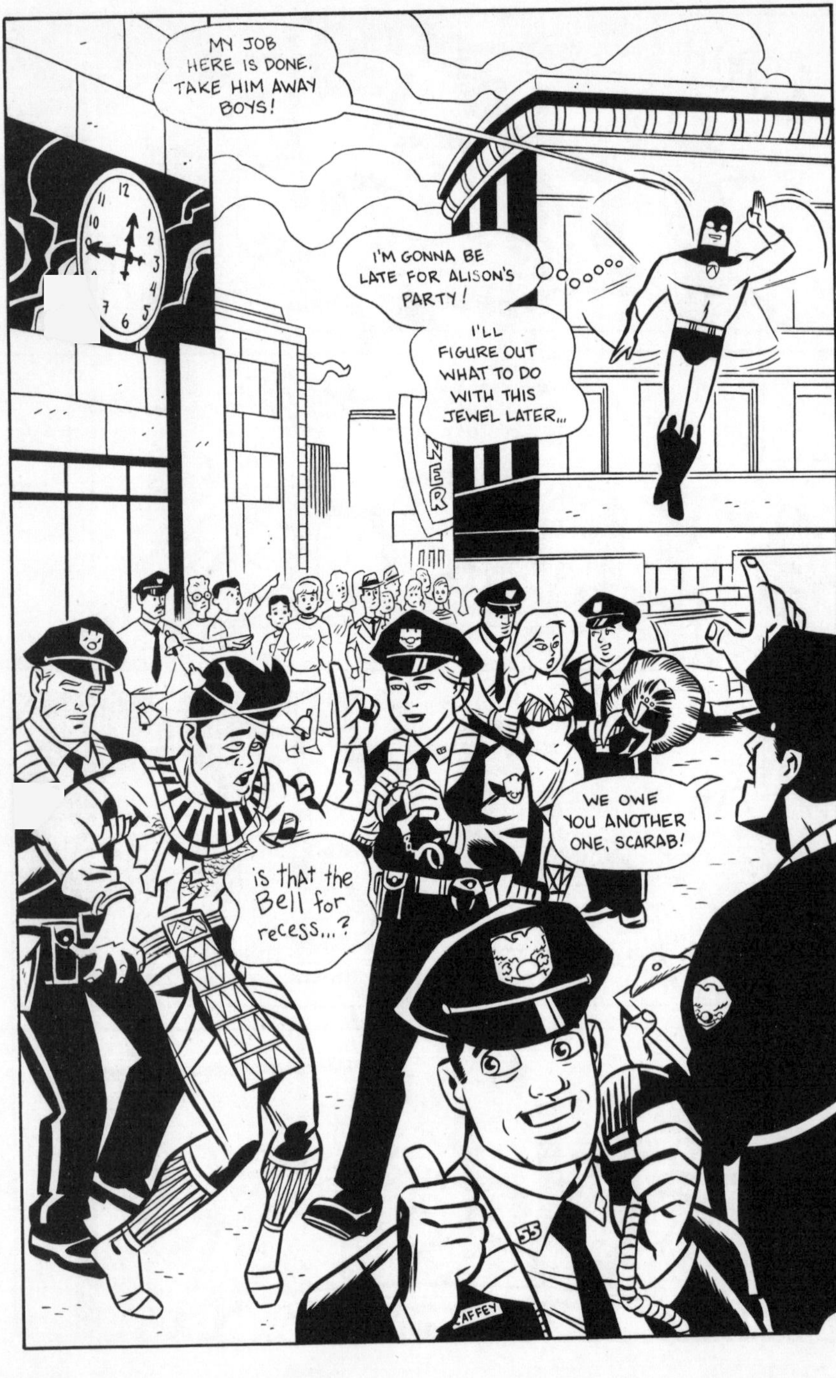
MY JOB
HERE IS DONE.
TAKE HIM AWAY
BOYS!
I'M GONNA BE
LATE FOR ALISON'S
PARTY!
I'LL
FIGURE OUT
WHAT TO DO
WITH THIS
JEWEL LATER...
WE OWE
YOU ANOTHER
ONE, SCARAB!
is that the
Bell for
recess...?

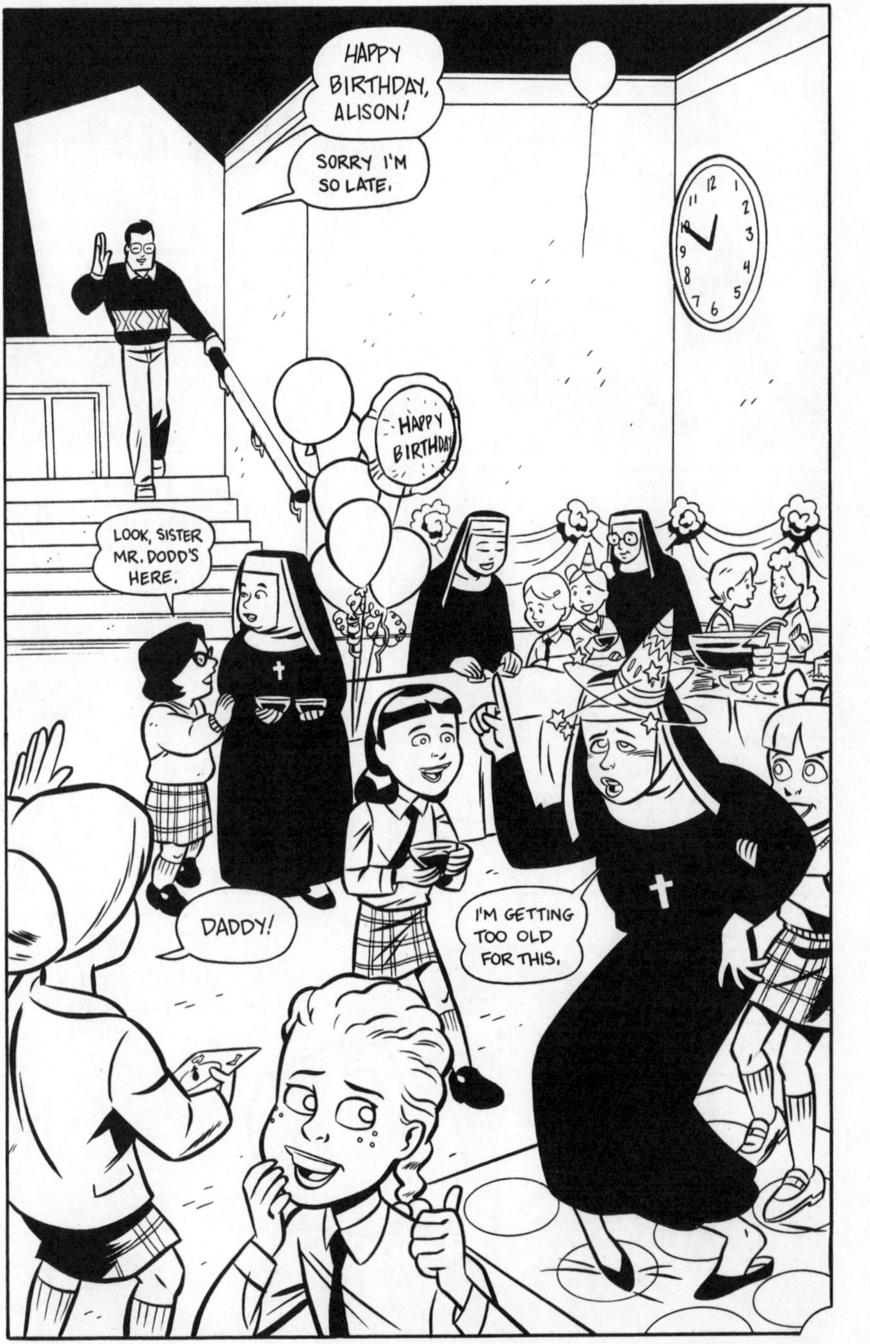
HAPPY BIRTHDAY, ALISON!
SORRY I'M SO LATE.
HAPPY BIRTHDAY
LOOK, SISTER MR. DODD'S HERE.
DADDY!
I'M GETTING TOO OLD FOR THIS.

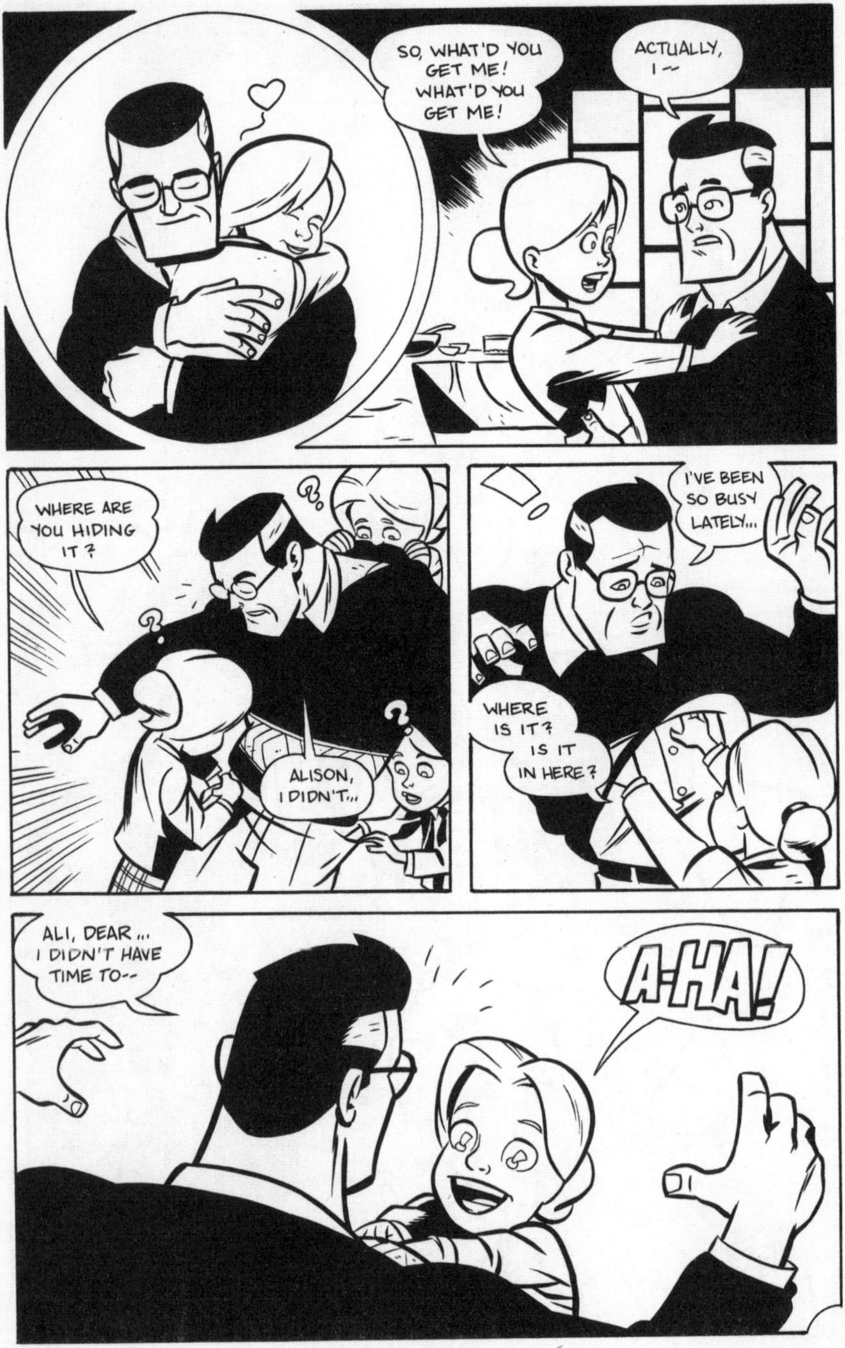
SO, WHAT'D YOU GET ME! WHAT'D YOU GET ME!
ACTUALLY, I --
WHERE ARE YOU HIDING IT?
ALISON, I DIDN'T...
I'VE BEEN SO BUSY LATELY...
WHERE IS IT? IS IT IN HERE?
ALI, DEAR... I DIDN'T HAVE TIME TO--
A-HA!

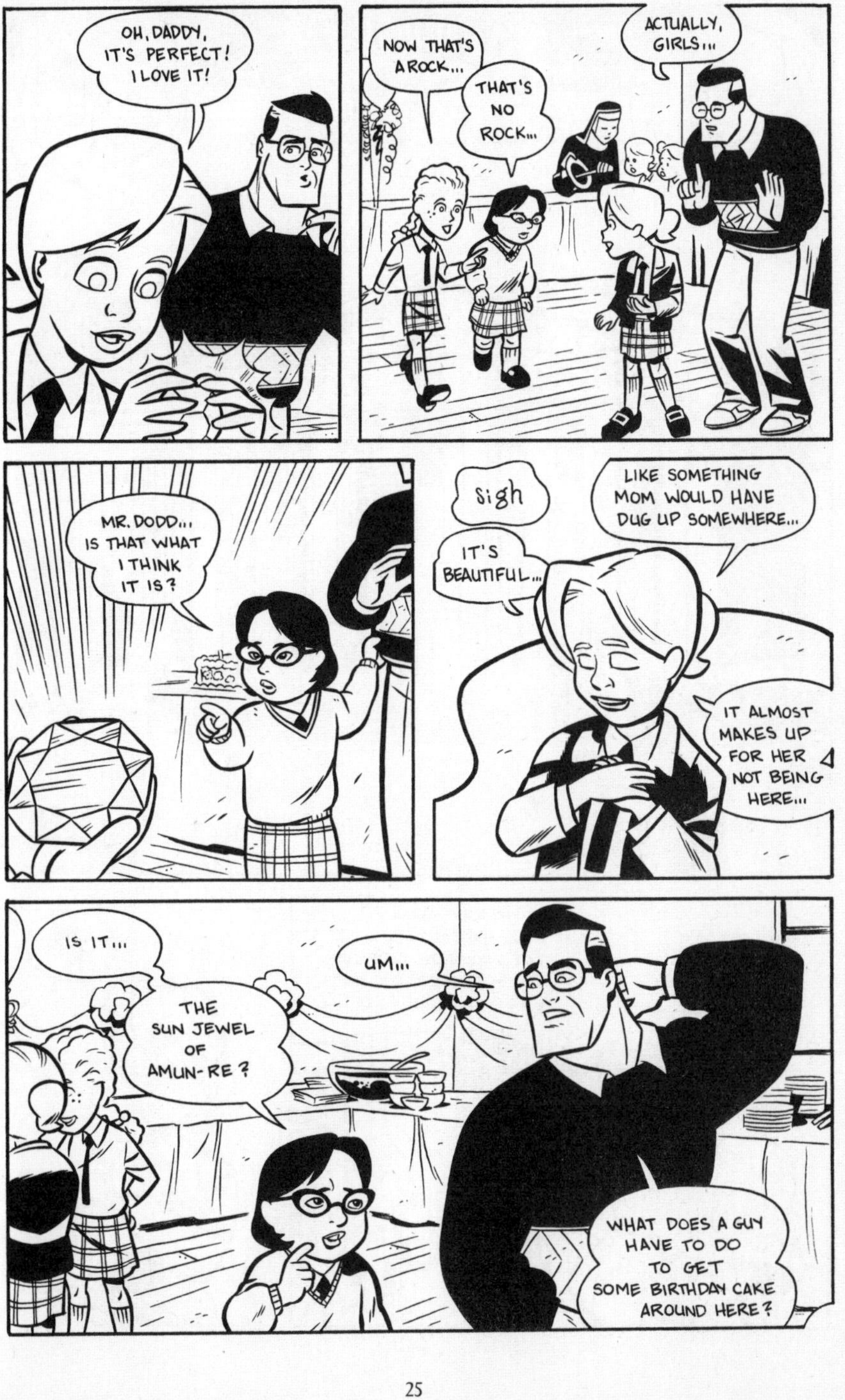
OH, DADDY, IT'S PERFECT! I LOVE IT!
NOW THAT'S A ROCK...
THAT'S NO ROCK...
ACTUALLY, GIRLS...
MR. DODD... IS THAT WHAT I THINK IT IS?
sigh
IT'S BEAUTIFUL...
LIKE SOMETHING MOM WOULD HAVE DUG UP SOMEWHERE...
IT ALMOST MAKES UP FOR HER NOT BEING HERE...
IS IT...
THE SUN JEWEL OF AMUN-RE?
UM...
WHAT DOES A GUY HAVE TO DO TO GET SOME BIRTHDAY CAKE AROUND HERE?

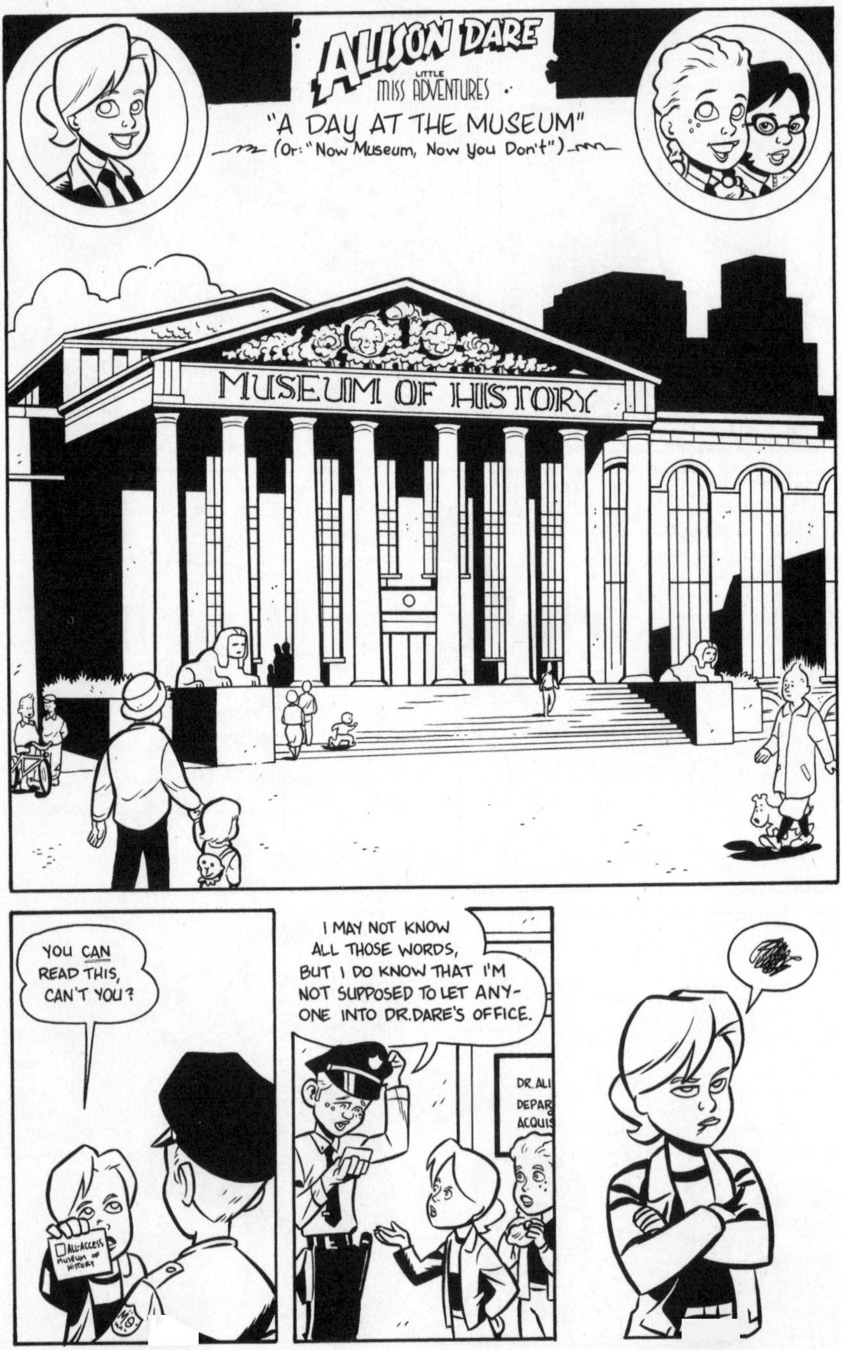
ALISON DARE
LITTLE MISS ADVENTURES
"A DAY AT THE MUSEUM"
(Or: "Now Museum, Now You Don't")
MUSEUM OF HISTORY
YOU CAN READ THIS, CAN'T YOU?
ALL-ACCESS MUSEUM OF HISTORY
I MAY NOT KNOW ALL THOSE WORDS, BUT I DO KNOW THAT I'M NOT SUPPOSED TO LET ANYONE INTO DR. DARE'S OFFICE.

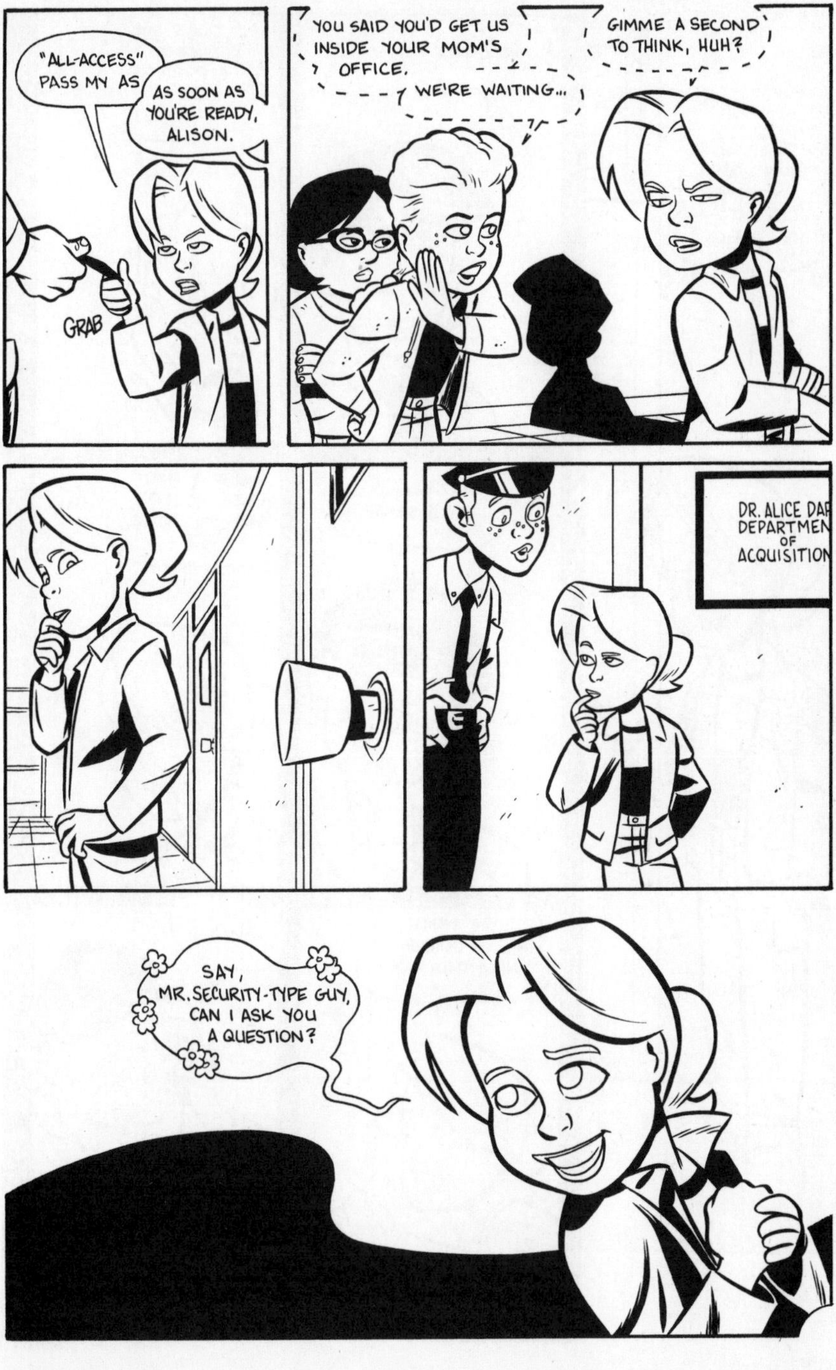
"ALL-ACCESS" PASS MY AS
AS SOON AS YOU'RE READY, ALISON.
GRAB
YOU SAID YOU'D GET US INSIDE YOUR MOM'S OFFICE.
WE'RE WAITING...
GIMME A SECOND TO THINK, HUH?
DR. ALICE DA
DEPARTMEN
OF
ACQUISITION
SAY, MR. SECURITY-TYPE GUY, CAN I ASK YOU A QUESTION?

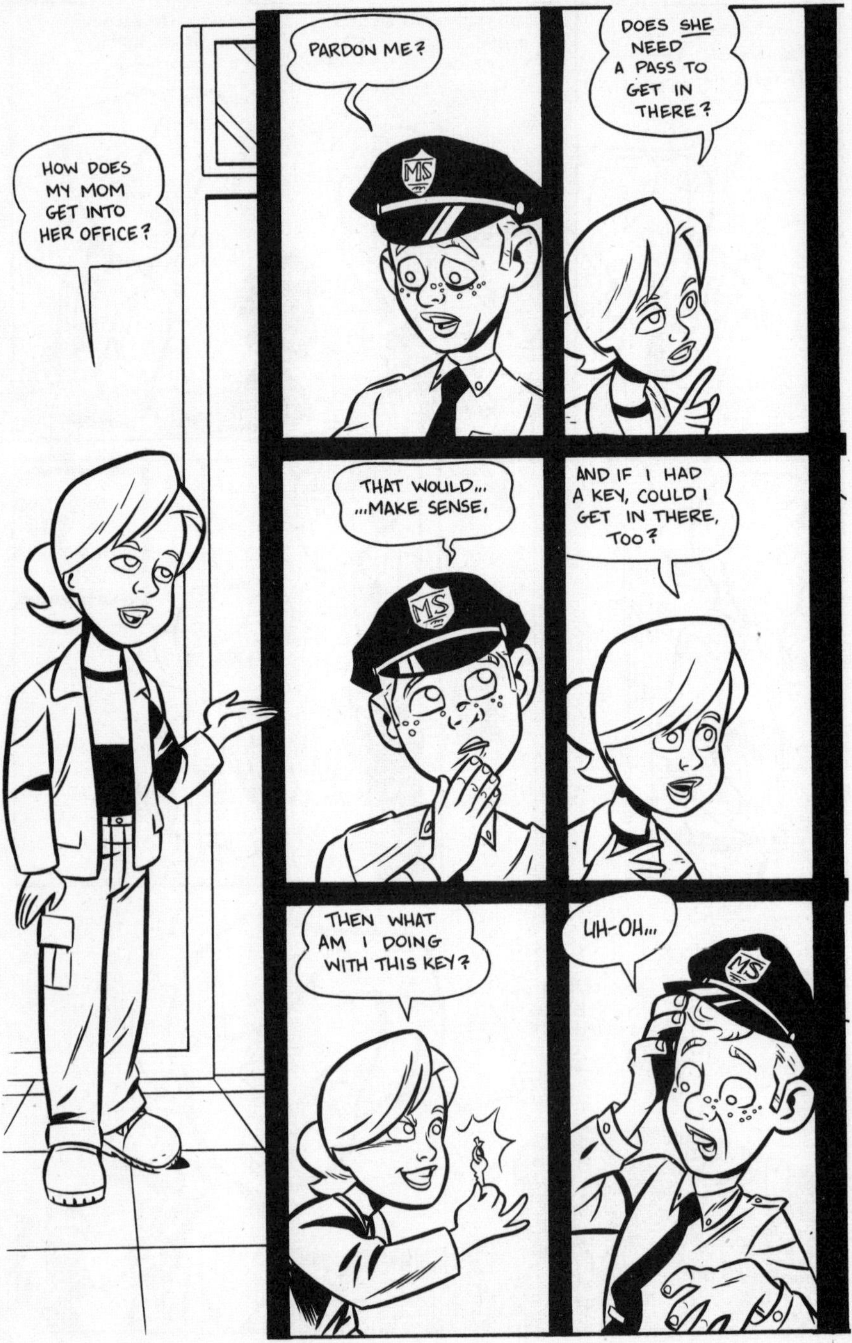
HOW DOES MY MOM GET INTO HER OFFICE?
PARDON ME?
DOES SHE NEED A PASS TO GET IN THERE?
THAT WOULD... ...MAKE SENSE.
AND IF I HAD A KEY, COULD I GET IN THERE, TOO?
THEN WHAT AM I DOING WITH THIS KEY?
UH-OH...

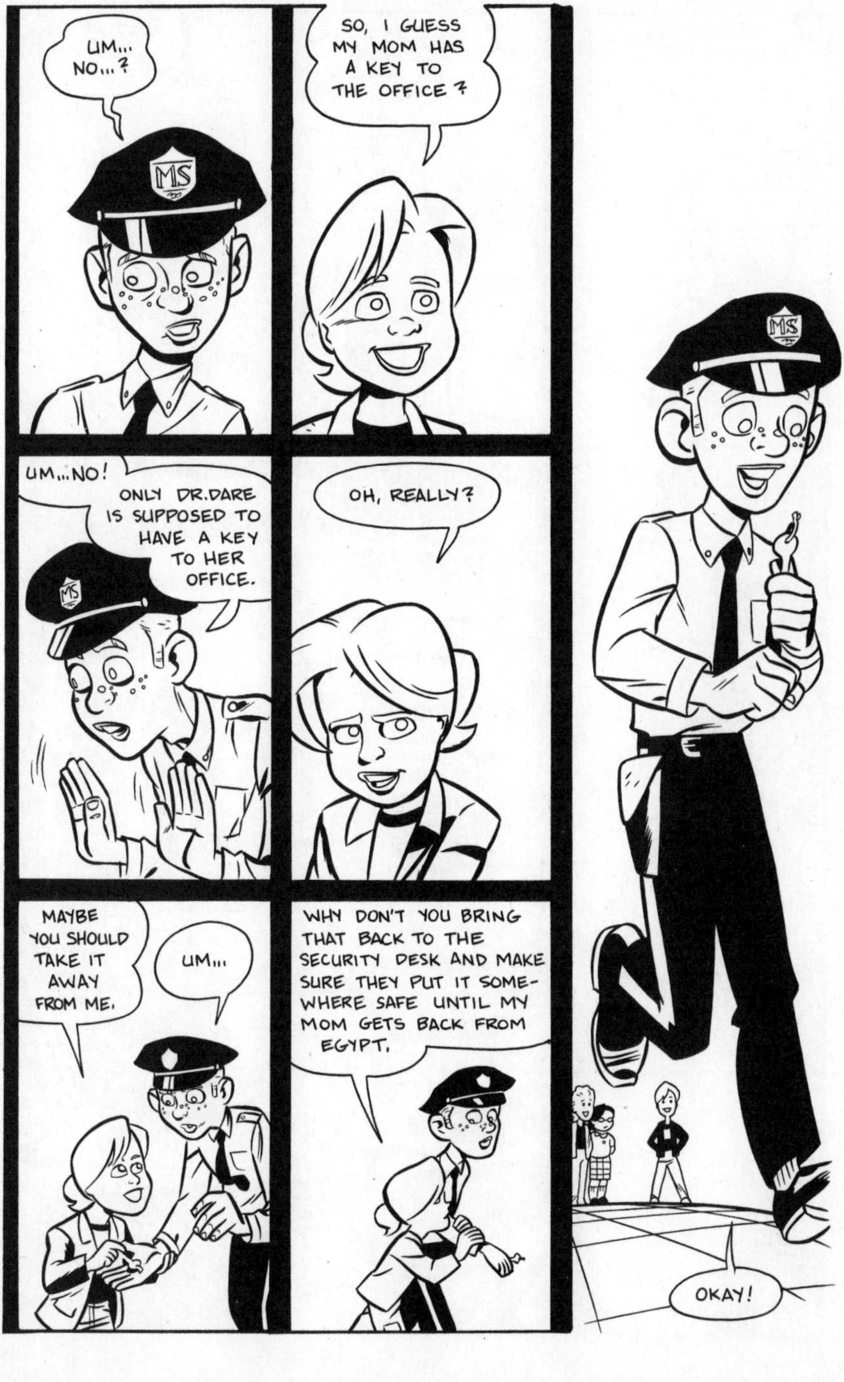
UM... NO...?
SO, I GUESS MY MOM HAS A KEY TO THE OFFICE?
UM...NO! ONLY DR.DARE IS SUPPOSED TO HAVE A KEY TO HER OFFICE.
OH, REALLY?
MAYBE YOU SHOULD TAKE IT AWAY FROM ME.
UM...
WHY DON'T YOU BRING THAT BACK TO THE SECURITY DESK AND MAKE SURE THEY PUT IT SOME-WHERE SAFE UNTIL MY MOM GETS BACK FROM EGYPT.
OKAY!

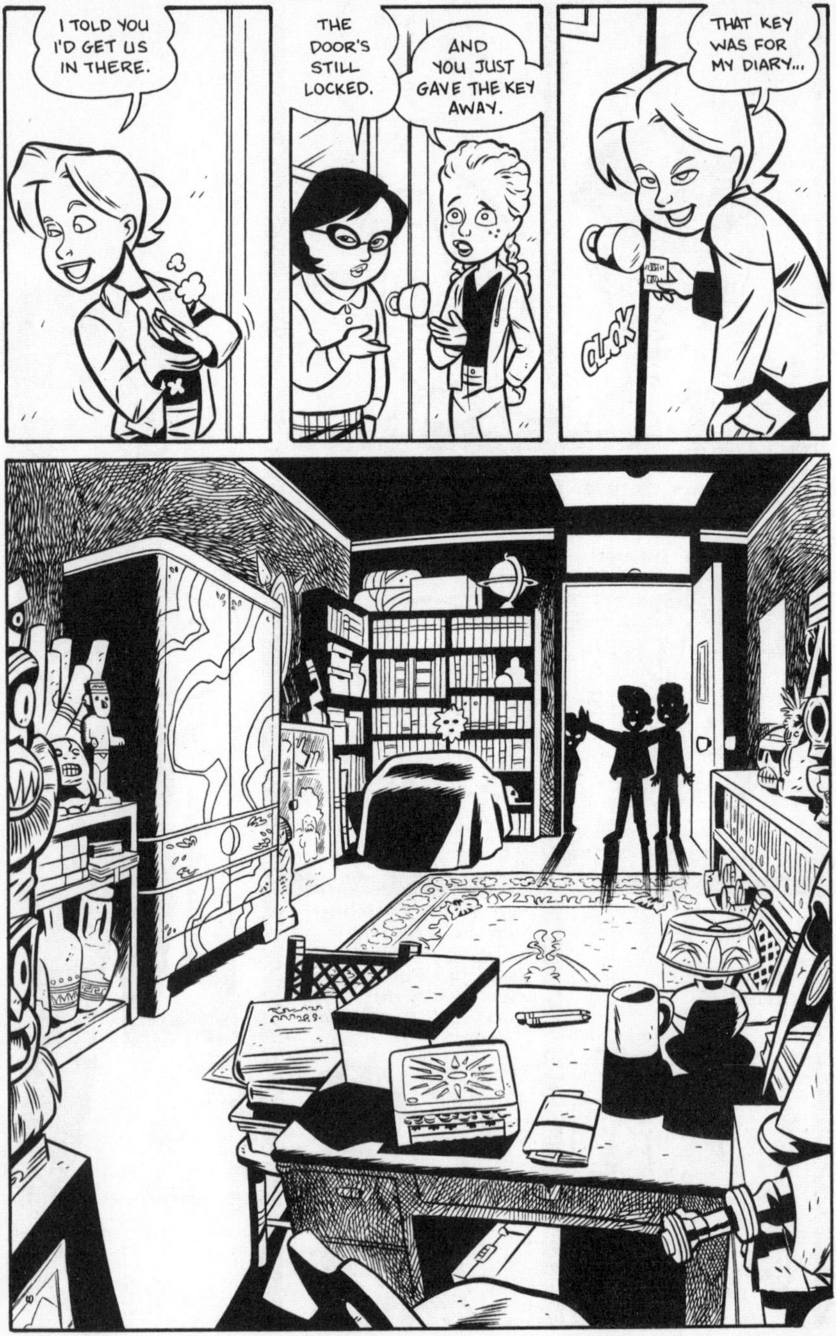
I TOLD YOU I'D GET US IN THERE.
THE DOOR'S STILL LOCKED.
AND YOU JUST GAVE THE KEY AWAY.
THAT KEY WAS FOR MY DIARY...
CLICK

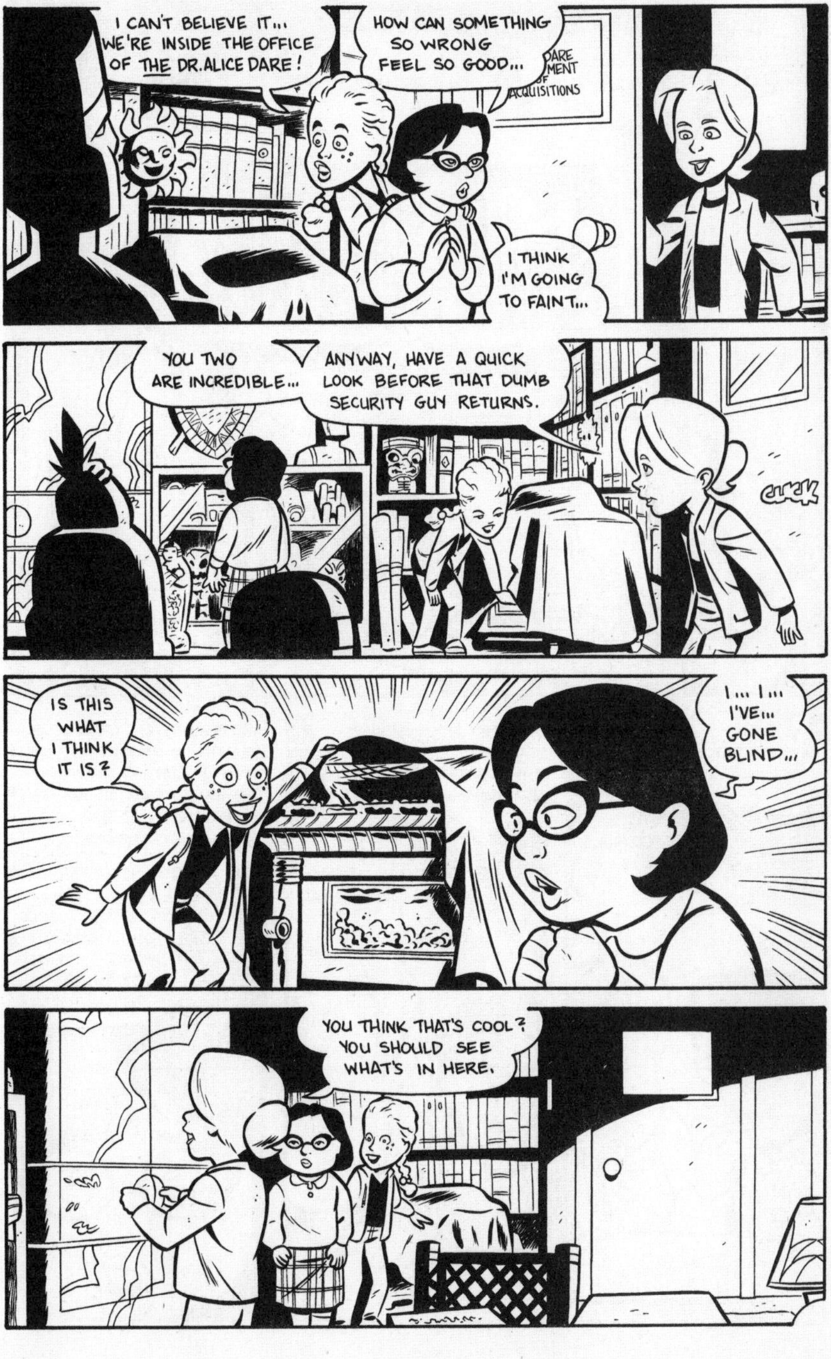
I CAN'T BELIEVE IT... WE'RE INSIDE THE OFFICE OF THE DR. ALICE DARE!
HOW CAN SOMETHING SO WRONG FEEL SO GOOD...
I THINK I'M GOING TO FAINT...
YOU TWO ARE INCREDIBLE...
ANYWAY, HAVE A QUICK LOOK BEFORE THAT DUMB SECURITY GUY RETURNS.
CLICK
IS THIS WHAT I THINK IT IS?
I... I... I'VE... GONE BLIND...
YOU THINK THAT'S COOL? YOU SHOULD SEE WHAT'S IN HERE.

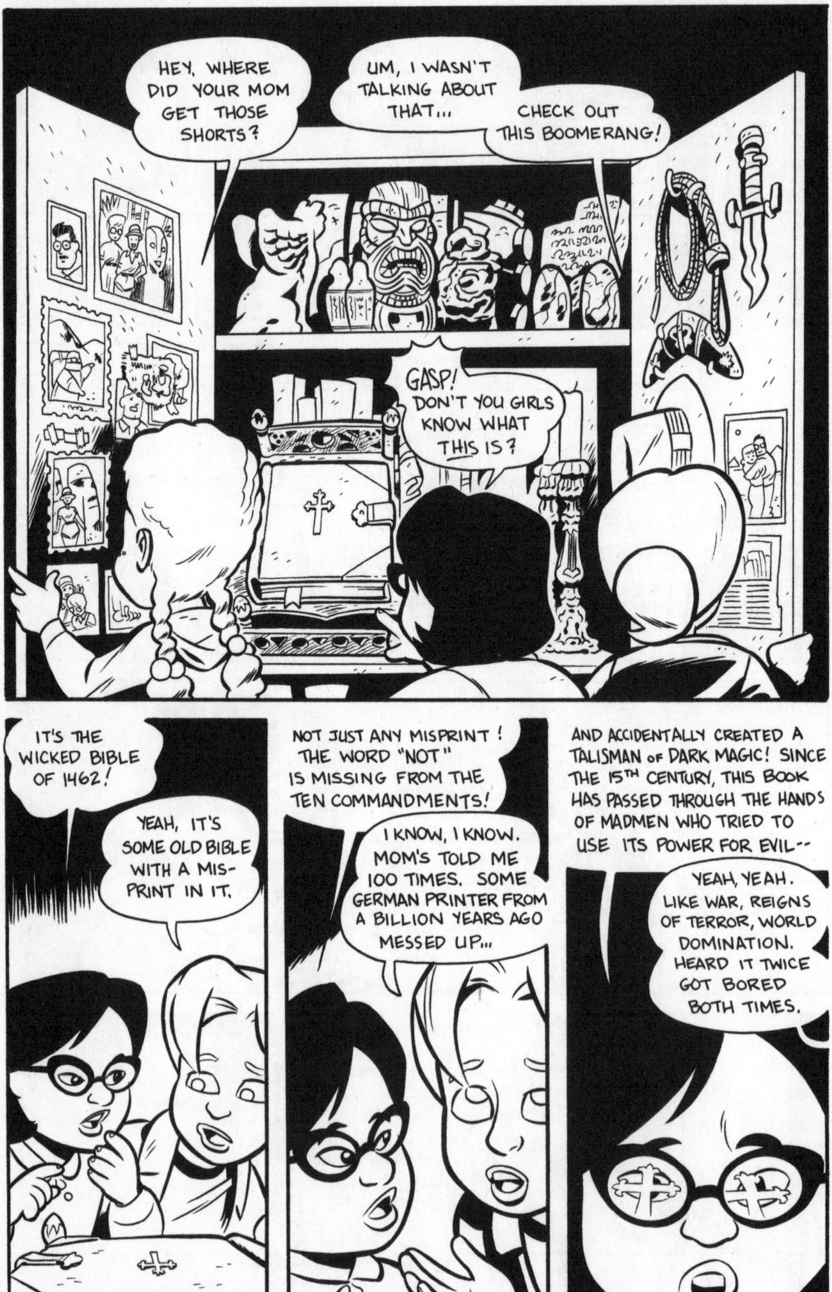
HEY, WHERE DID YOUR MOM GET THOSE SHORTS?
UM, I WASN'T TALKING ABOUT THAT...
CHECK OUT THIS BOOMERANG!
GASP! DON'T YOU GIRLS KNOW WHAT THIS IS?
IT'S THE WICKED BIBLE OF 1462!
YEAH, IT'S SOME OLD BIBLE WITH A MIS-PRINT IN IT.
NOT JUST ANY MISPRINT! THE WORD "NOT" IS MISSING FROM THE TEN COMMANDMENTS!
I KNOW, I KNOW. MOM'S TOLD ME 100 TIMES. SOME GERMAN PRINTER FROM A BILLION YEARS AGO MESSED UP...
AND ACCIDENTALLY CREATED A TALISMAN OF DARK MAGIC! SINCE THE 15TH CENTURY, THIS BOOK HAS PASSED THROUGH THE HANDS OF MADMEN WHO TRIED TO USE ITS POWER FOR EVIL--
YEAH, YEAH. LIKE WAR, REIGNS OF TERROR, WORLD DOMINATION. HEARD IT TWICE GOT BORED BOTH TIMES.

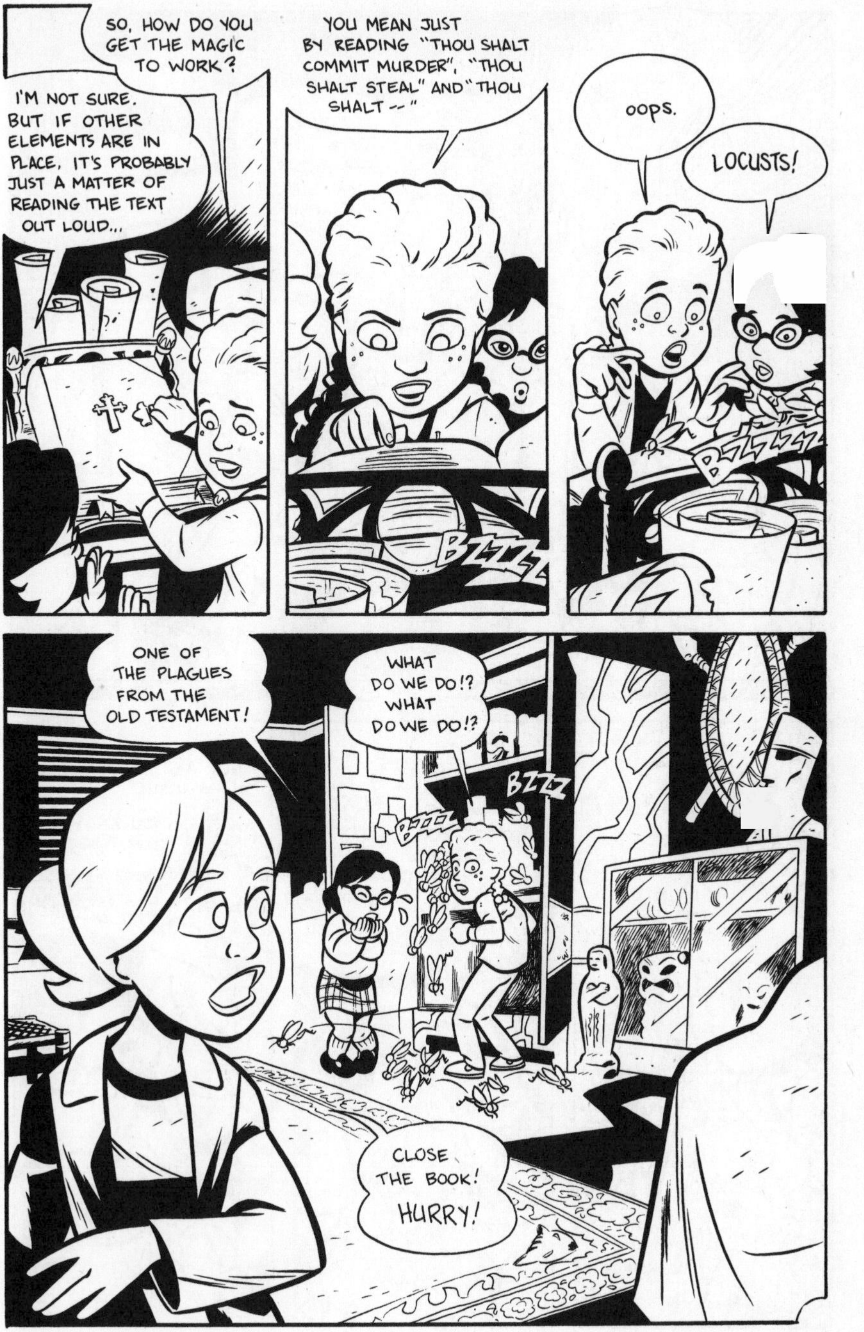
SO, HOW DO YOU GET THE MAGIC TO WORK?
I'M NOT SURE. BUT IF OTHER ELEMENTS ARE IN PLACE, IT'S PROBABLY JUST A MATTER OF READING THE TEXT OUT LOUD...
YOU MEAN JUST BY READING "THOU SHALT COMMIT MURDER", "THOU SHALT STEAL" AND "THOU SHALT --"
BZZZZ
oops.
LOCUSTS!
BZZZZZ
ONE OF THE PLAGUES FROM THE OLD TESTAMENT!
WHAT DO WE DO!? WHAT DO WE DO!?
BZZZ
BZZZ
CLOSE THE BOOK! HURRY!

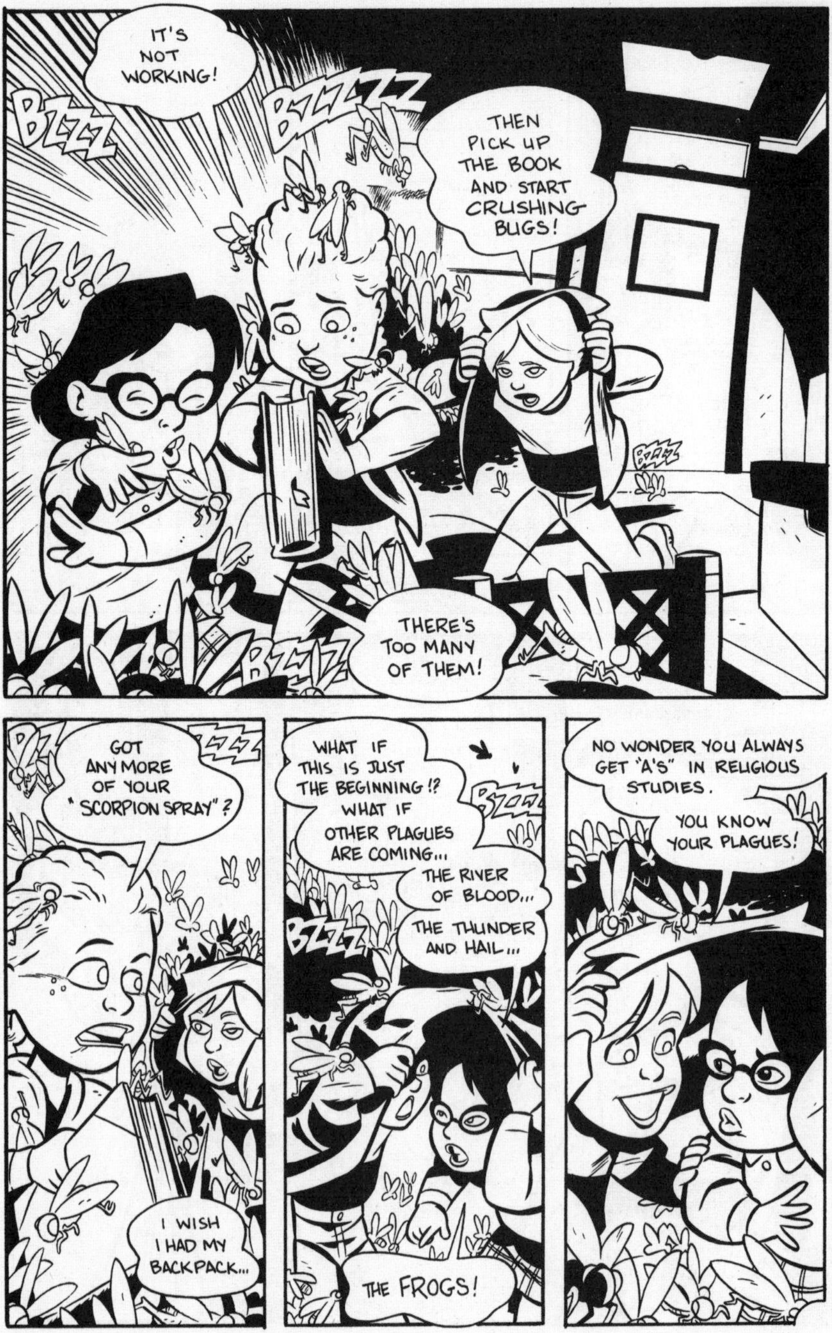
IT'S NOT WORKING!
BZZZ
BZZZZZ
THEN PICK UP THE BOOK AND START CRUSHING BUGS!
BZZZ
BZZZ
THERE'S TOO MANY OF THEM!
GOT ANYMORE OF YOUR "SCORPION SPRAY"?
I WISH I HAD MY BACKPACK...
WHAT IF THIS IS JUST THE BEGINNING!? WHAT IF OTHER PLAGUES ARE COMING...
THE RIVER OF BLOOD...
THE THUNDER AND HAIL...
BZZZZ
THE FROGS!
NO WONDER YOU ALWAYS GET "A'S" IN RELIGIOUS STUDIES.
YOU KNOW YOUR PLAGUES!

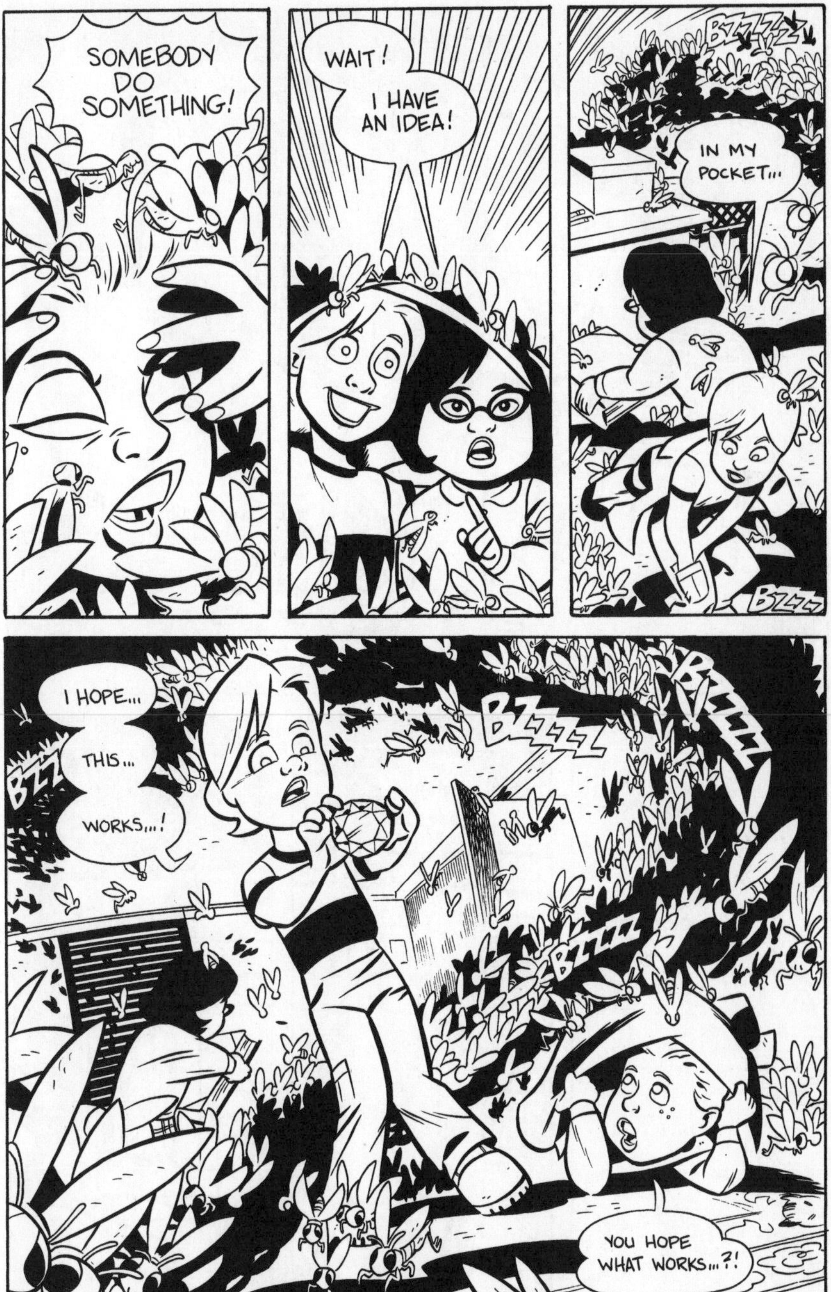
SOMEBODY DO SOMETHING!
WAIT!
I HAVE AN IDEA!
BZZZZZ
IN MY POCKET...
BZZZ
I HOPE...
THIS...
WORKS...!
BZZZZ
BZZZZ
BZZZ
BZZZZ
YOU HOPE WHAT WORKS...?!

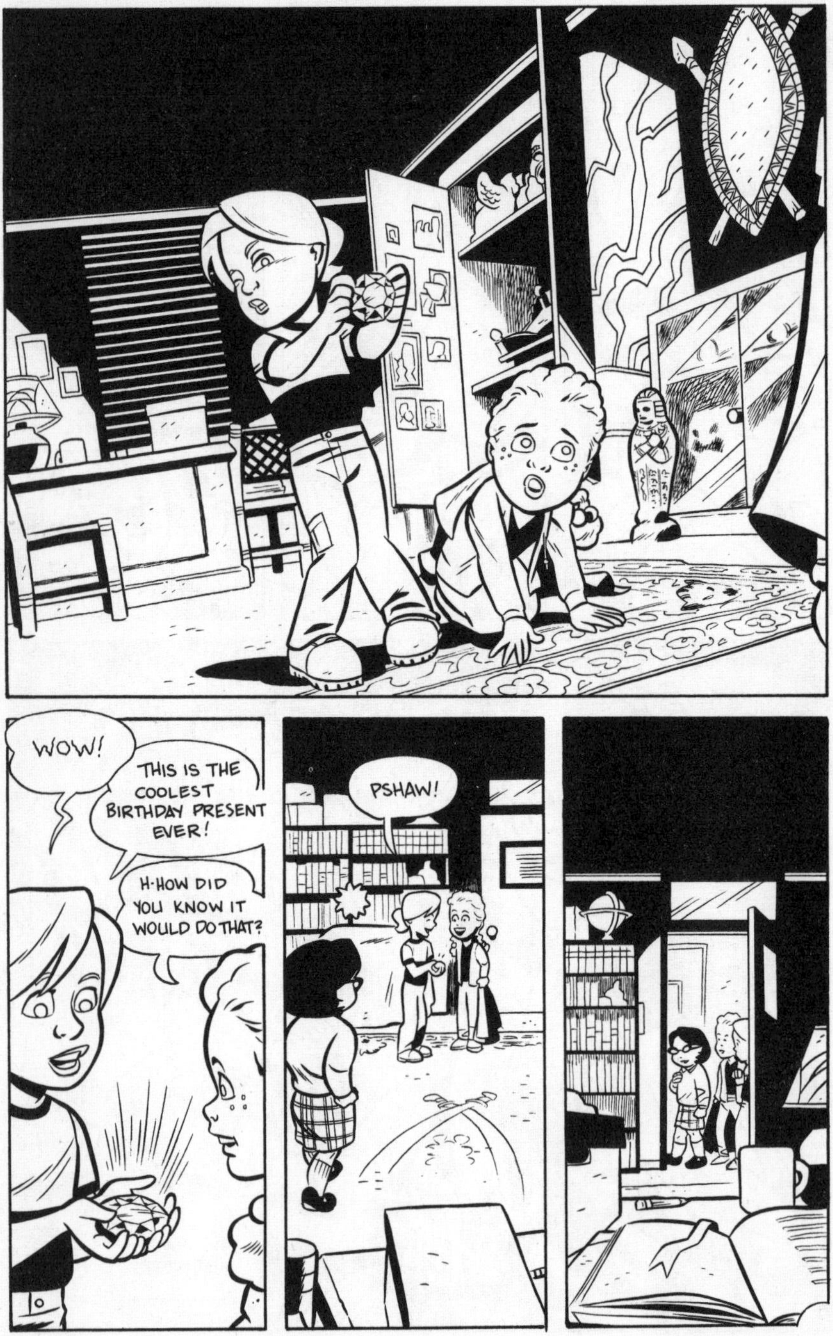
WOW!
THIS IS THE COOLEST BIRTHDAY PRESENT EVER!
H-HOW DID YOU KNOW IT WOULD DO THAT?
PSHAW!

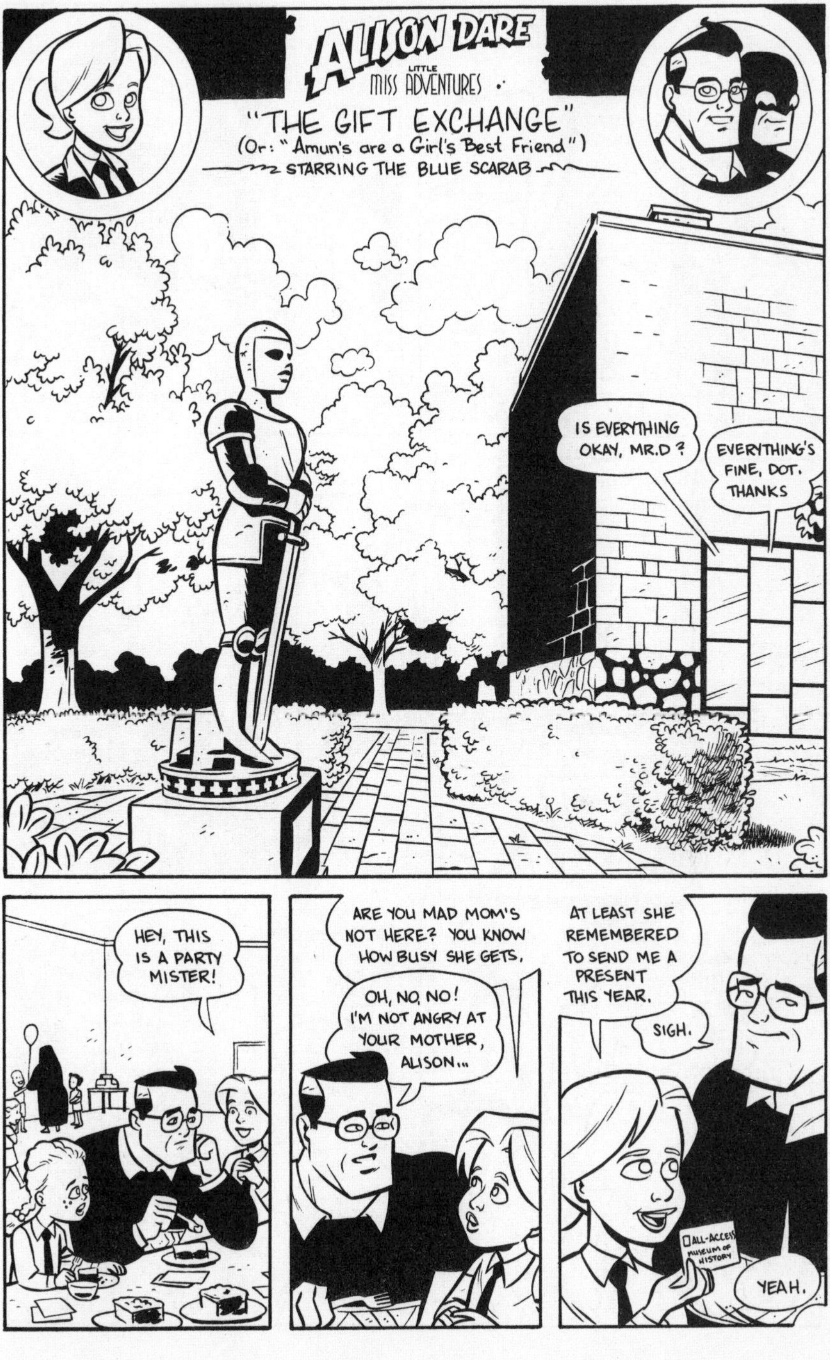
ALISON DARE
LITTLE MISS ADVENTURES
"THE GIFT EXCHANGE"
(Or: "Amun's are a Girl's Best Friend")
STARRING THE BLUE SCARAB
IS EVERYTHING OKAY, MR.D?
EVERYTHING'S FINE, DOT. THANKS
HEY, THIS IS A PARTY MISTER!
ARE YOU MAD MOM'S NOT HERE? YOU KNOW HOW BUSY SHE GETS.
OH, NO, NO! I'M NOT ANGRY AT YOUR MOTHER, ALISON...
AT LEAST SHE REMEMBERED TO SEND ME A PRESENT THIS YEAR.
SIGH.
ALL-ACCESS MUSEUM OF HISTORY
YEAH.

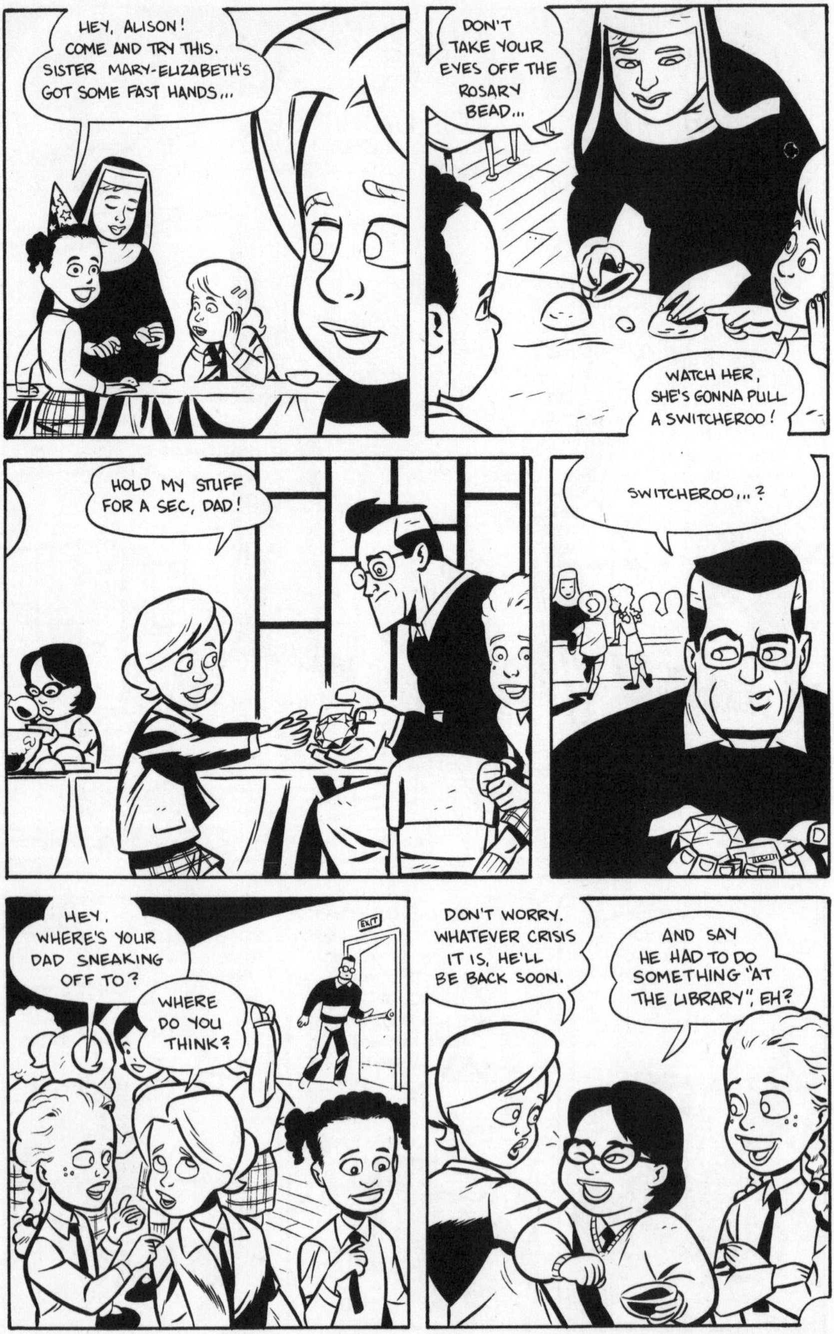
HEY, ALISON! COME AND TRY THIS. SISTER MARY-ELIZABETH'S GOT SOME FAST HANDS...
DON'T TAKE YOUR EYES OFF THE ROSARY BEAD...
WATCH HER, SHE'S GONNA PULL A SWITCHEROO!
HOLD MY STUFF FOR A SEC, DAD!
SWITCHEROO...?
HEY. WHERE'S YOUR DAD SNEAKING OFF TO?
EXIT
WHERE DO YOU THINK?
DON'T WORRY. WHATEVER CRISIS IT IS, HE'LL BE BACK SOON.
AND SAY HE HAD TO DO SOMETHING "AT THE LIBRARY", EH?

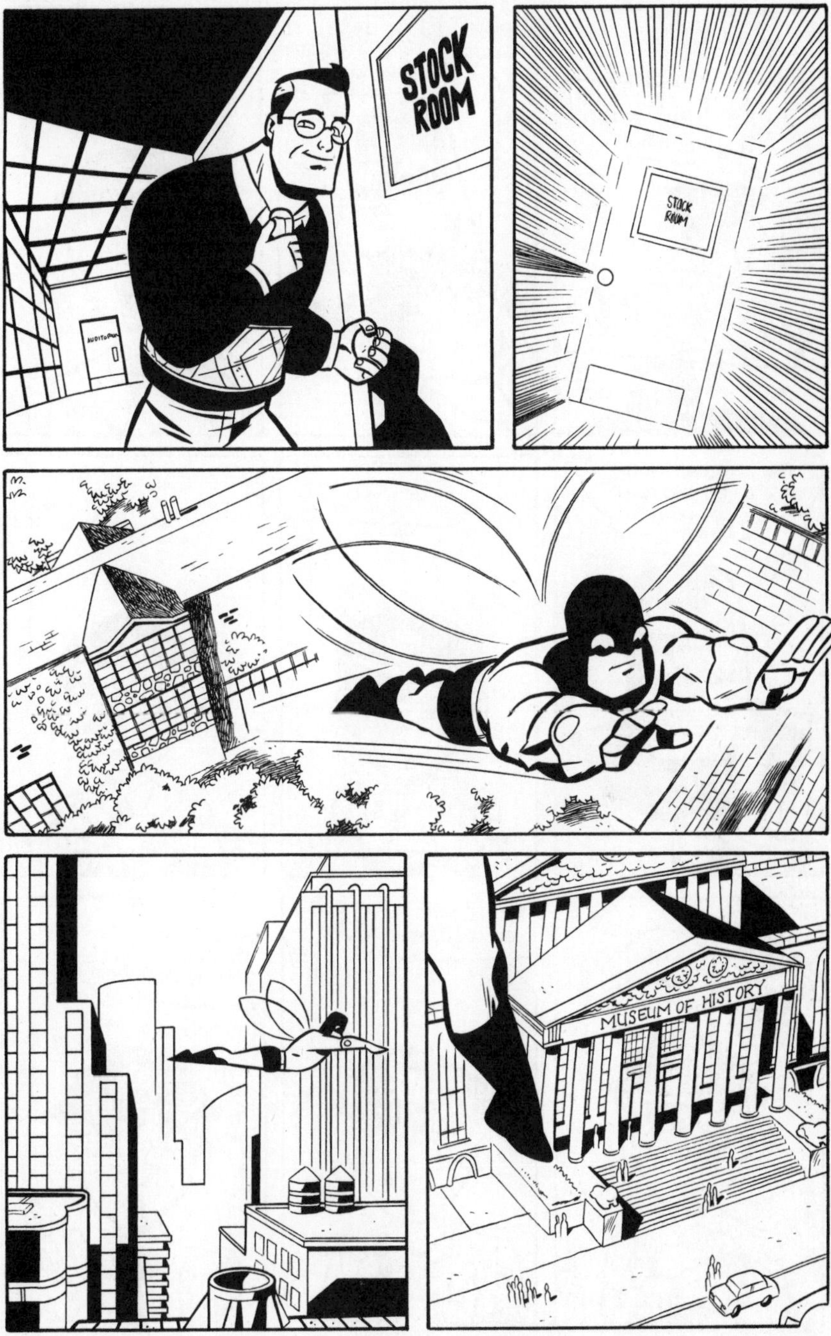
STOCK ROOM
STOCK ROOM
MUSEUM OF HISTORY

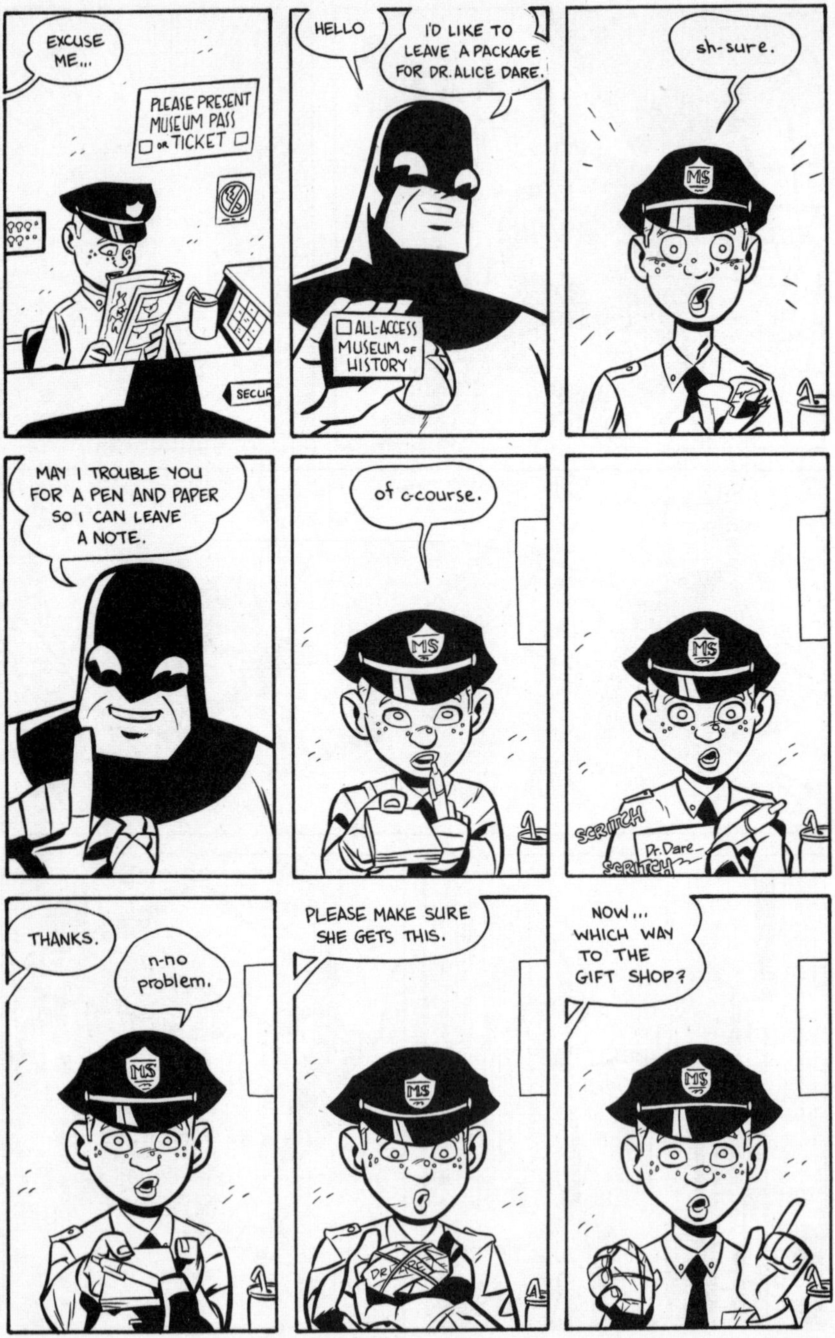
EXCUSE ME...
PLEASE PRESENT MUSEUM PASS OR TICKET
SECUR
HELLO
I'D LIKE TO LEAVE A PACKAGE FOR DR. ALICE DARE.
ALL-ACCESS MUSEUM OF HISTORY
sh-sure.
MS
MAY I TROUBLE YOU FOR A PEN AND PAPER SO I CAN LEAVE A NOTE.
of c-course.
SCRITCH
Dr. Dare
SCRITCH
THANKS.
n-no problem.
PLEASE MAKE SURE SHE GETS THIS.
NOW... WHICH WAY TO THE GIFT SHOP?

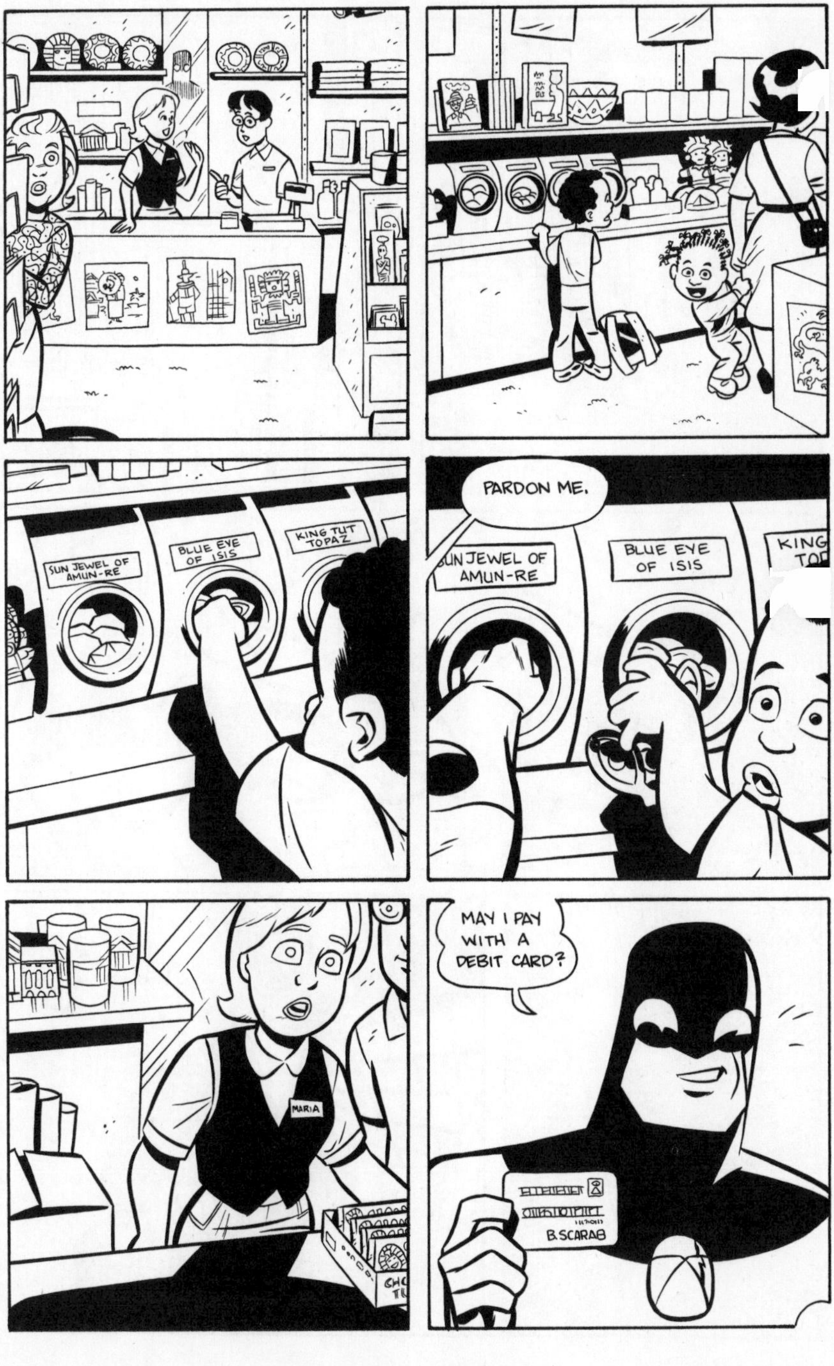
SUN JEWEL OF AMUN-RE
BLUE EYE OF ISIS
KING TUT TOPAZ
PARDON ME.
SUN JEWEL OF AMUN-RE
BLUE EYE OF ISIS
MARIA
MAY I PAY WITH A DEBIT CARD?
B.SCARAB

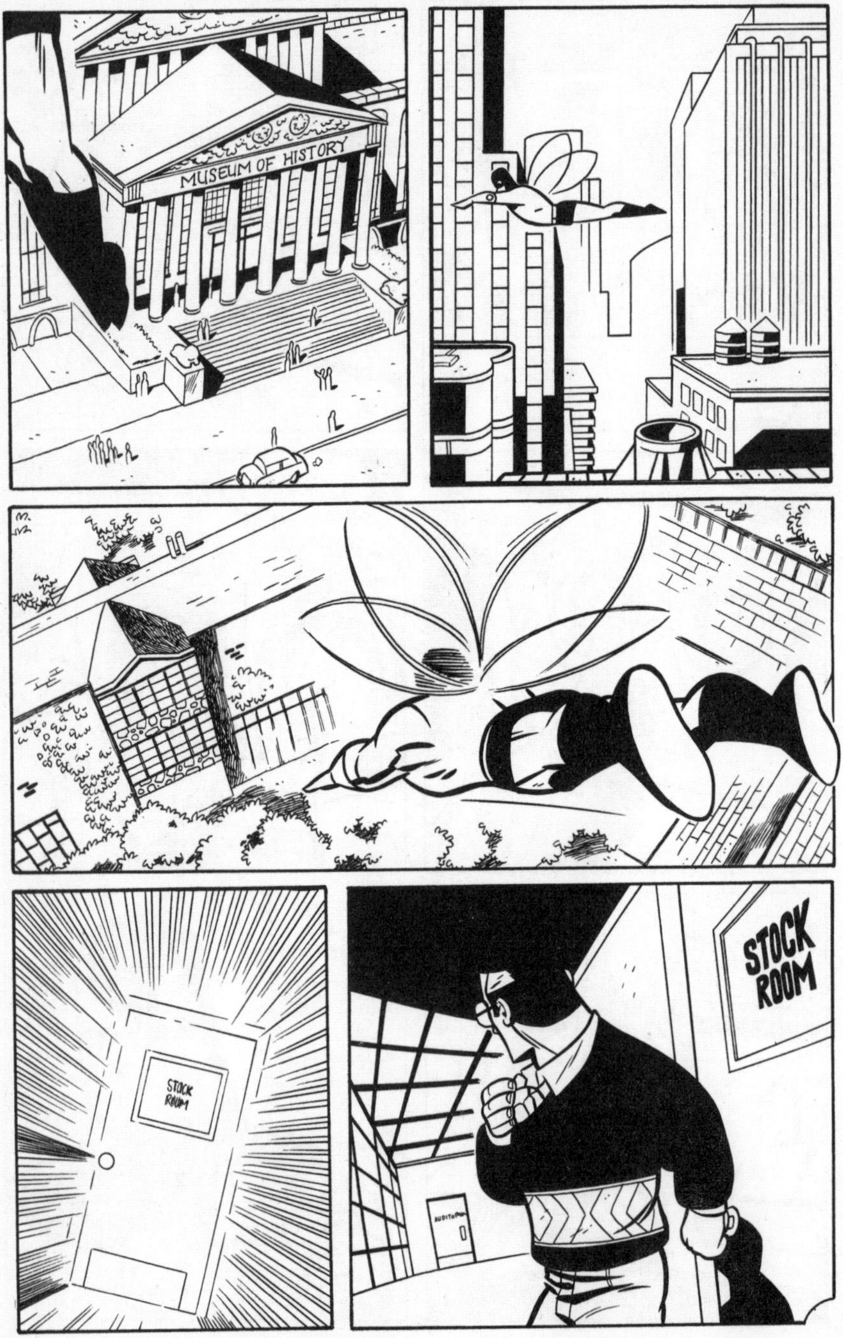
MUSEUM OF HISTORY
STOCK ROOM
STOCK ROOM

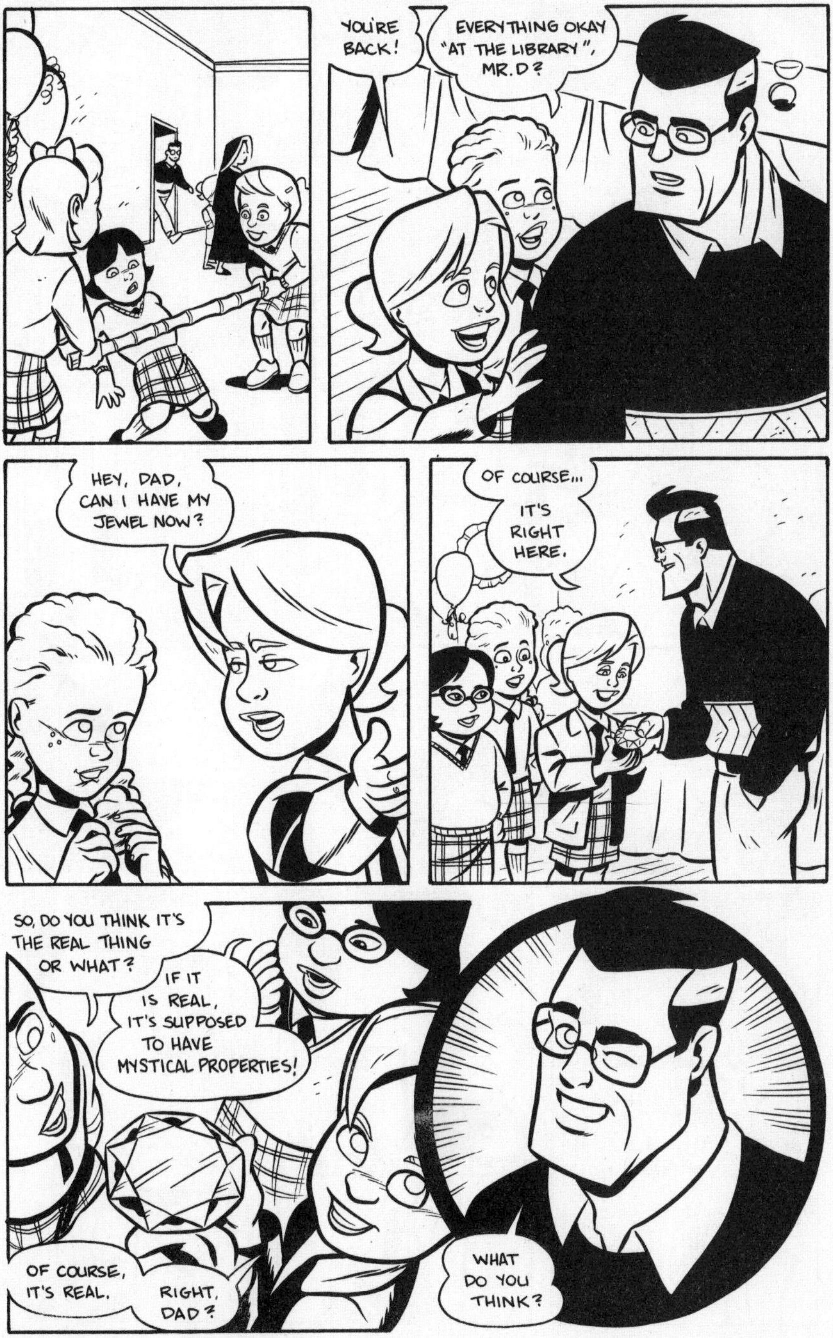
YOU'RE BACK!
EVERYTHING OKAY "AT THE LIBRARY", MR. D?
HEY, DAD, CAN I HAVE MY JEWEL NOW?
OF COURSE...
IT'S RIGHT HERE.
SO, DO YOU THINK IT'S THE REAL THING OR WHAT?
IF IT IS REAL, IT'S SUPPOSED TO HAVE MYSTICAL PROPERTIES!
OF COURSE, IT'S REAL.
RIGHT, DAD?
WHAT DO YOU THINK?

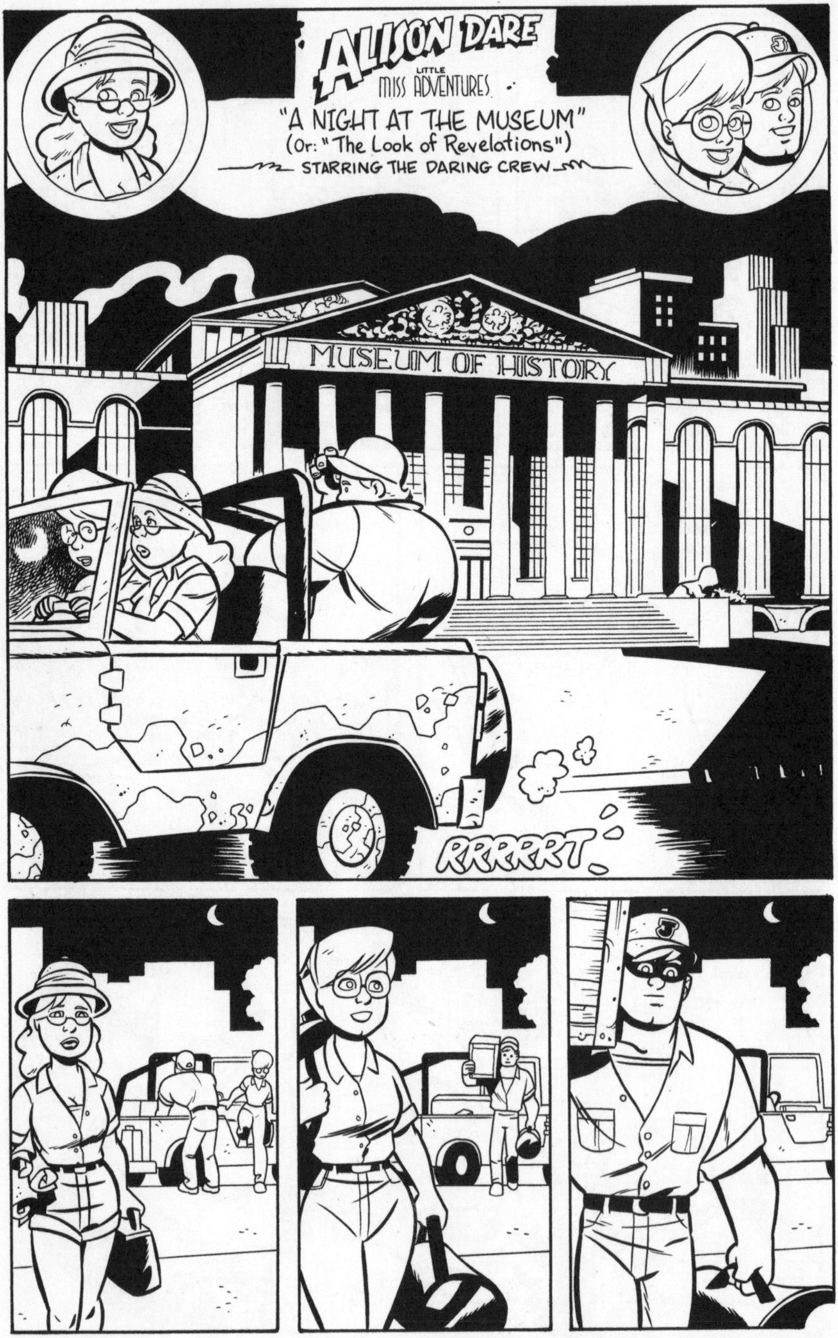
ALISON DARE
LITTLE MISS ADVENTURES
"A NIGHT AT THE MUSEUM"
(Or: "The Look of Revelations")
STARRING THE DARING CREW
MUSEUM OF HISTORY
RRRRRT

STAFF ONLY
GAYLE GIBSON
EGYPTOLOGIST
DR. ALICE DARE
DEPARTMENT
OF
ACQUISITIONS

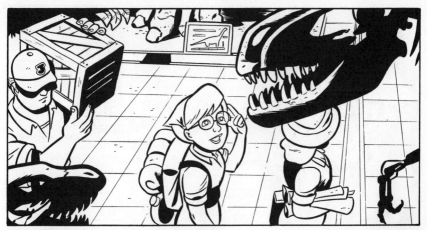

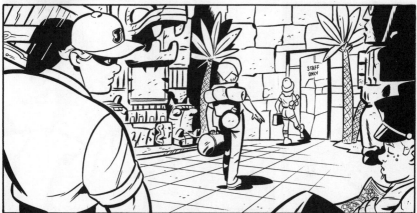

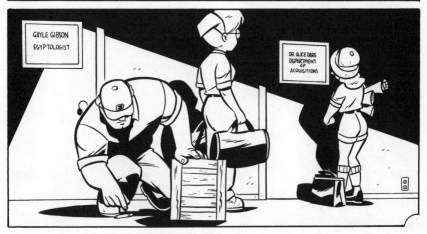

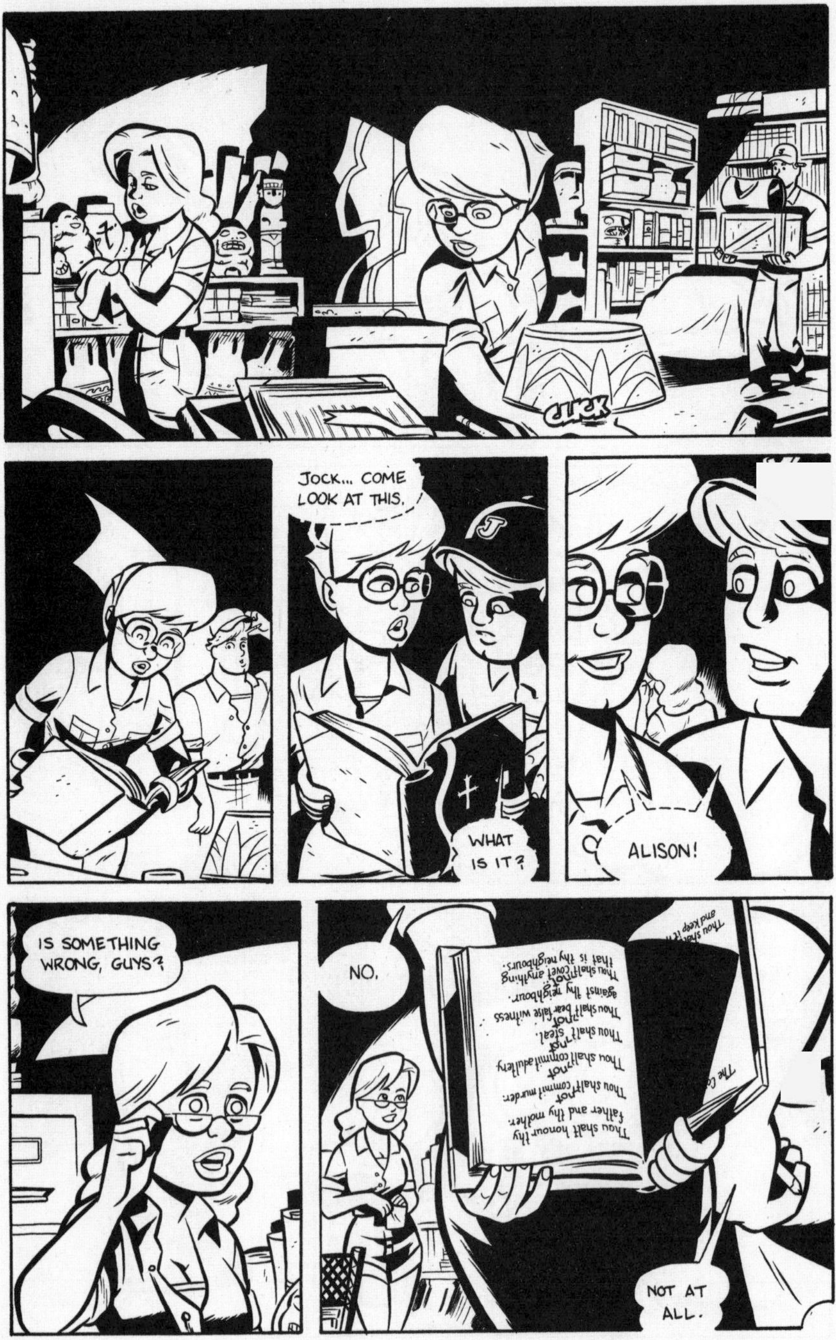
CLICK
JOCK... COME LOOK AT THIS.
WHAT IS IT?
ALISON!
IS SOMETHING WRONG, GUYS?
NO.
Thou shalt honour thy father and thy mother.
Thou shalt not commit murder.
Thou shalt not commit adultery.
Thou shalt not steal.
Thou shalt not bear false witness against thy neighbour.
Thou shalt not covet anything that is thy neighbours.
NOT AT ALL.

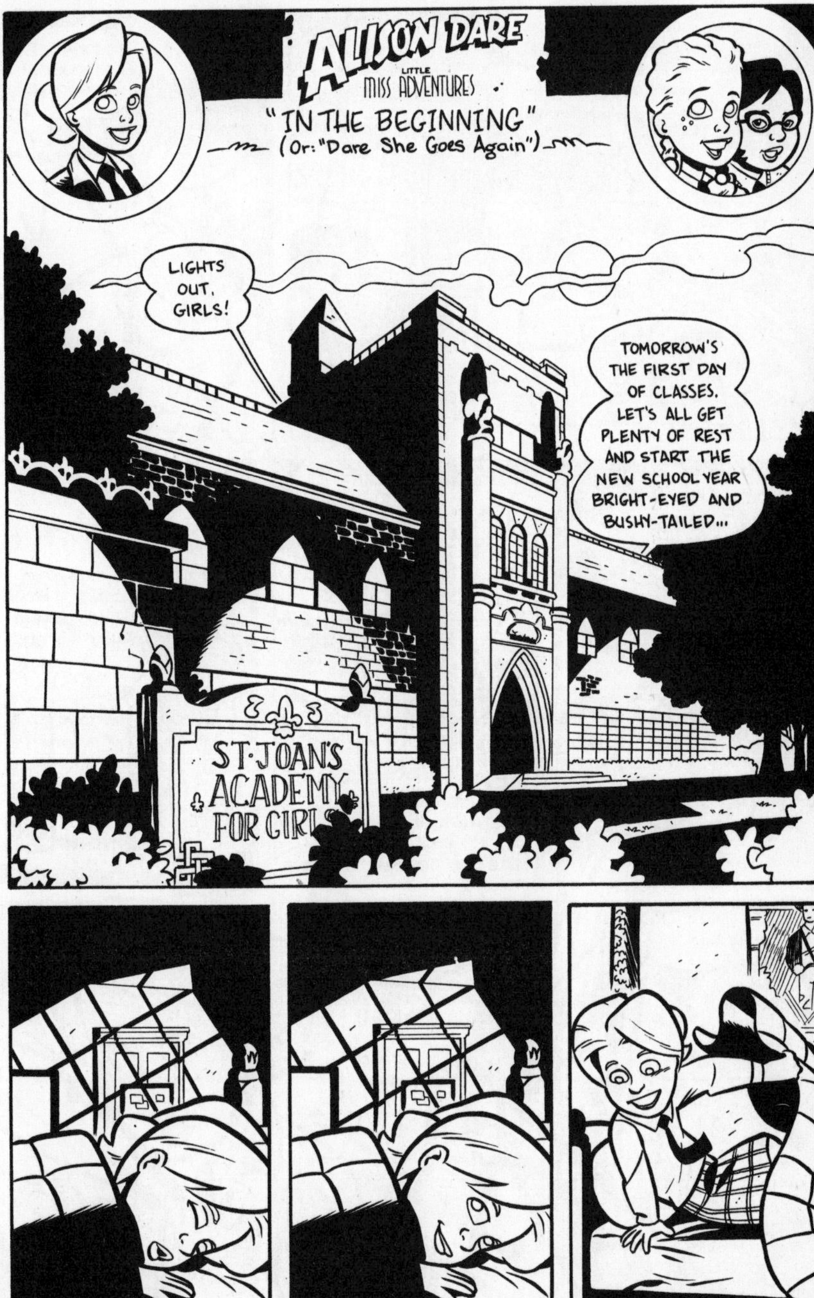
ALISON DARE
LITTLE MISS ADVENTURES
"IN THE BEGINNING"
(Or: "Dare She Goes Again")
LIGHTS OUT, GIRLS!
TOMORROW'S THE FIRST DAY OF CLASSES. LET'S ALL GET PLENTY OF REST AND START THE NEW SCHOOL YEAR BRIGHT-EYED AND BUSHY-TAILED...
ST. JOAN'S ACADEMY FOR GIRLS

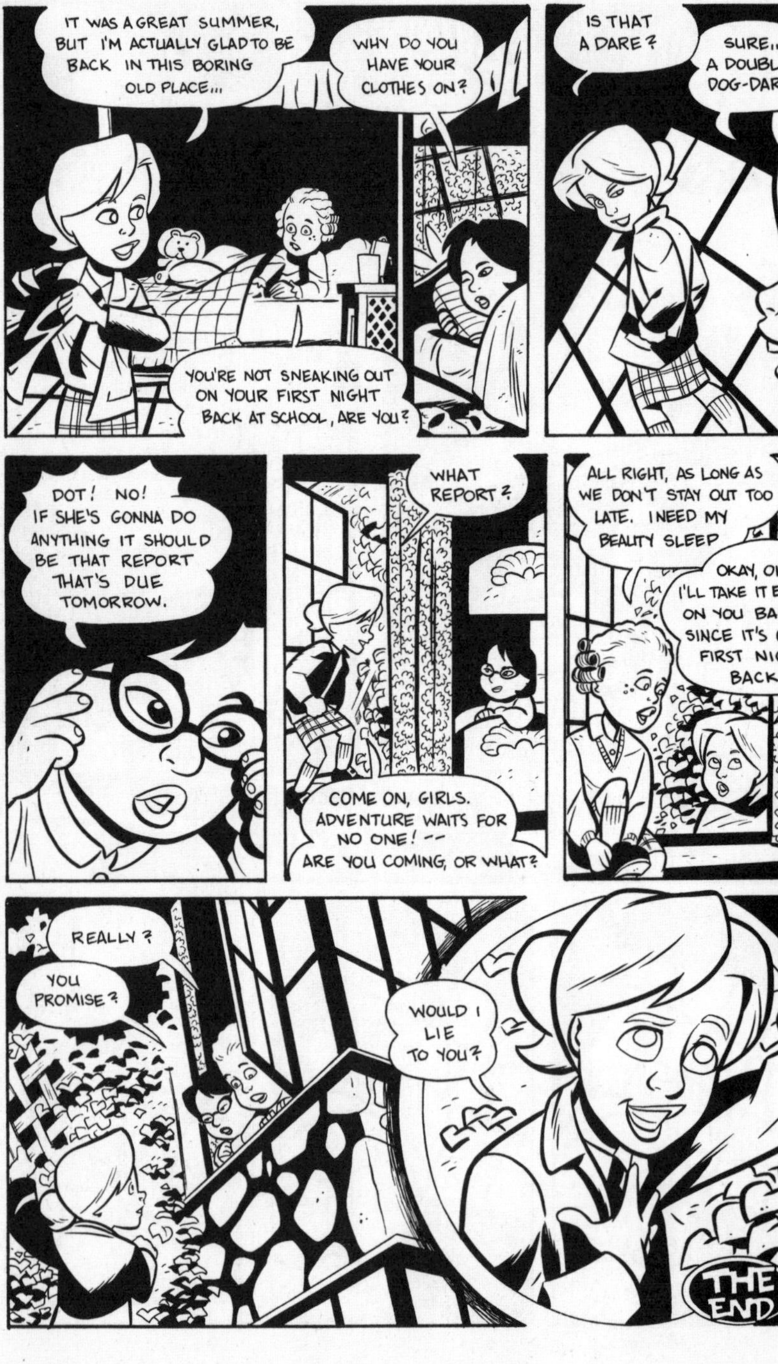
IT WAS A GREAT SUMMER, BUT I'M ACTUALLY GLAD TO BE BACK IN THIS BORING OLD PLACE...
WHY DO YOU HAVE YOUR CLOTHES ON?
YOU'RE NOT SNEAKING OUT ON YOUR FIRST NIGHT BACK AT SCHOOL, ARE YOU?
IS THAT A DARE?
SURE... A DOUBLE-DOG-DARE!
DOT! NO! IF SHE'S GONNA DO ANYTHING IT SHOULD BE THAT REPORT THAT'S DUE TOMORROW.
WHAT REPORT?
COME ON, GIRLS. ADVENTURE WAITS FOR NO ONE! -- ARE YOU COMING, OR WHAT?
ALL RIGHT, AS LONG AS WE DON'T STAY OUT TOO LATE. I NEED MY BEAUTY SLEEP
OKAY, OKAY. I'LL TAKE IT EASY ON YOU BABIES SINCE IT'S OUR FIRST NIGHT BACK.
REALLY?
YOU PROMISE?
WOULD I LIE TO YOU?
THE END

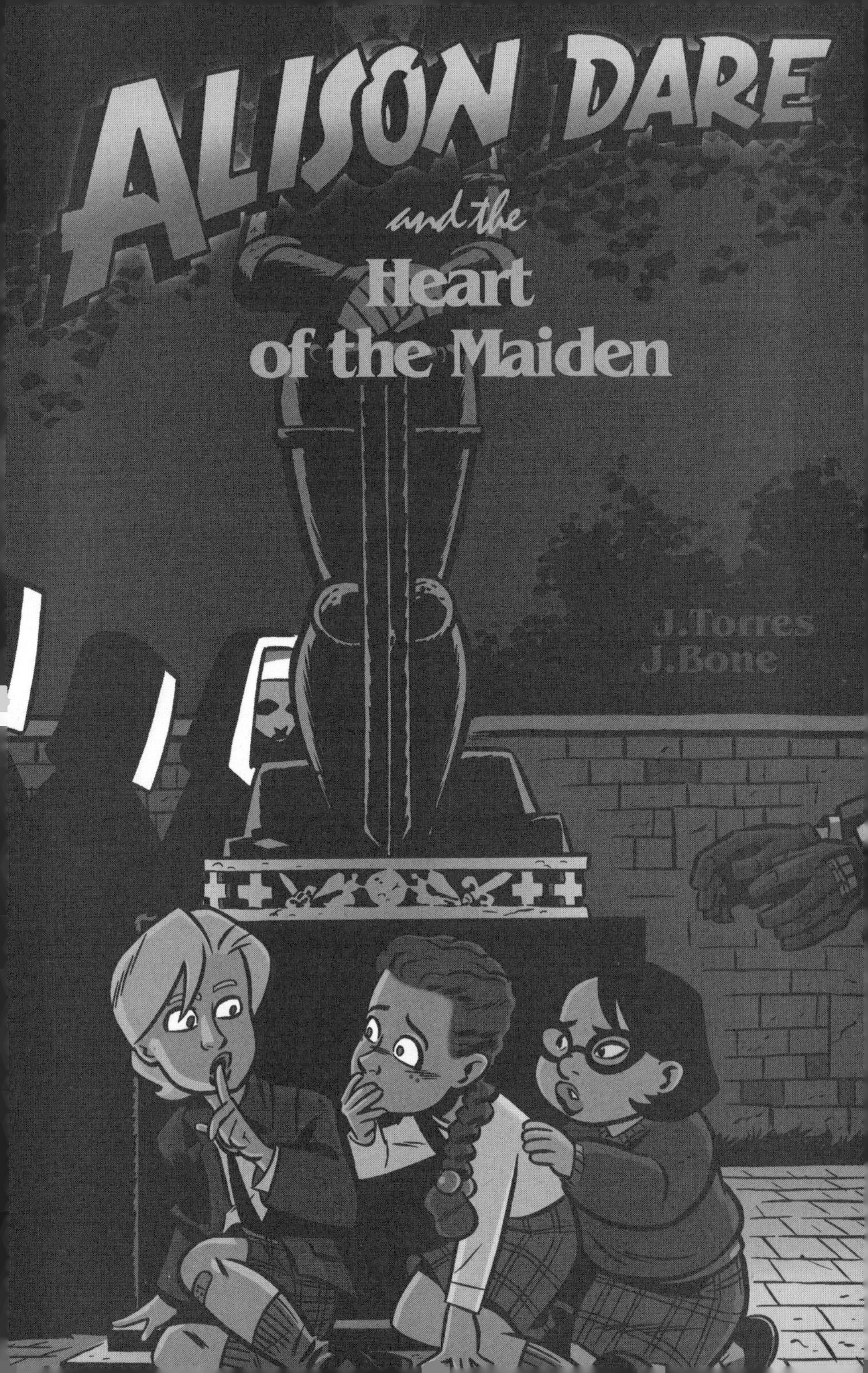
ALISON DARE
and the
Heart of the Maiden
J.Torres
J.Bone

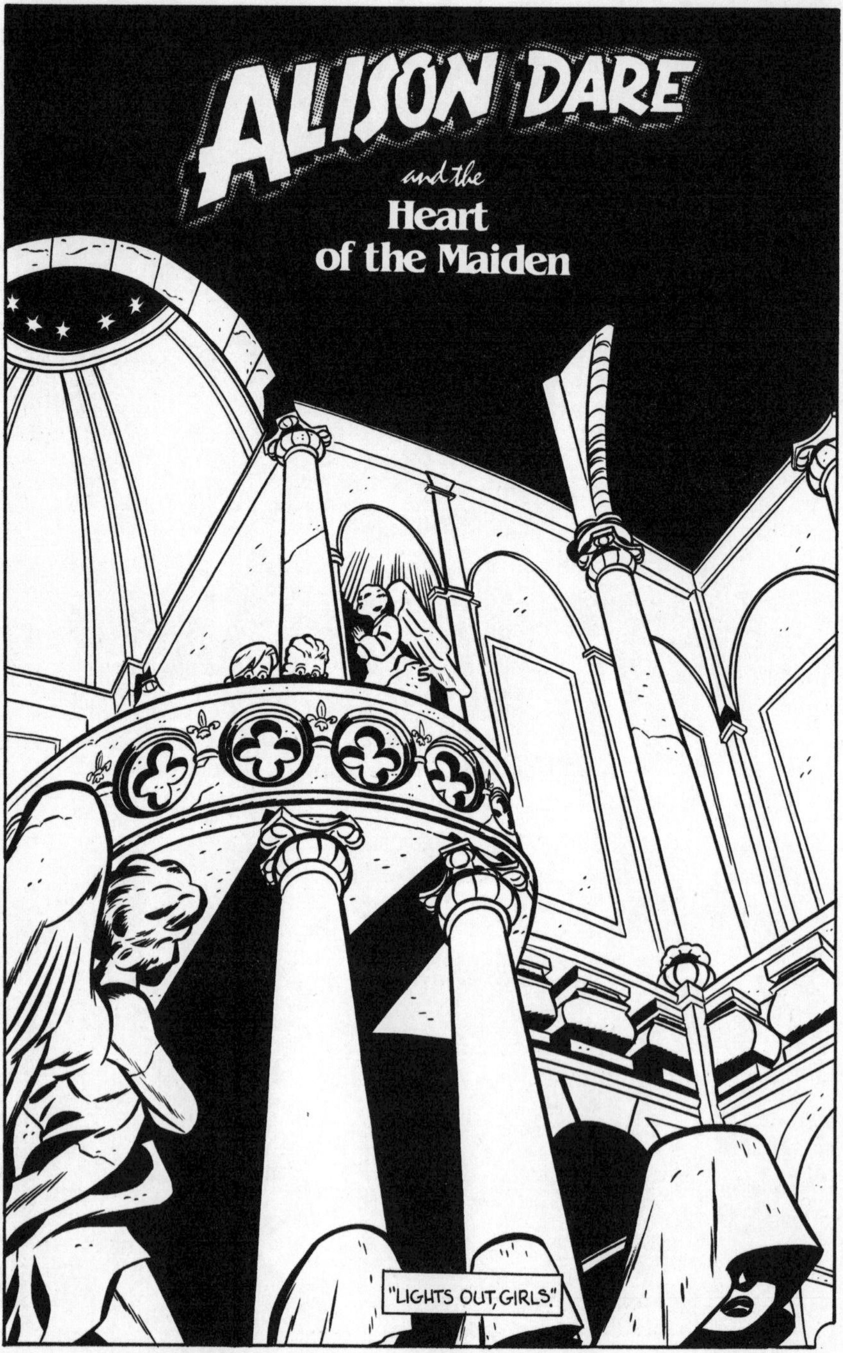
ALISON DARE
and the
Heart
of the Maiden
"LIGHTS OUT, GIRLS."

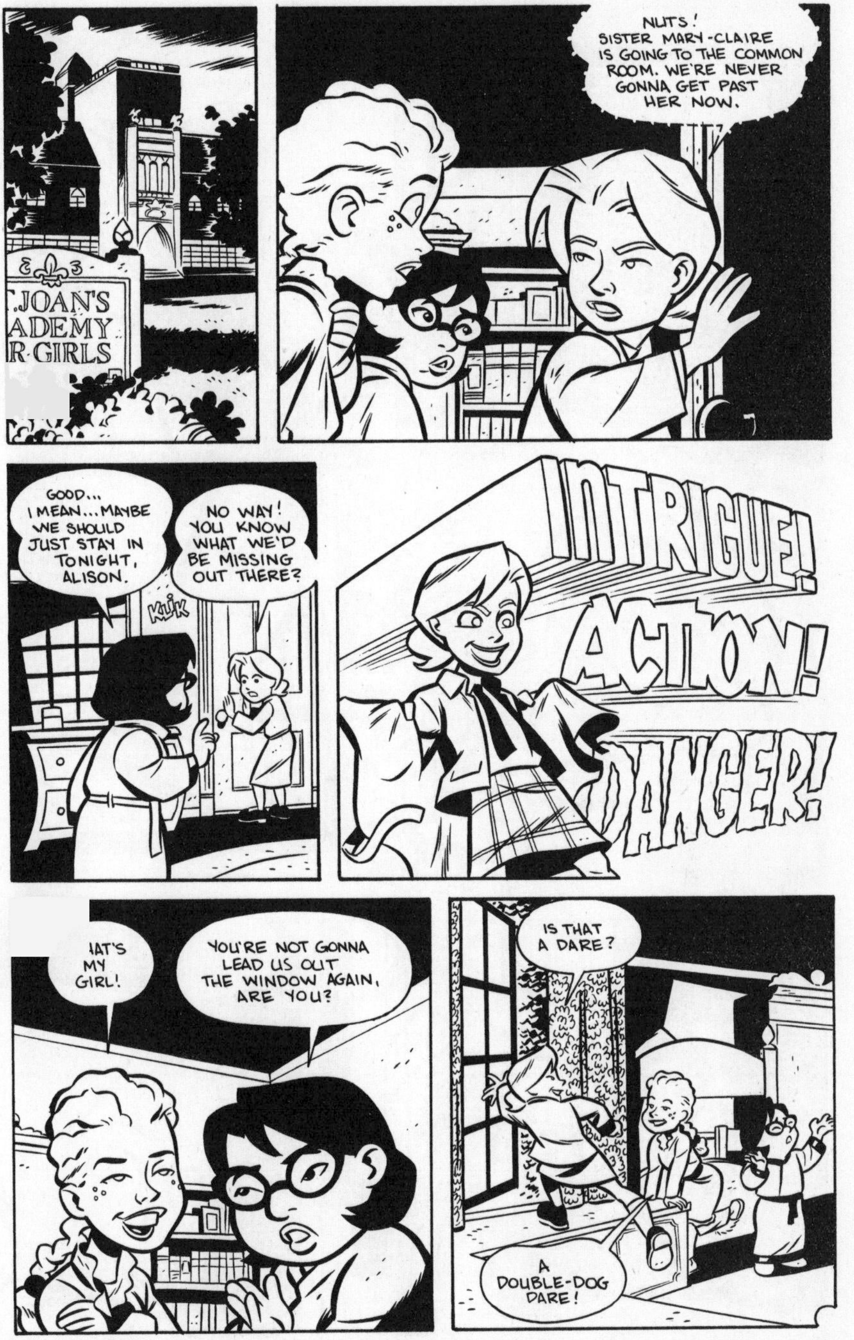

T.JOAN'S
ADEMY
R-GIRLS
NUTS! SISTER MARY-CLAIRE IS GOING TO THE COMMON ROOM. WE'RE NEVER GONNA GET PAST HER NOW.
GOOD... I MEAN... MAYBE WE SHOULD JUST STAY IN TONIGHT, ALISON.
KLIK
NO WAY! YOU KNOW WHAT WE'D BE MISSING OUT THERE?
INTRIGUE!
ACTION!
DANGER!
HAT'S MY GIRL!
YOU'RE NOT GONNA LEAD US OUT THE WINDOW AGAIN, ARE YOU?
IS THAT A DARE?
A DOUBLE-DOG DARE!

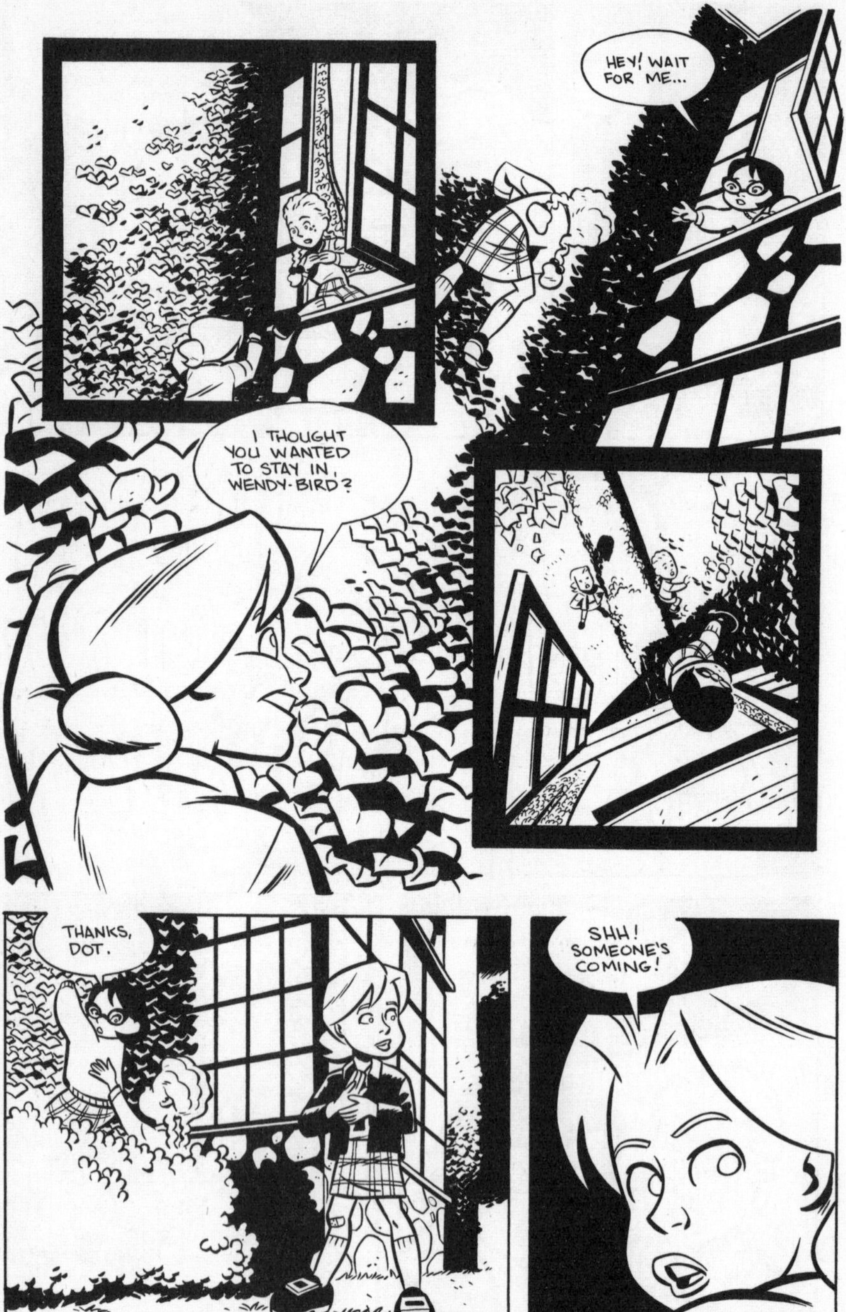
HEY! WAIT FOR ME...
I THOUGHT YOU WANTED TO STAY IN, WENDY-BIRD?
THANKS, DOT.
SHH! SOMEONE'S COMING!

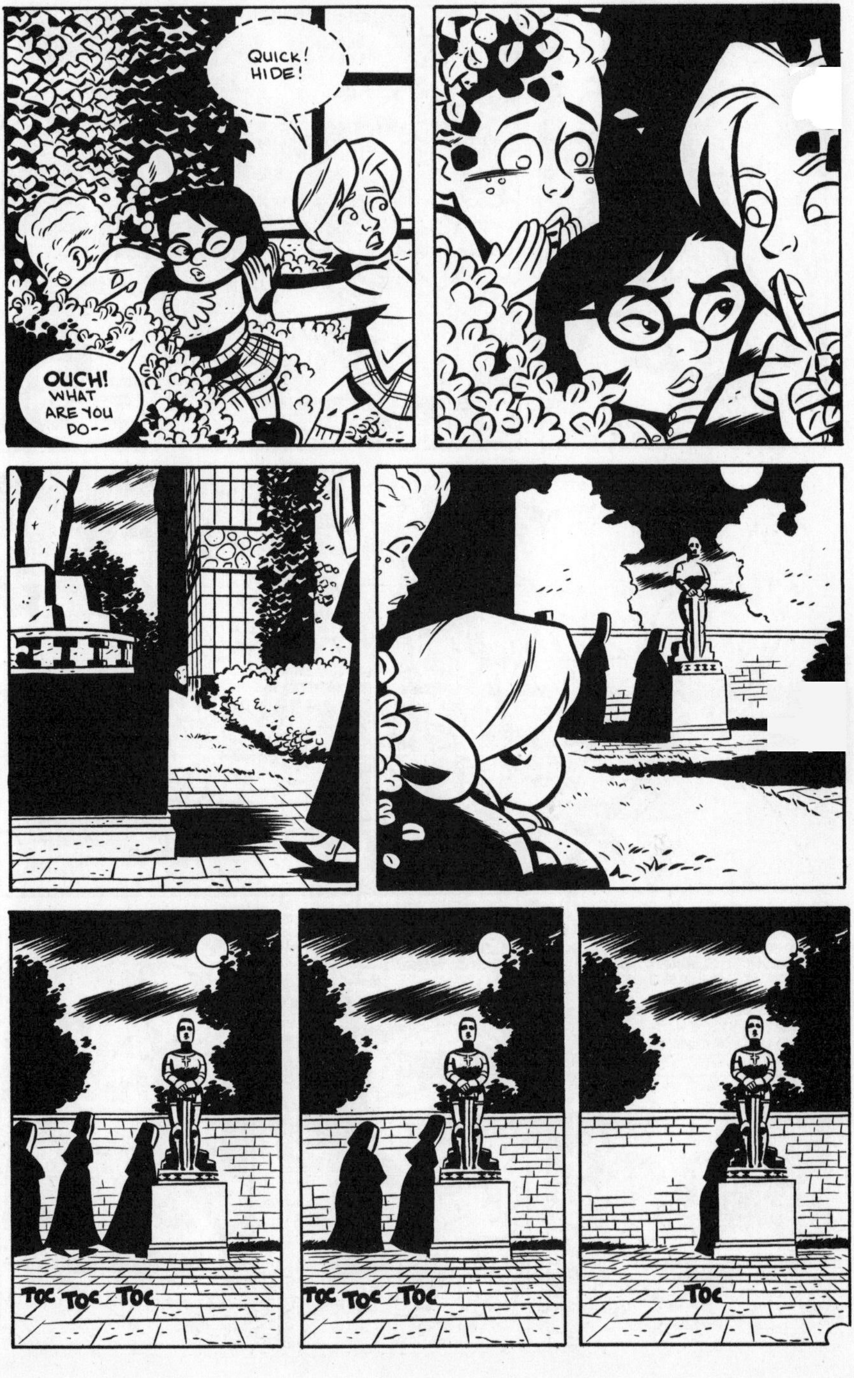

QUICK! HIDE!
OUCH! WHAT ARE YOU DO--
TOC TOC TOC
TOC TOC TOC
TOC

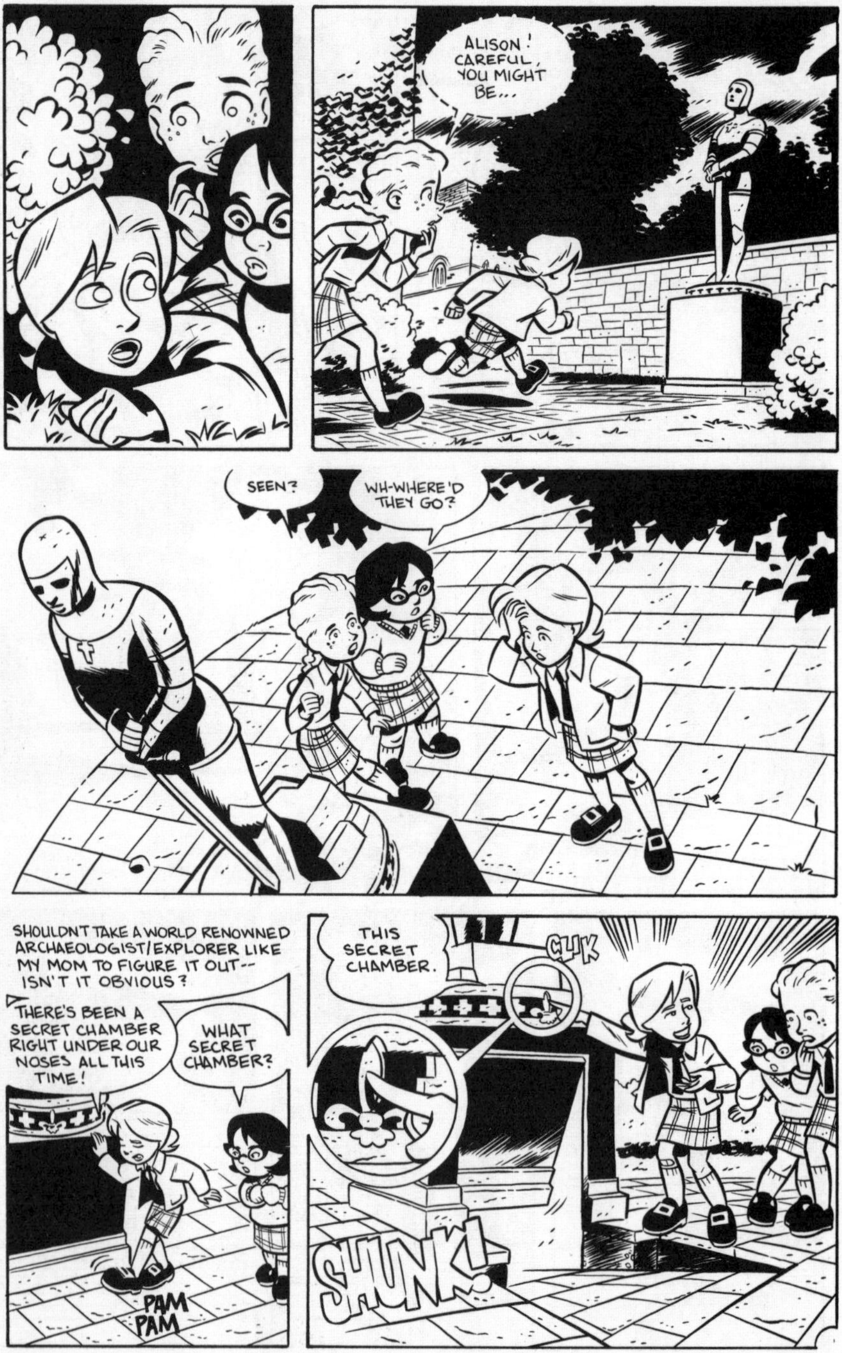
ALISON! CAREFUL, YOU MIGHT BE...
SEEN?
WH-WHERE'D THEY GO?
SHOULDN'T TAKE A WORLD RENOWNED ARCHAEOLOGIST/EXPLORER LIKE MY MOM TO FIGURE IT OUT-- ISN'T IT OBVIOUS?
THERE'S BEEN A SECRET CHAMBER RIGHT UNDER OUR NOSES ALL THIS TIME!
WHAT SECRET CHAMBER?
PAM PAM
THIS SECRET CHAMBER.
CLIK
SHUNK!

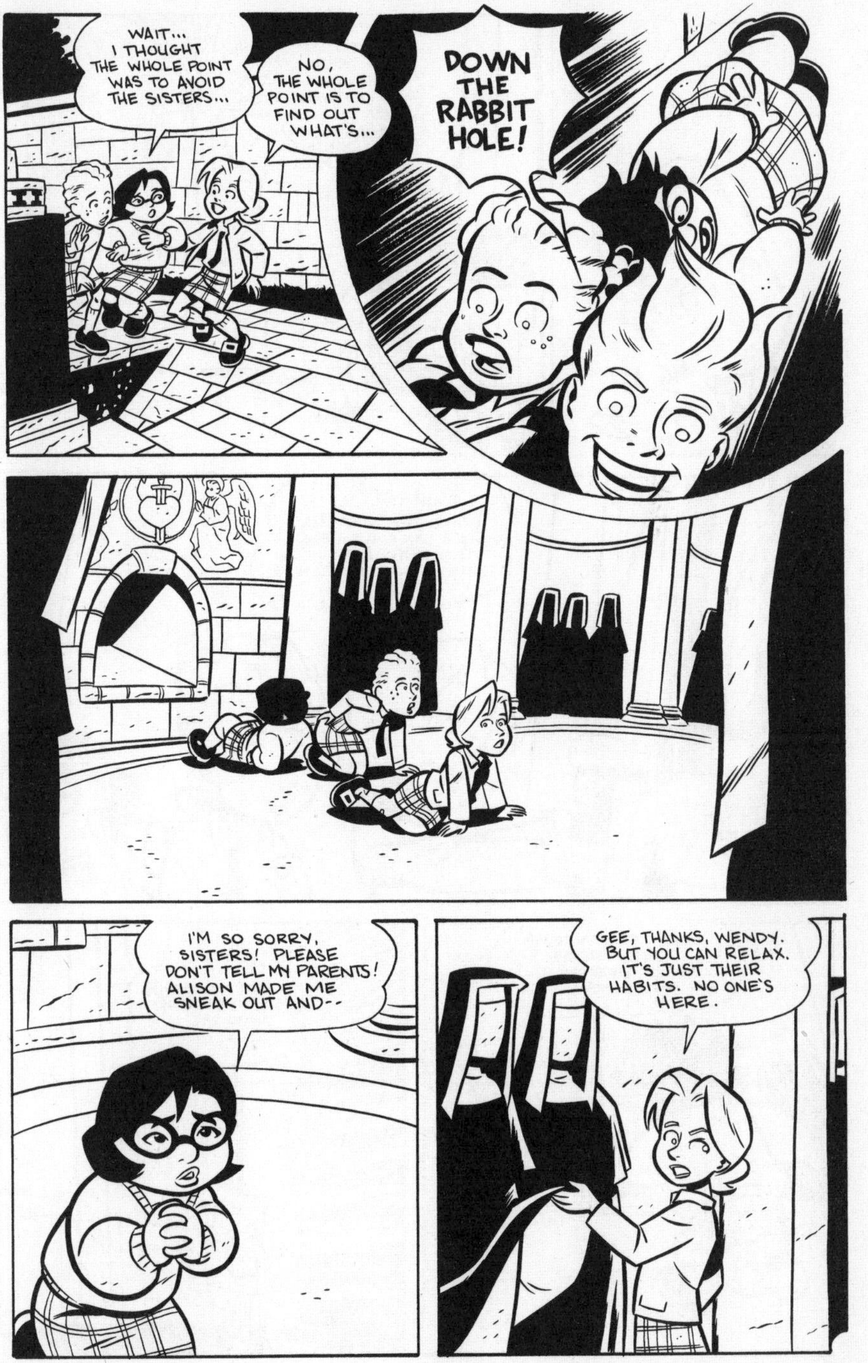
WAIT... I THOUGHT THE WHOLE POINT WAS TO AVOID THE SISTERS...
NO, THE WHOLE POINT IS TO FIND OUT WHAT'S...
DOWN THE RABBIT HOLE!
I'M SO SORRY, SISTERS! PLEASE DON'T TELL MY PARENTS! ALISON MADE ME SNEAK OUT AND--
GEE, THANKS, WENDY. BUT YOU CAN RELAX. IT'S JUST THEIR HABITS. NO ONE'S HERE.

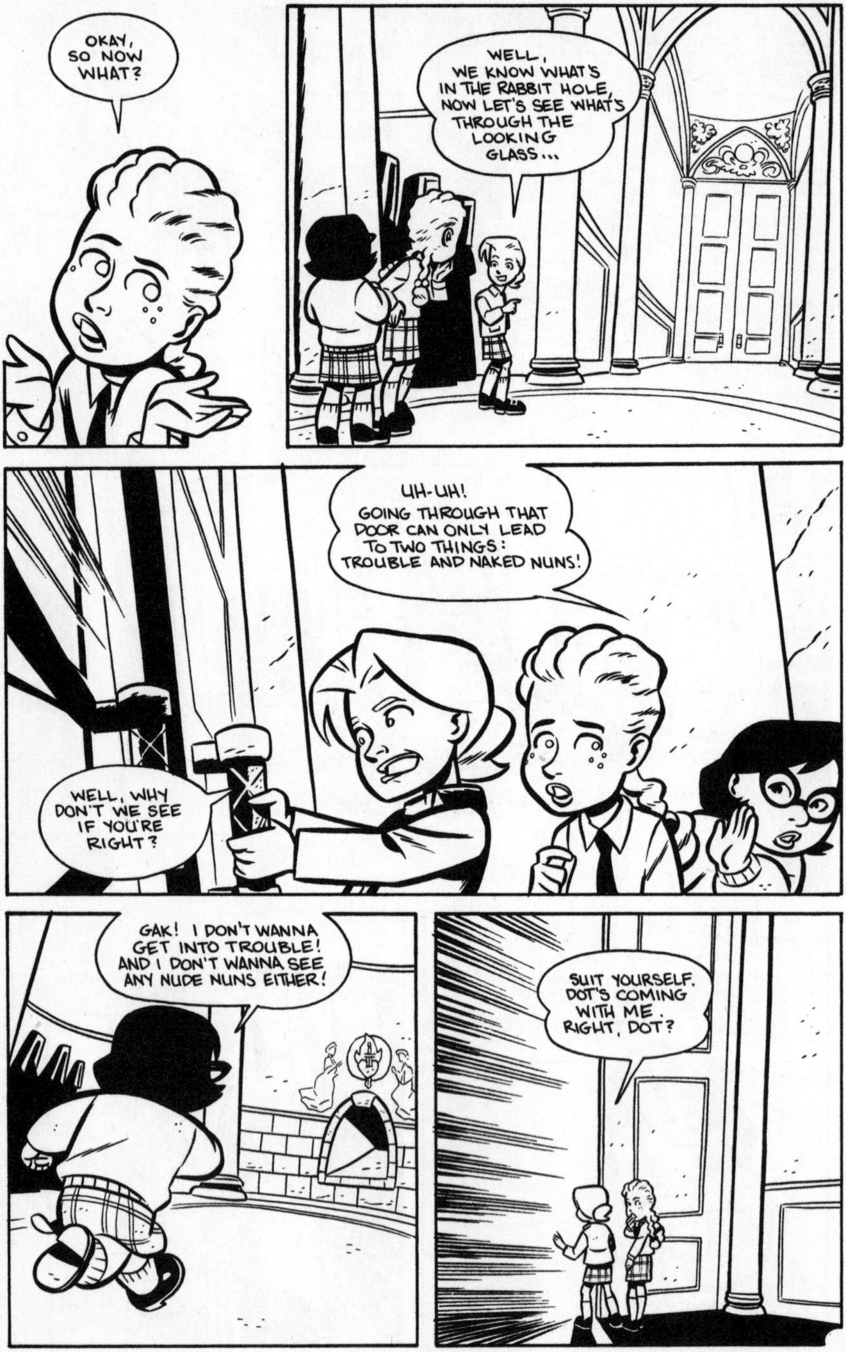
OKAY, SO NOW WHAT?
WELL, WE KNOW WHAT'S IN THE RABBIT HOLE, NOW LET'S SEE WHAT'S THROUGH THE LOOKING GLASS...
UH-UH! GOING THROUGH THAT DOOR CAN ONLY LEAD TO TWO THINGS: TROUBLE AND NAKED NUNS!
WELL, WHY DON'T WE SEE IF YOU'RE RIGHT?
GAK! I DON'T WANNA GET INTO TROUBLE! AND I DON'T WANNA SEE ANY NUDE NUNS EITHER!
SUIT YOURSELF. DOT'S COMING WITH ME. RIGHT, DOT?

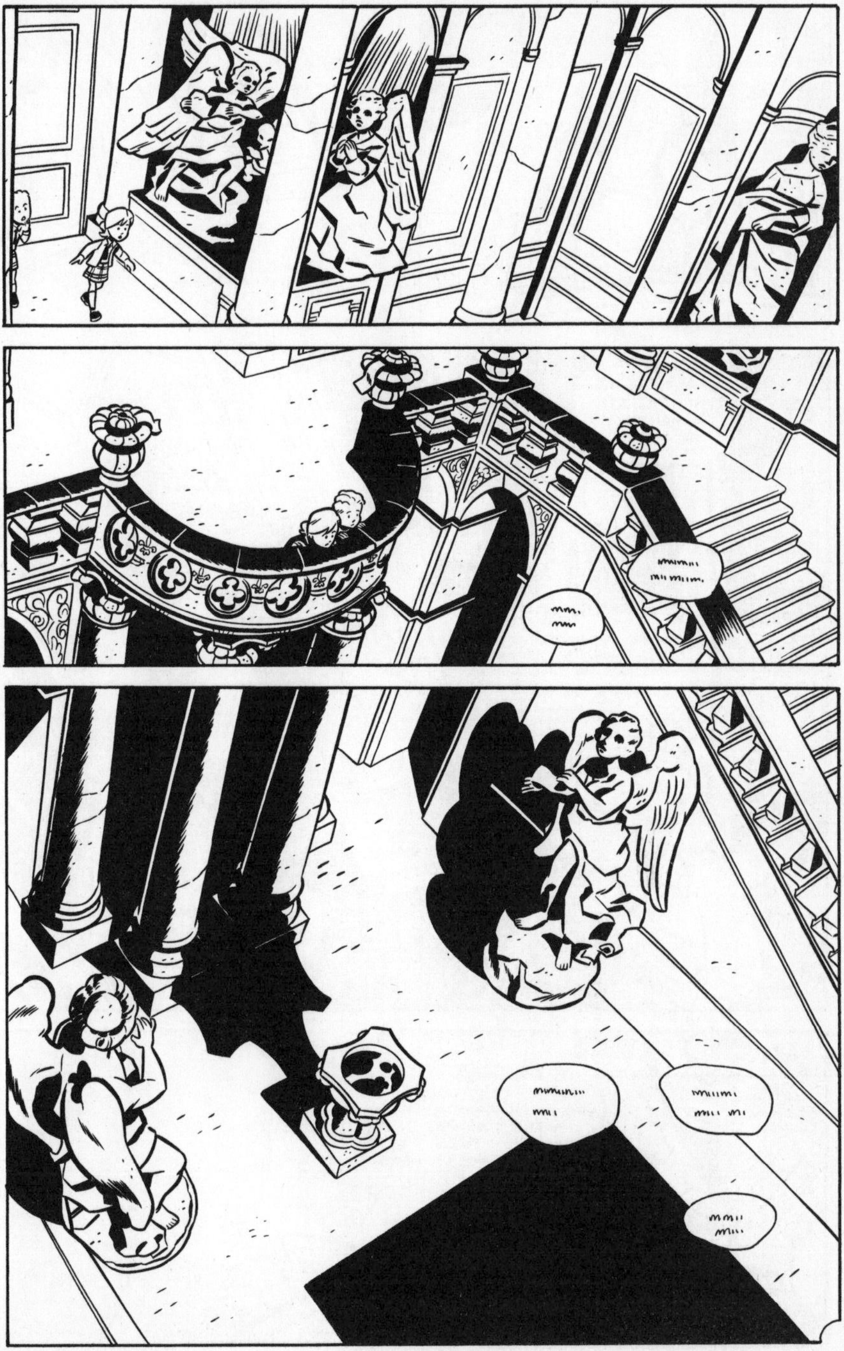

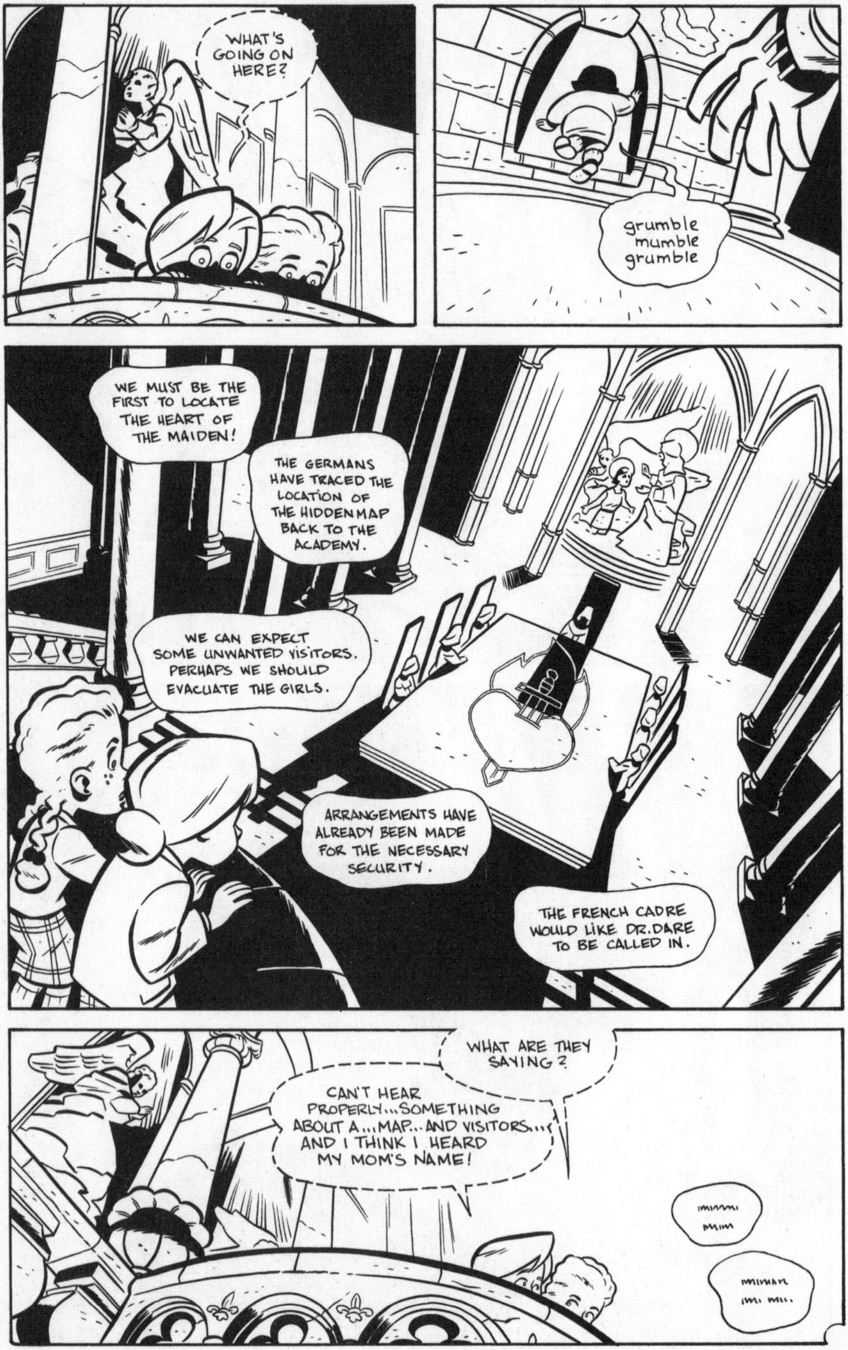
WHAT'S GOING ON HERE?
grumble mumble grumble
WE MUST BE THE FIRST TO LOCATE THE HEART OF THE MAIDEN!
THE GERMANS HAVE TRACED THE LOCATION OF THE HIDDEN MAP BACK TO THE ACADEMY.
WE CAN EXPECT SOME UNWANTED VISITORS. PERHAPS WE SHOULD EVACUATE THE GIRLS.
ARRANGEMENTS HAVE ALREADY BEEN MADE FOR THE NECESSARY SECURITY.
THE FRENCH CADRE WOULD LIKE DR. DARE TO BE CALLED IN.
WHAT ARE THEY SAYING?
CAN'T HEAR PROPERLY...SOMETHING ABOUT A...MAP...AND VISITORS... AND I THINK I HEARD MY MOM'S NAME!

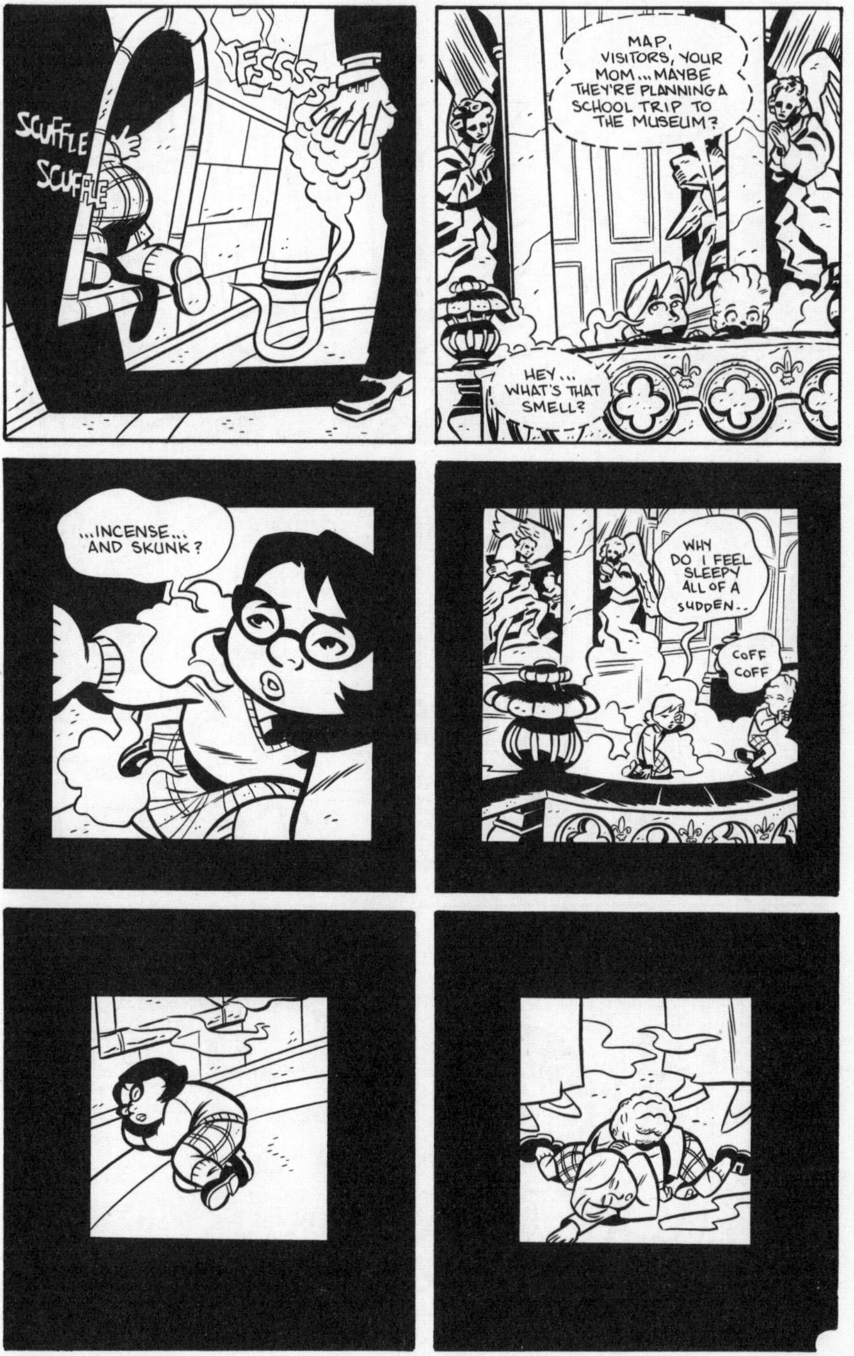
FSSSSS
SCUFFLE
SCUFFLE
MAP, VISITORS, YOUR MOM... MAYBE THEY'RE PLANNING A SCHOOL TRIP TO THE MUSEUM?
HEY... WHAT'S THAT SMELL?
...INCENSE... AND SKUNK?
WHY DO I FEEL SLEEPY ALL OF A SUDDEN..
COFF COFF

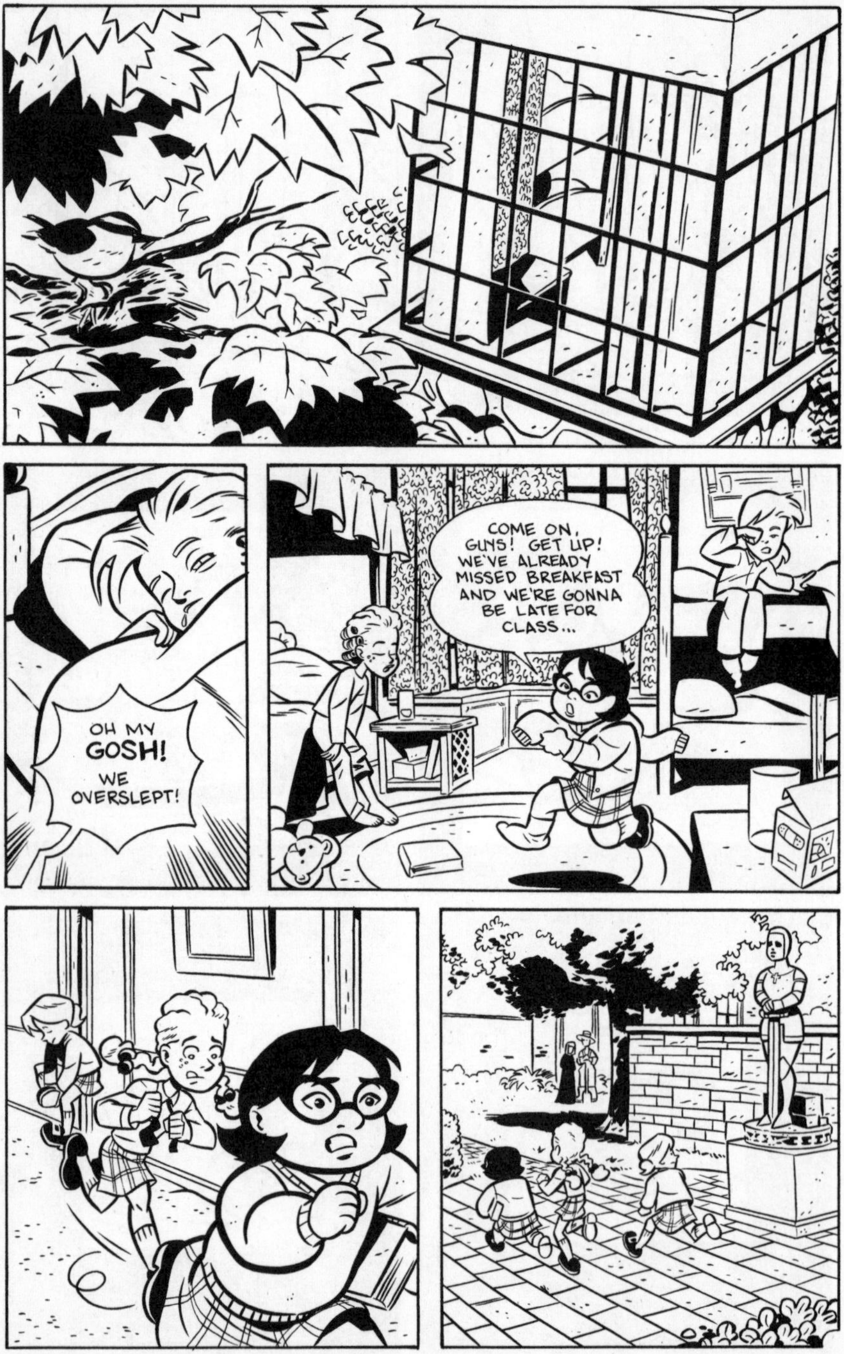
OH MY GOSH! WE OVERSLEPT!
COME ON, GUYS! GET UP! WE'VE ALREADY MISSED BREAKFAST AND WE'RE GONNA BE LATE FOR CLASS...

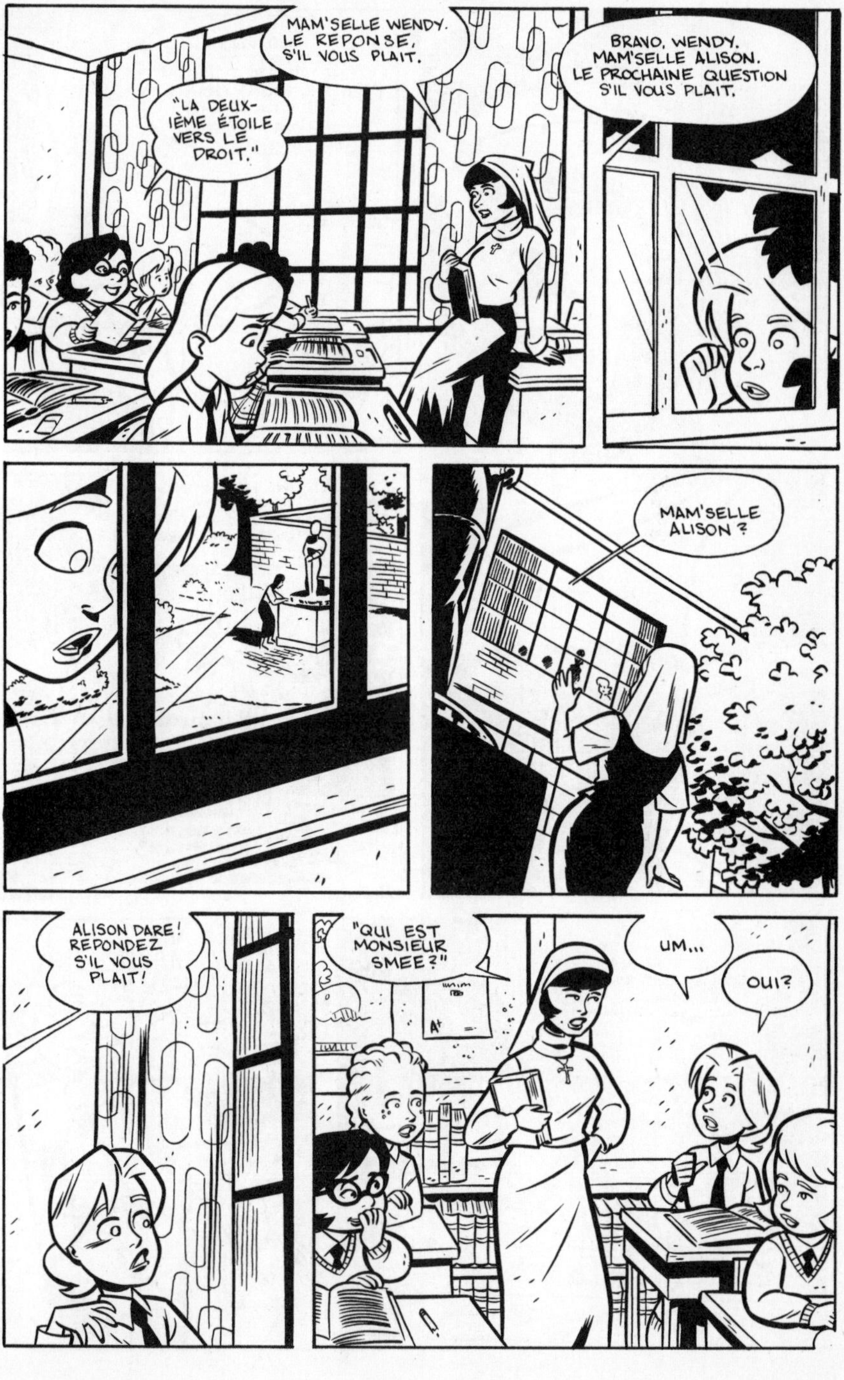
MAM'SELLE WENDY. LE REPONSE, S'IL VOUS PLAIT.
"LA DEUXIÈME ÉTOILE VERS LE DROIT."
BRAVO, WENDY. MAM'SELLE ALISON. LE PROCHAINE QUESTION S'IL VOUS PLAIT.
MAM'SELLE ALISON?
ALISON DARE! REPONDEZ S'IL VOUS PLAIT!
"QUI EST MONSIEUR SMEE?"
UM...
OUI?

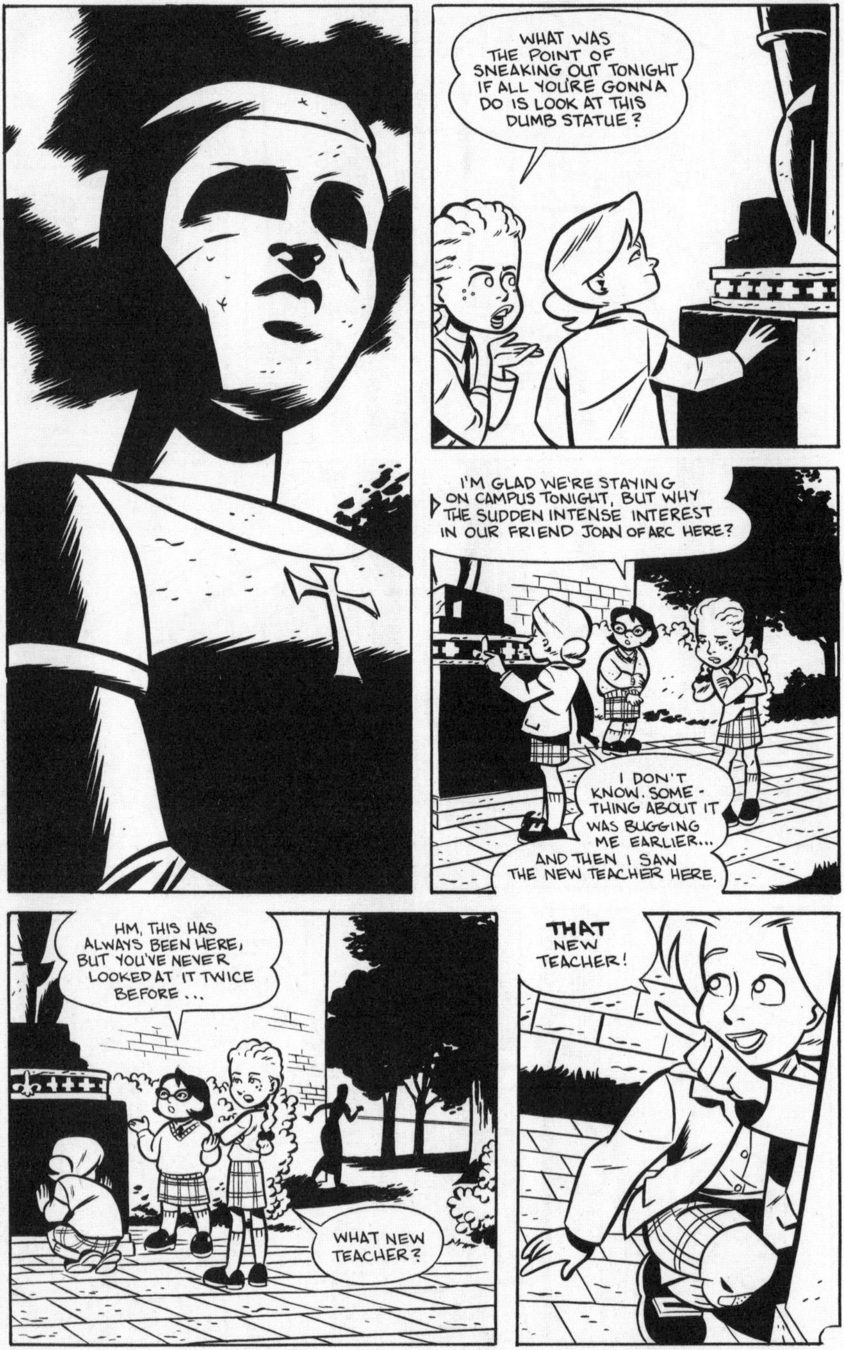

WHAT WAS THE POINT OF SNEAKING OUT TONIGHT IF ALL YOU'RE GONNA DO IS LOOK AT THIS DUMB STATUE?
I'M GLAD WE'RE STAYING ON CAMPUS TONIGHT, BUT WHY THE SUDDEN INTENSE INTEREST IN OUR FRIEND JOAN OF ARC HERE?
I DON'T KNOW. SOME-THING ABOUT IT WAS BUGGING ME EARLIER...
AND THEN I SAW THE NEW TEACHER HERE.
HM, THIS HAS ALWAYS BEEN HERE, BUT YOU'VE NEVER LOOKED AT IT TWICE BEFORE...
WHAT NEW TEACHER?
THAT NEW TEACHER!

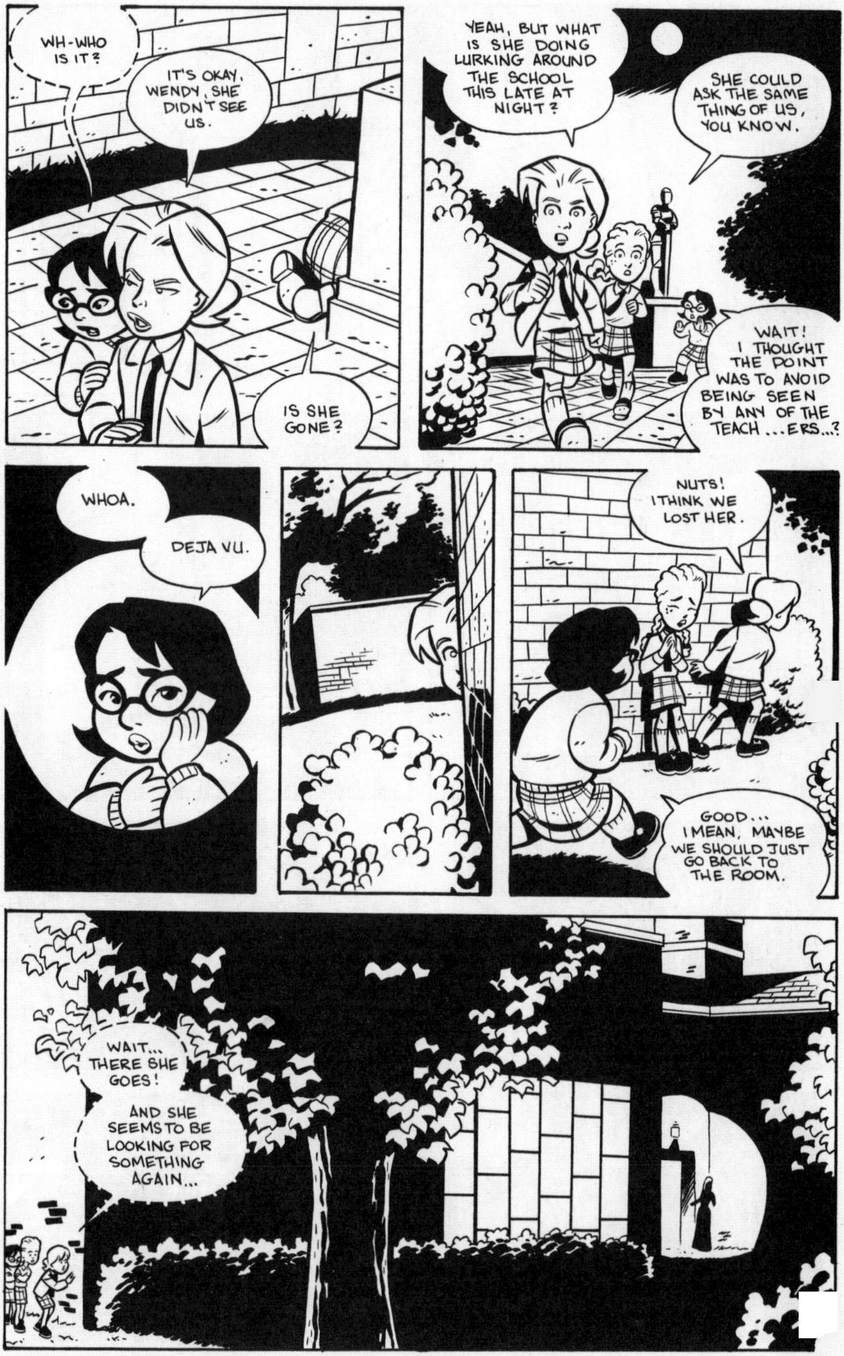
WH-WHO IS IT?
IT'S OKAY, WENDY, SHE DIDN'T SEE US.
IS SHE GONE?
YEAH, BUT WHAT IS SHE DOING LURKING AROUND THE SCHOOL THIS LATE AT NIGHT?
SHE COULD ASK THE SAME THING OF US, YOU KNOW.
WAIT! I THOUGHT THE POINT WAS TO AVOID BEING SEEN BY ANY OF THE TEACH...ERS...?
WHOA.
DEJA VU.
NUTS! I THINK WE LOST HER.
GOOD... I MEAN, MAYBE WE SHOULD JUST GO BACK TO THE ROOM.
WAIT... THERE SHE GOES!
AND SHE SEEMS TO BE LOOKING FOR SOMETHING AGAIN...

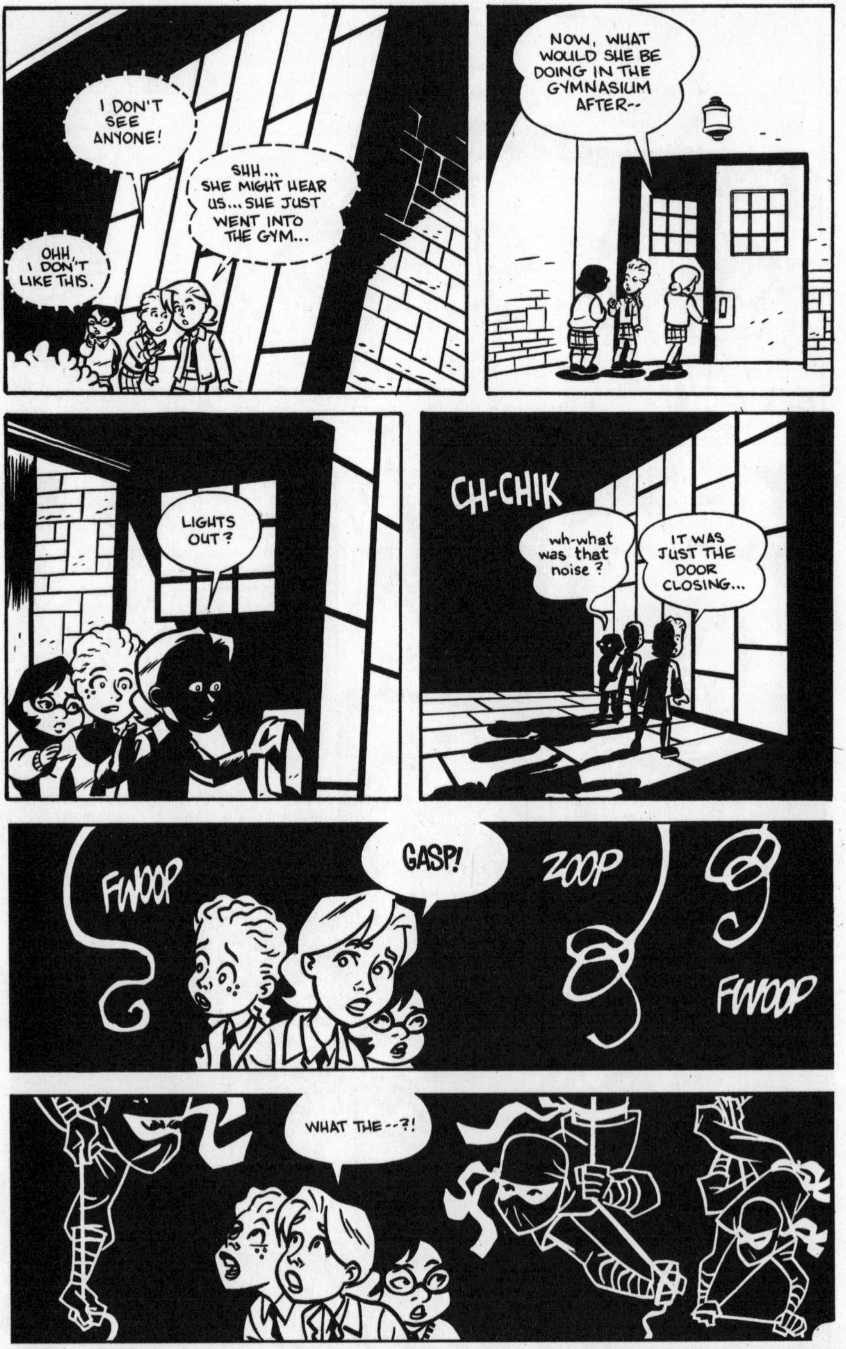
I DON'T SEE ANYONE!
SHH... SHE MIGHT HEAR US... SHE JUST WENT INTO THE GYM...
OHH, I DON'T LIKE THIS.
NOW, WHAT WOULD SHE BE DOING IN THE GYMNASIUM AFTER--
LIGHTS OUT?
CH-CHIK
wh-what was that noise?
IT WAS JUST THE DOOR CLOSING...
FWOOP
GASP!
ZOOP
FWOOP
WHAT THE--?!

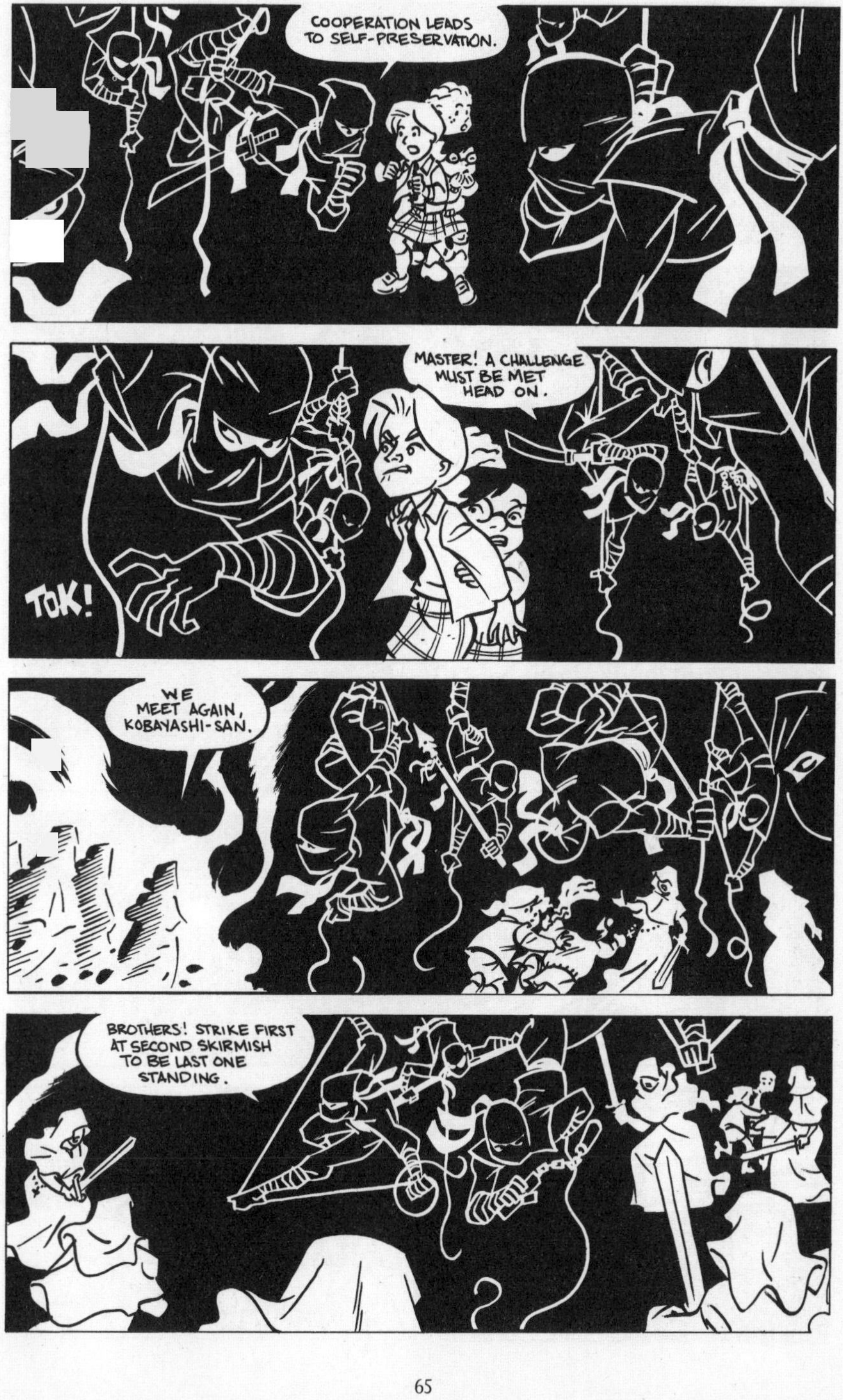
COOPERATION LEADS TO SELF-PRESERVATION.
MASTER! A CHALLENGE MUST BE MET HEAD ON.
TOK!
WE MEET AGAIN, KOBAYASHI-SAN.
BROTHERS! STRIKE FIRST AT SECOND SKIRMISH TO BE LAST ONE STANDING.

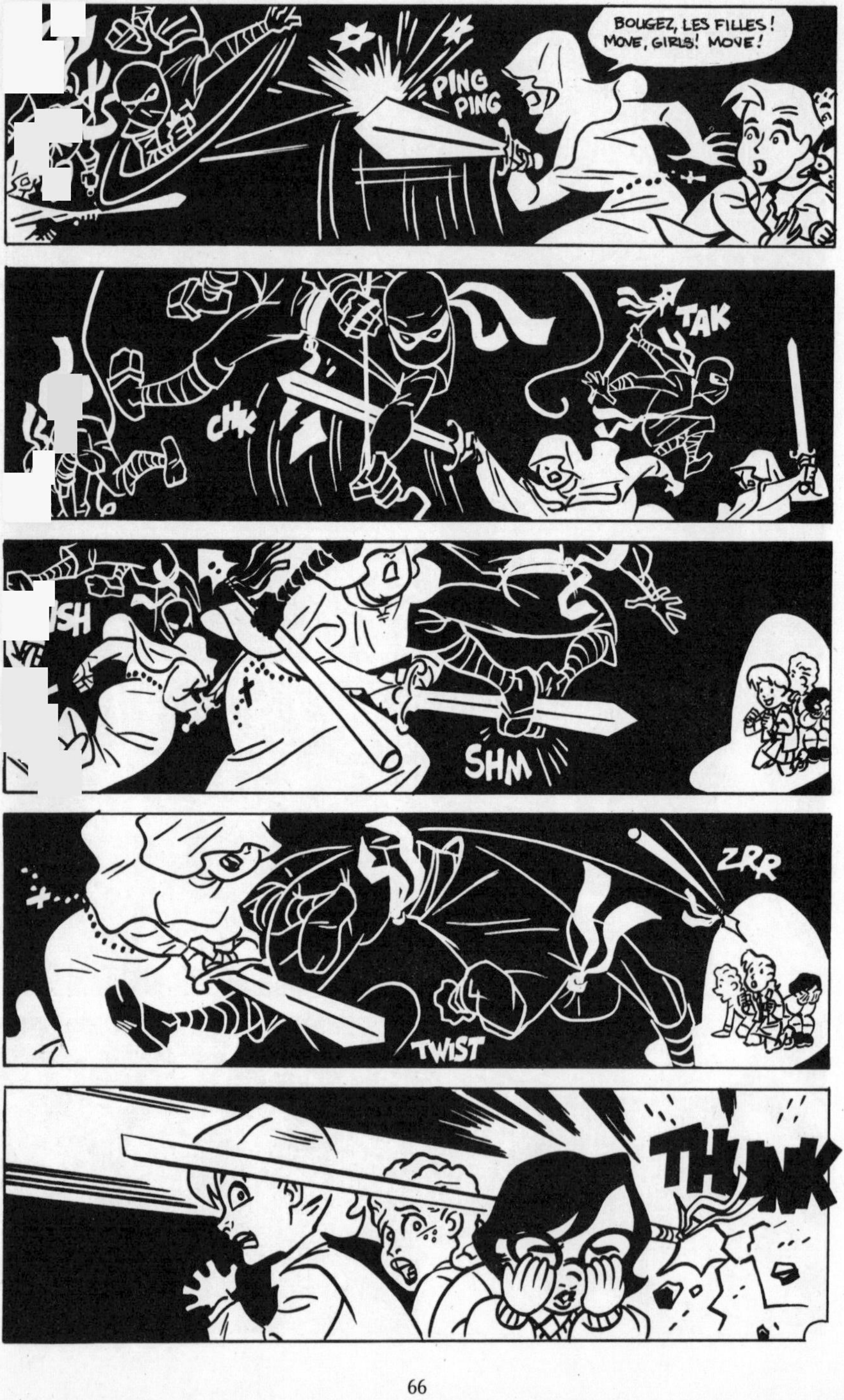
BOUGEZ, LES FILLES!
MOVE, GIRLS! MOVE!
PING
PING
TAK
CHK
SHM
ZRR
TWIST

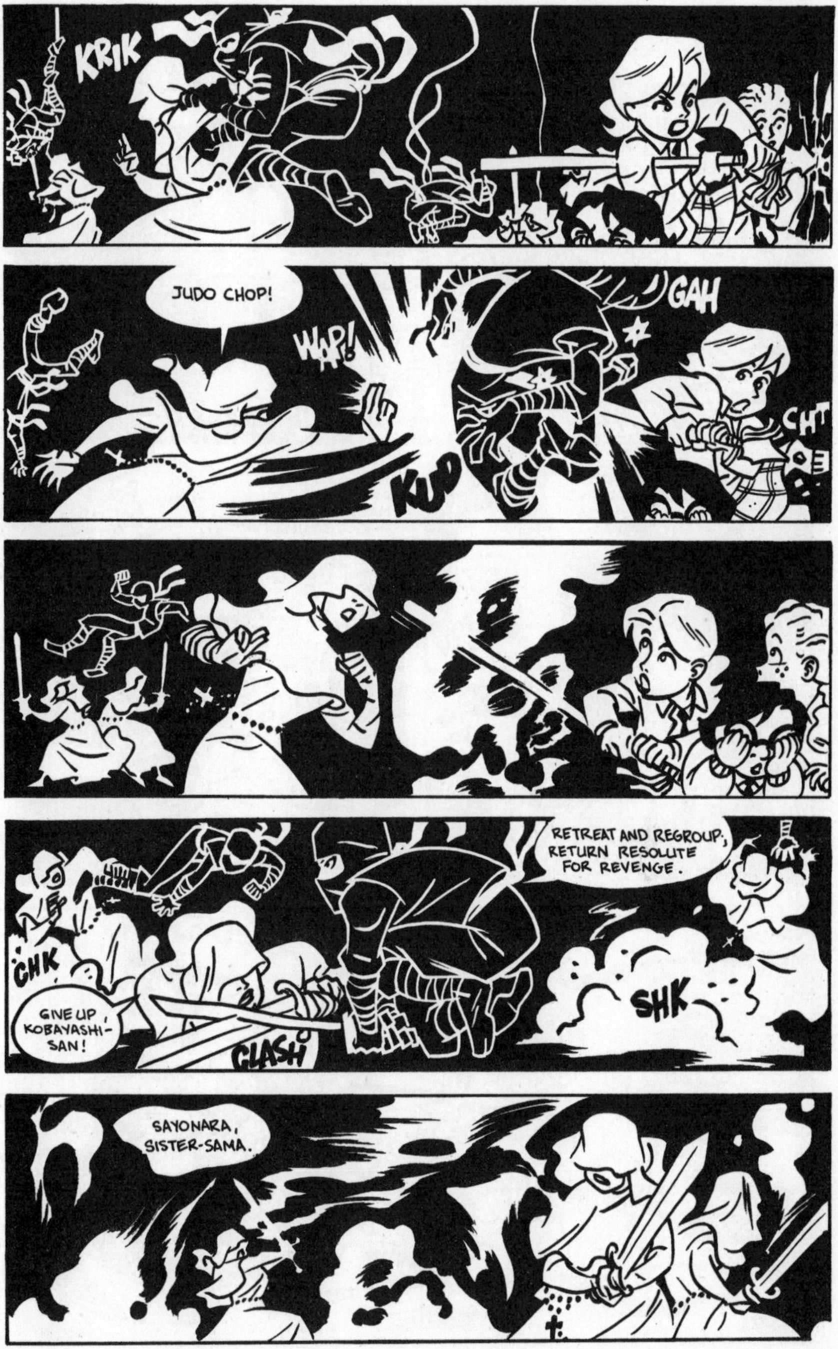
KRIK
JUDO CHOP!
WAP!
GAH
KUD
CHT
RETREAT AND REGROUP; RETURN RESOLUTE FOR REVENGE.
CHK
GIVE UP KOBAYASHI-SAN!
CLASH
SHK
SAYONARA, SISTER-SAMA.

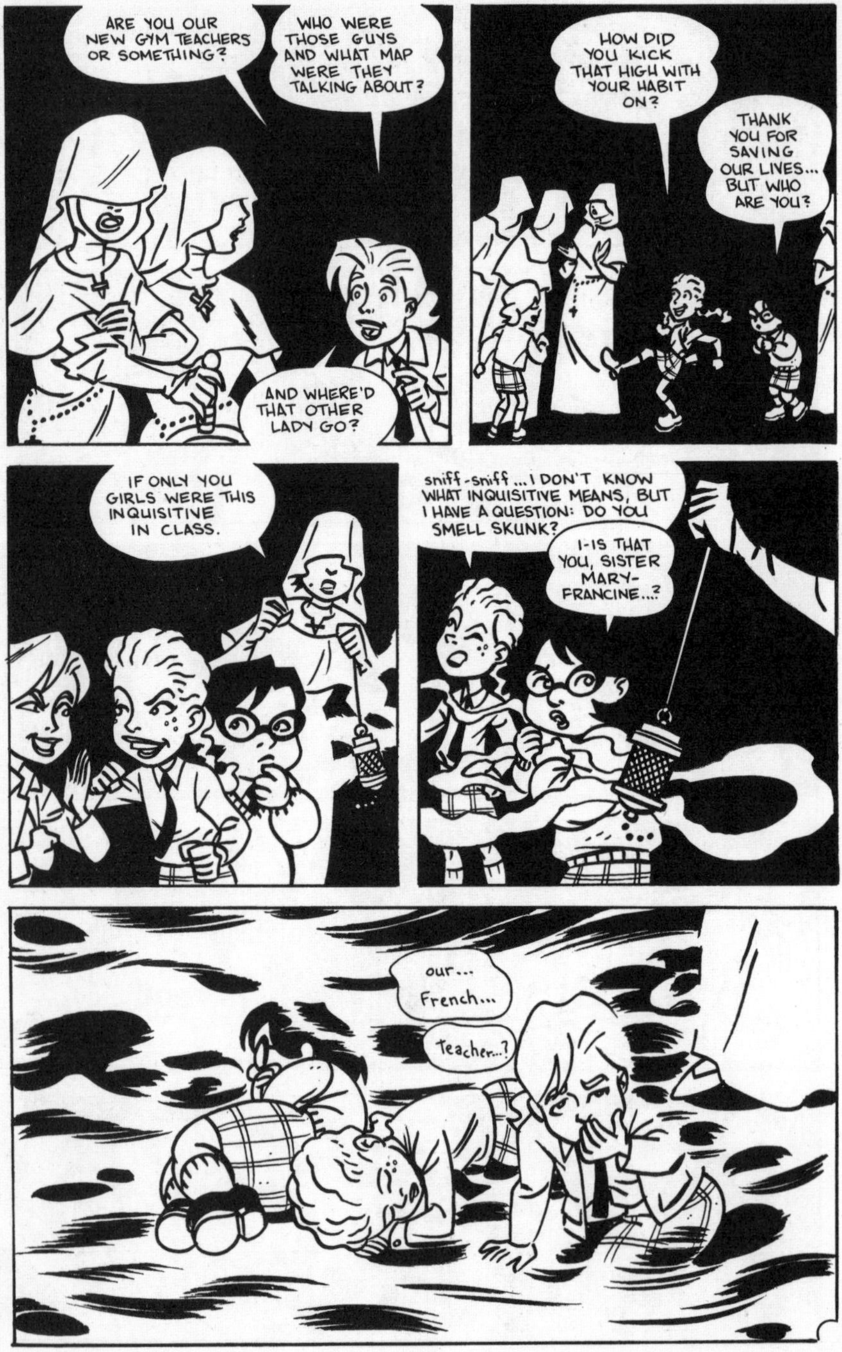

ARE YOU OUR NEW GYM TEACHERS OR SOMETHING?
WHO WERE THOSE GUYS AND WHAT MAP WERE THEY TALKING ABOUT?
AND WHERE'D THAT OTHER LADY GO?
HOW DID YOU KICK THAT HIGH WITH YOUR HABIT ON?
THANK YOU FOR SAVING OUR LIVES... BUT WHO ARE YOU?
IF ONLY YOU GIRLS WERE THIS INQUISITIVE IN CLASS.
sniff-sniff ... I DON'T KNOW WHAT INQUISITIVE MEANS, BUT I HAVE A QUESTION: DO YOU SMELL SKUNK?
I-IS THAT YOU, SISTER MARY-FRANCINE...?
our...
French...
teacher...?

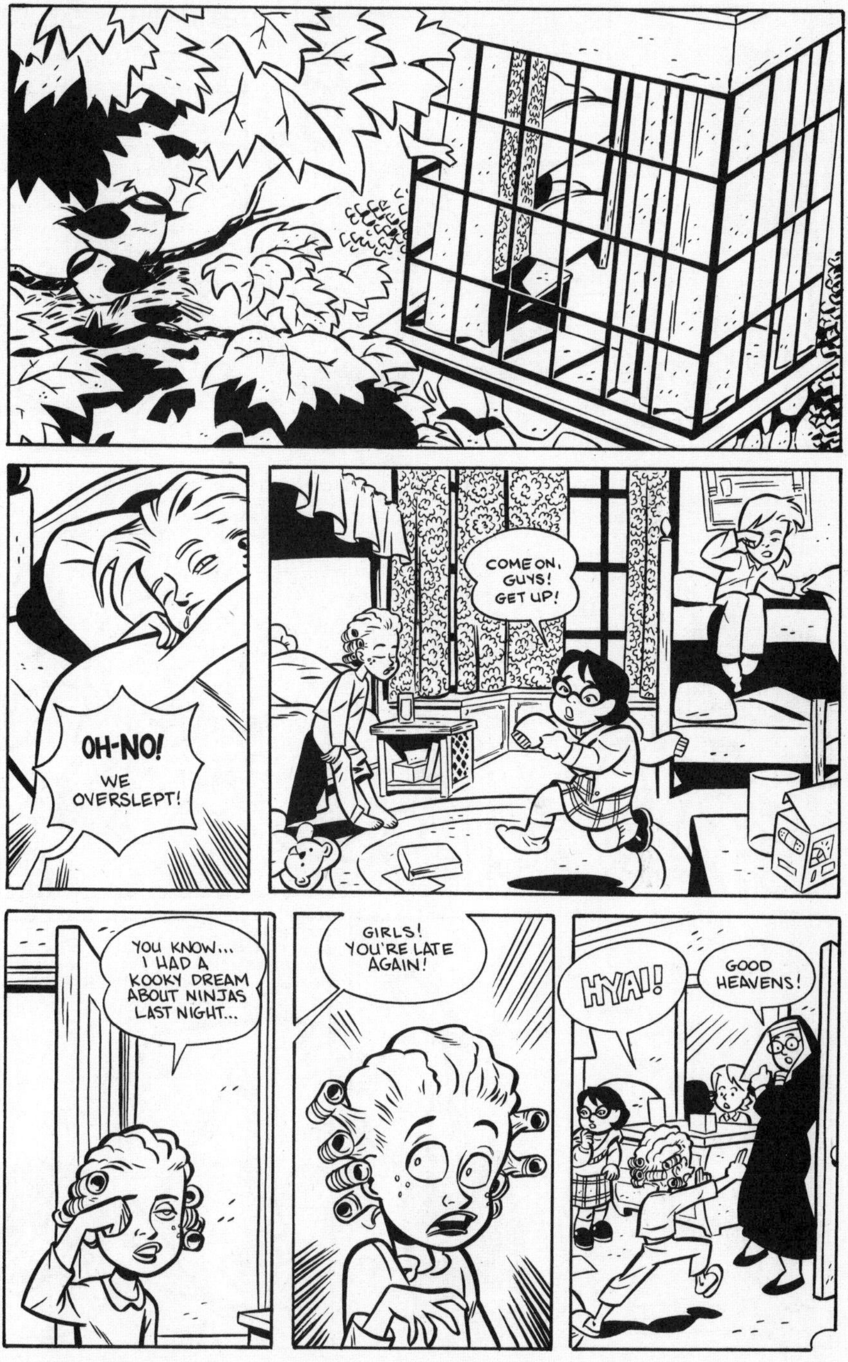
OH-NO!
WE OVERSLEPT!
COME ON, GUYS! GET UP!
YOU KNOW... I HAD A KOOKY DREAM ABOUT NINJAS LAST NIGHT...
GIRLS! YOU'RE LATE AGAIN!
HYA!!
GOOD HEAVENS!

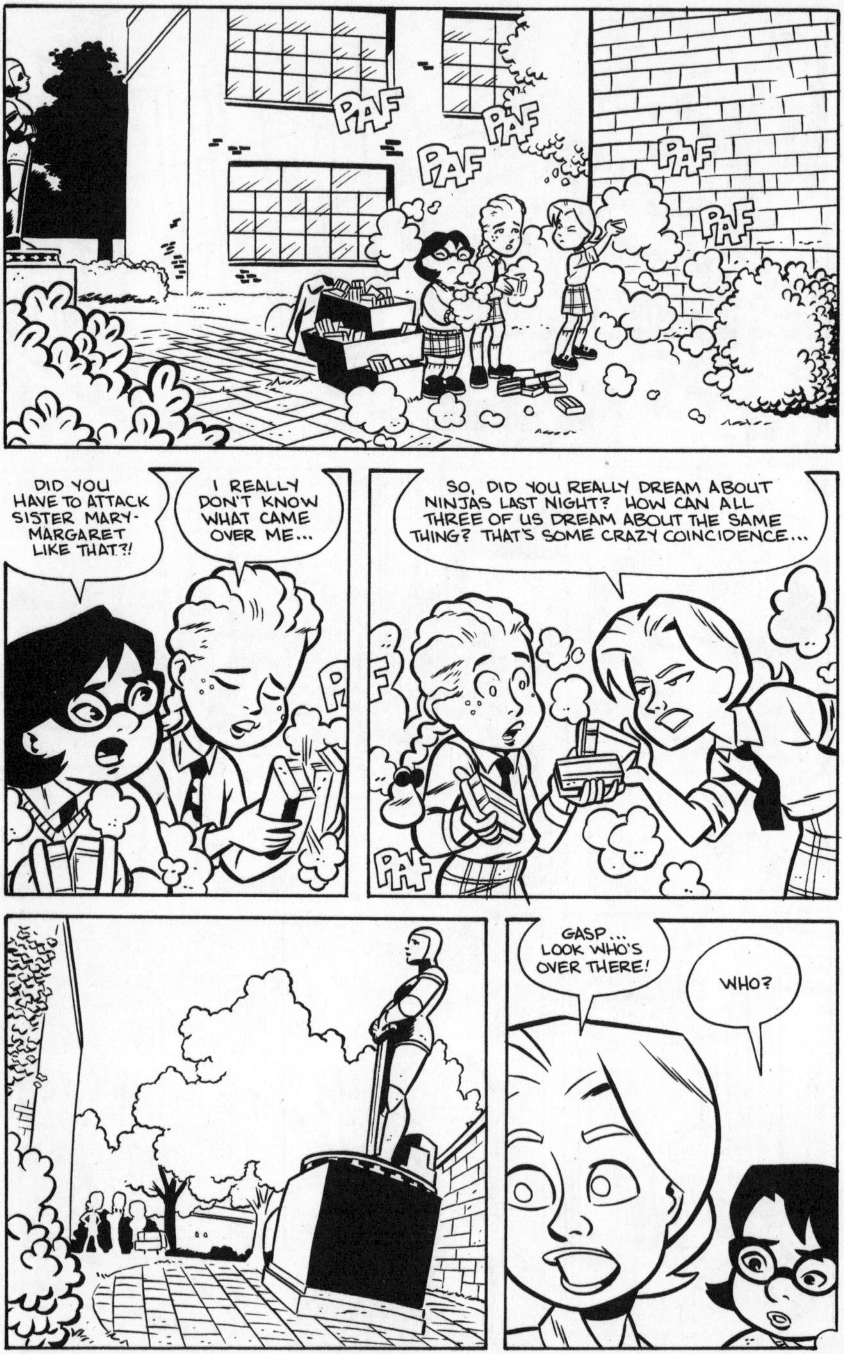
PAF
PAF
PAF
PAF
PAF
DID YOU HAVE TO ATTACK SISTER MARY-MARGARET LIKE THAT?!
I REALLY DON'T KNOW WHAT CAME OVER ME...
PAF
SO, DID YOU REALLY DREAM ABOUT NINJAS LAST NIGHT? HOW CAN ALL THREE OF US DREAM ABOUT THE SAME THING? THAT'S SOME CRAZY COINCIDENCE...
PAF
GASP... LOOK WHO'S OVER THERE!
WHO?

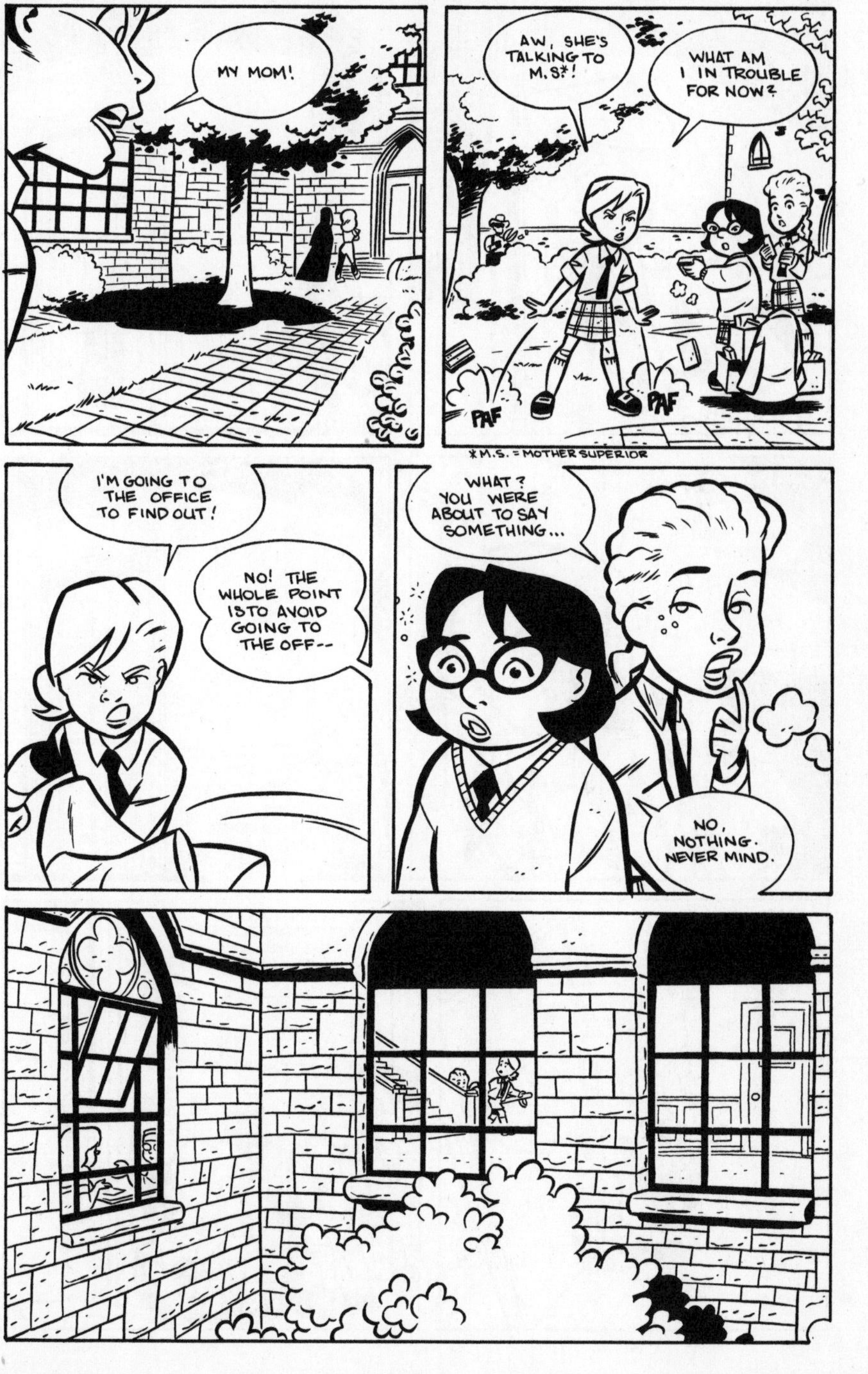
MY MOM!
AW, SHE'S TALKING TO M.S*!
WHAT AM I IN TROUBLE FOR NOW?
PAF
PAF
*M.S. = MOTHER SUPERIOR
I'M GOING TO THE OFFICE TO FIND OUT!
NO! THE WHOLE POINT IS TO AVOID GOING TO THE OFF--
WHAT? YOU WERE ABOUT TO SAY SOMETHING...
NO, NOTHING. NEVER MIND.

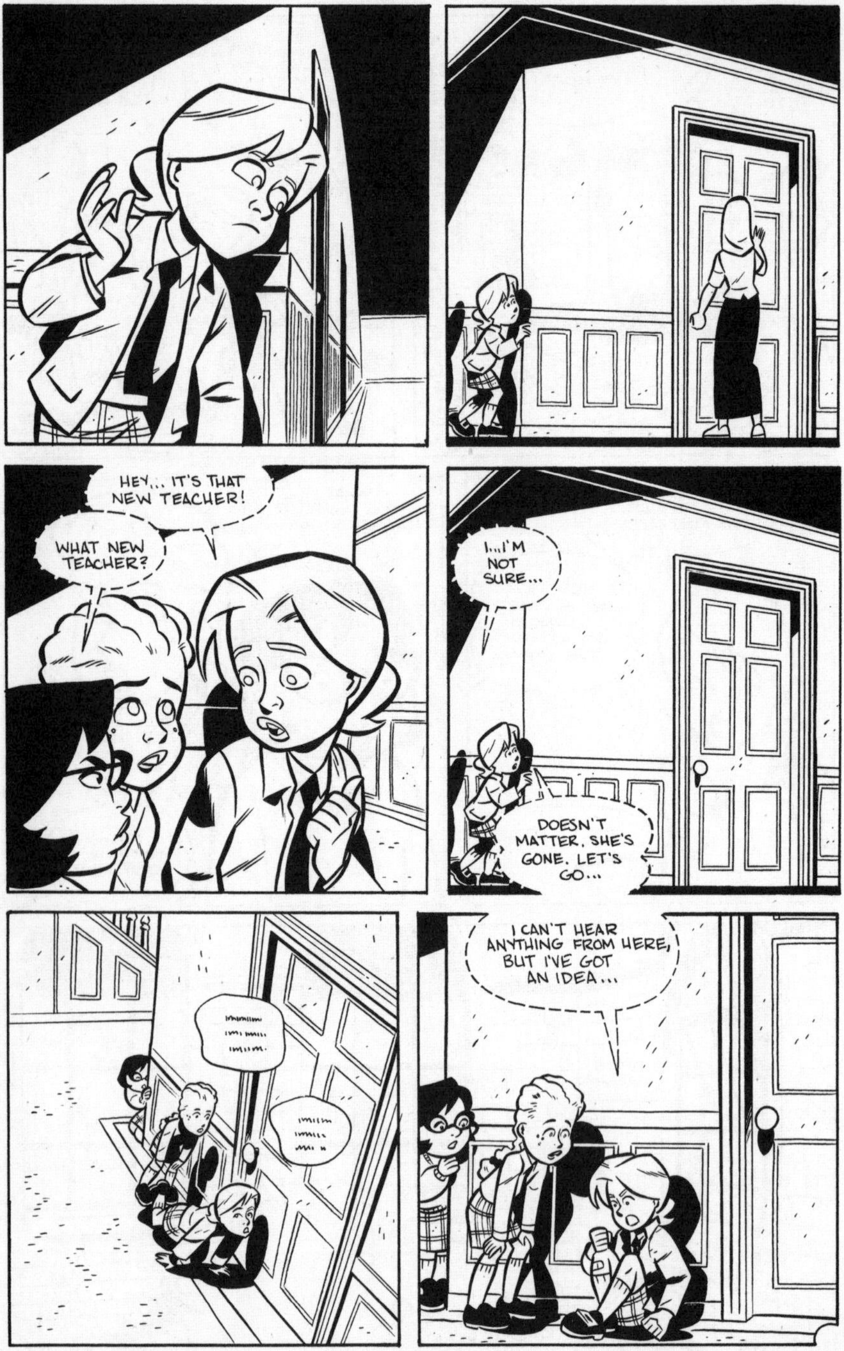
HEY... IT'S THAT NEW TEACHER!
WHAT NEW TEACHER?
I...I'M NOT SURE...
DOESN'T MATTER. SHE'S GONE. LET'S GO...
I CAN'T HEAR ANYTHING FROM HERE, BUT I'VE GOT AN IDEA...

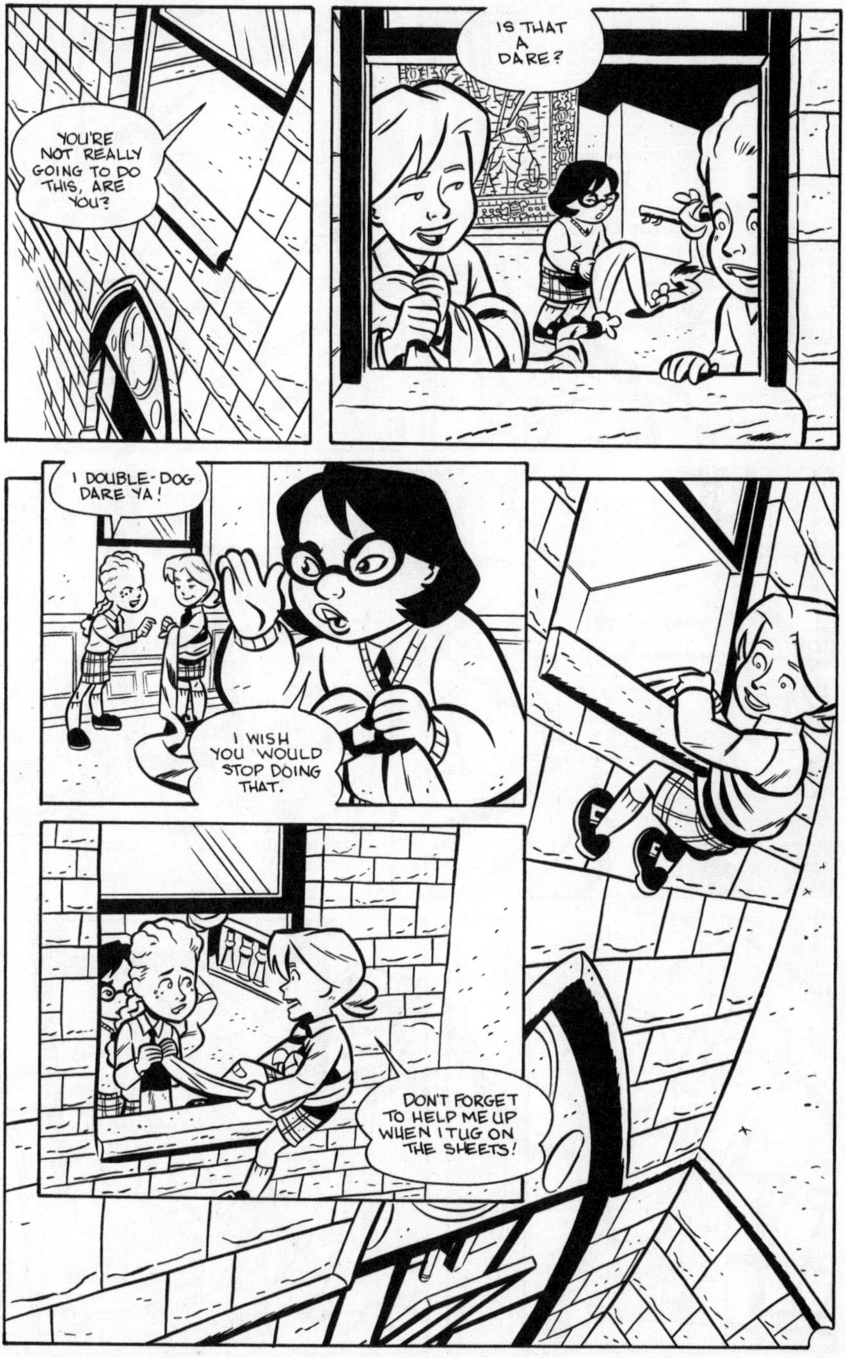
YOU'RE NOT REALLY GOING TO DO THIS, ARE YOU?
IS THAT A DARE?
I DOUBLE-DOG DARE YA!
I WISH YOU WOULD STOP DOING THAT.
DON'T FORGET TO HELP ME UP WHEN I TUG ON THE SHEETS!

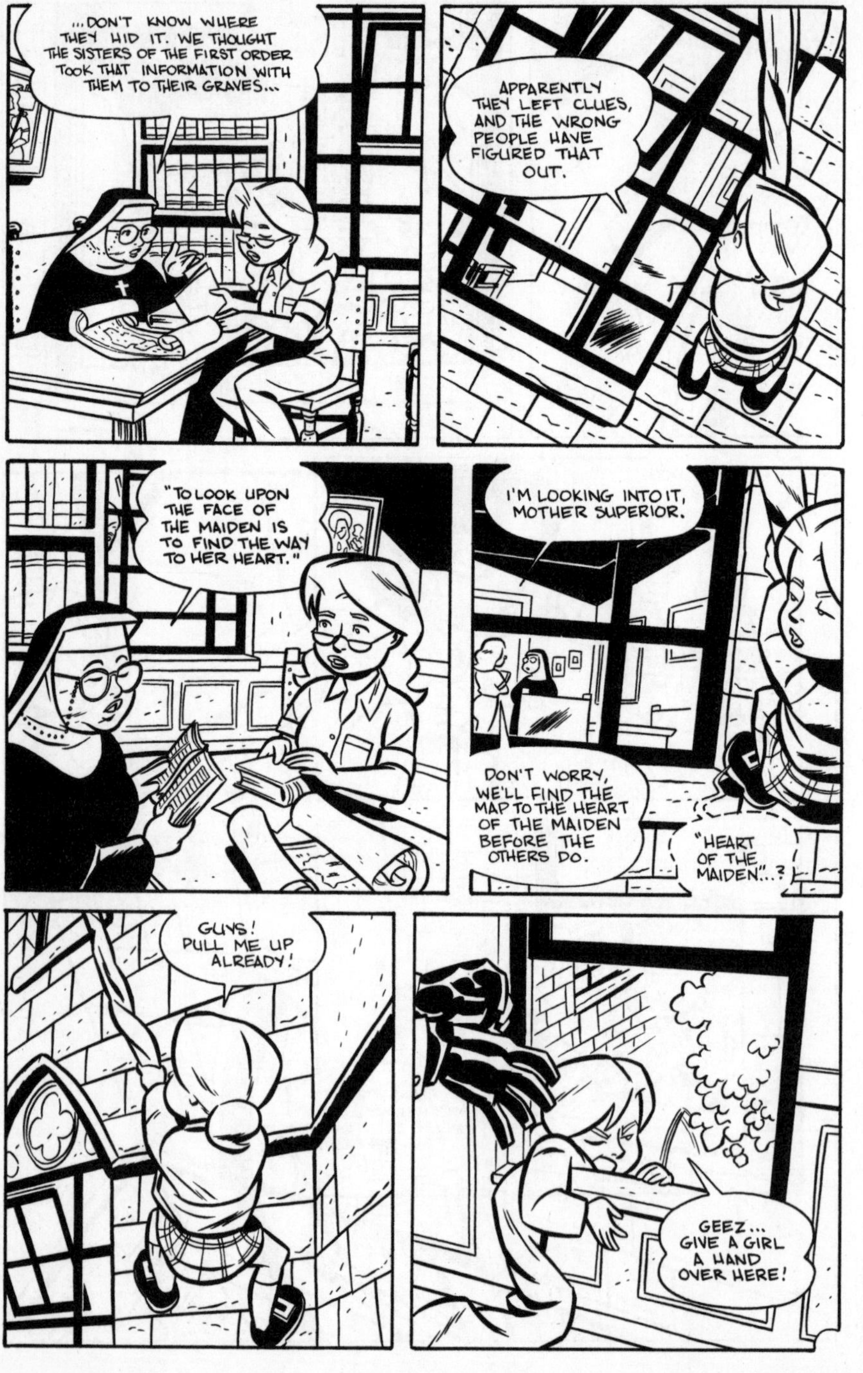
...DON'T KNOW WHERE THEY HID IT. WE THOUGHT THE SISTERS OF THE FIRST ORDER TOOK THAT INFORMATION WITH THEM TO THEIR GRAVES...
APPARENTLY THEY LEFT CLUES, AND THE WRONG PEOPLE HAVE FIGURED THAT OUT.
"TO LOOK UPON THE FACE OF THE MAIDEN IS TO FIND THE WAY TO HER HEART."
I'M LOOKING INTO IT, MOTHER SUPERIOR.
DON'T WORRY, WE'LL FIND THE MAP TO THE HEART OF THE MAIDEN BEFORE THE OTHERS DO.
"HEART OF THE MAIDEN"...?
GUYS! PULL ME UP ALREADY!
GEEZ... GIVE A GIRL A HAND OVER HERE!

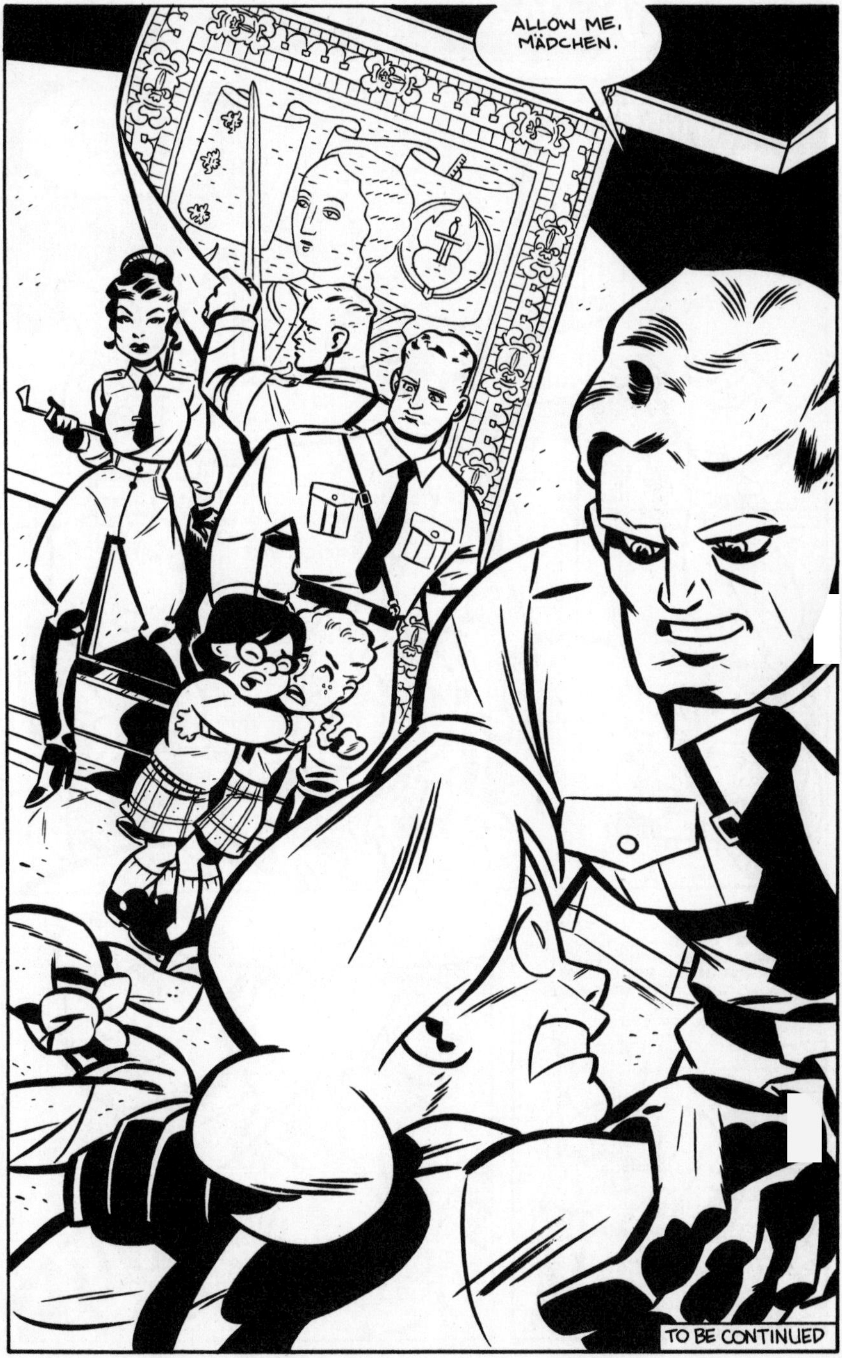
ALLOW ME, MÄDCHEN.
TO BE CONTINUED

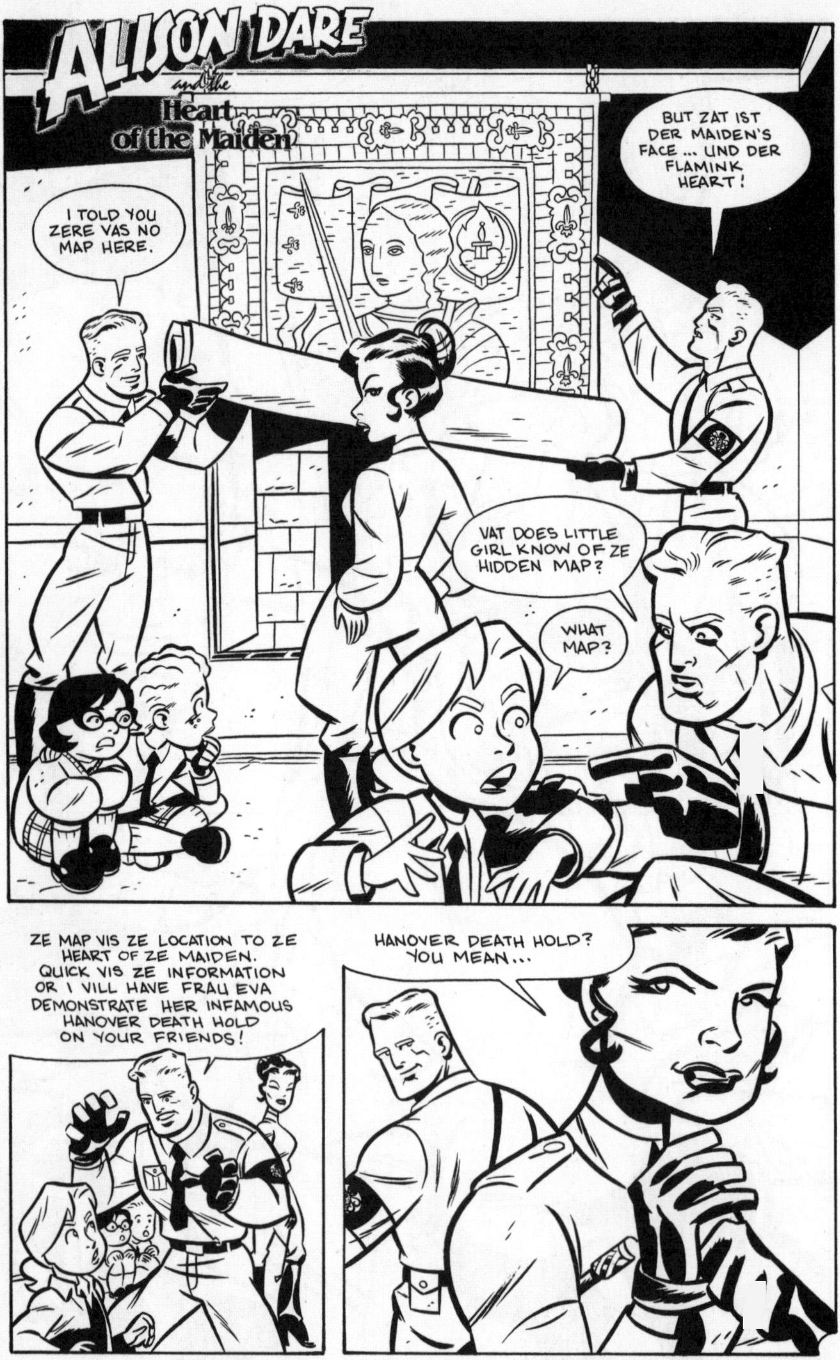
ALISON DARE
and the Heart of the Maiden
I TOLD YOU ZERE VAS NO MAP HERE.
BUT ZAT IST DER MAIDEN'S FACE ... UND DER FLAMINK HEART!
VAT DOES LITTLE GIRL KNOW OF ZE HIDDEN MAP?
WHAT MAP?
ZE MAP VIS ZE LOCATION TO ZE HEART OF ZE MAIDEN. QUICK VIS ZE INFORMATION OR I VILL HAVE FRAU EVA DEMONSTRATE HER INFAMOUS HANOVER DEATH HOLD ON YOUR FRIENDS!
HANOVER DEATH HOLD? YOU MEAN...

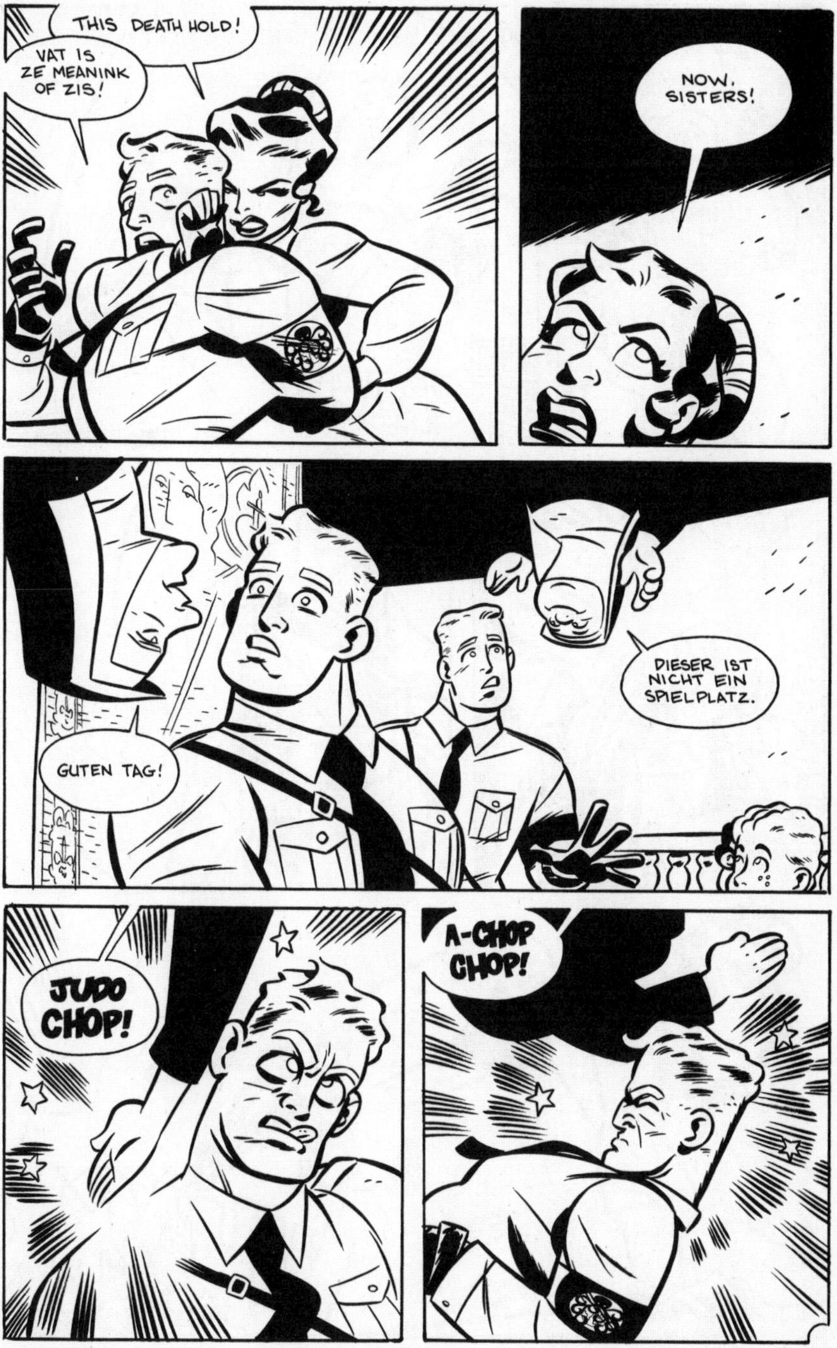
VAT IS ZE MEANINK OF ZIS!
THIS DEATH HOLD!
NOW, SISTERS!
GUTEN TAG!
DIESER IST NICHT EIN SPIELPLATZ.
JUDO CHOP!
A-CHOP CHOP!

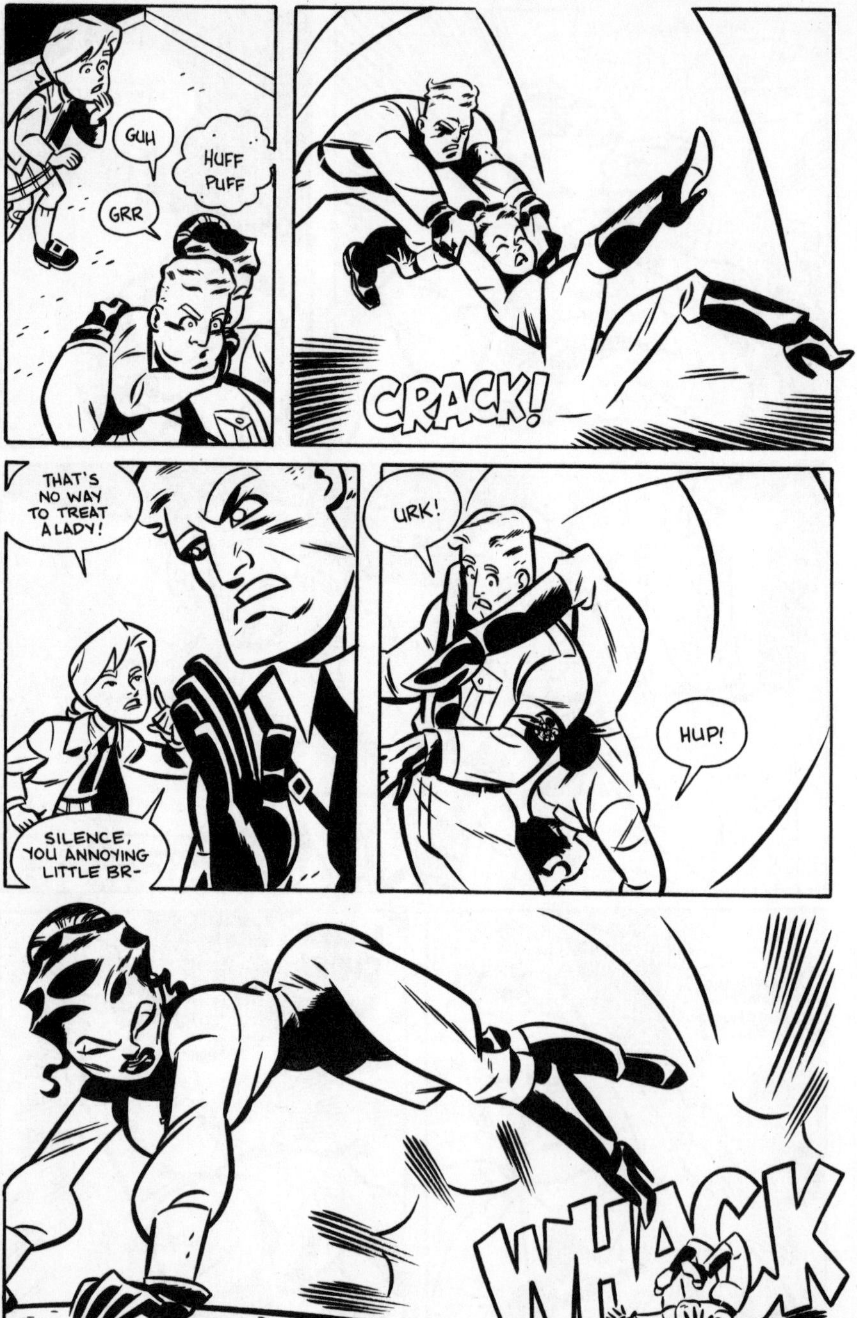
GUH
HUFF PUFF
GRR
CRACK!
THAT'S NO WAY TO TREAT A LADY!
SILENCE, YOU ANNOYING LITTLE BR-
URK!
HUP!
WHACK

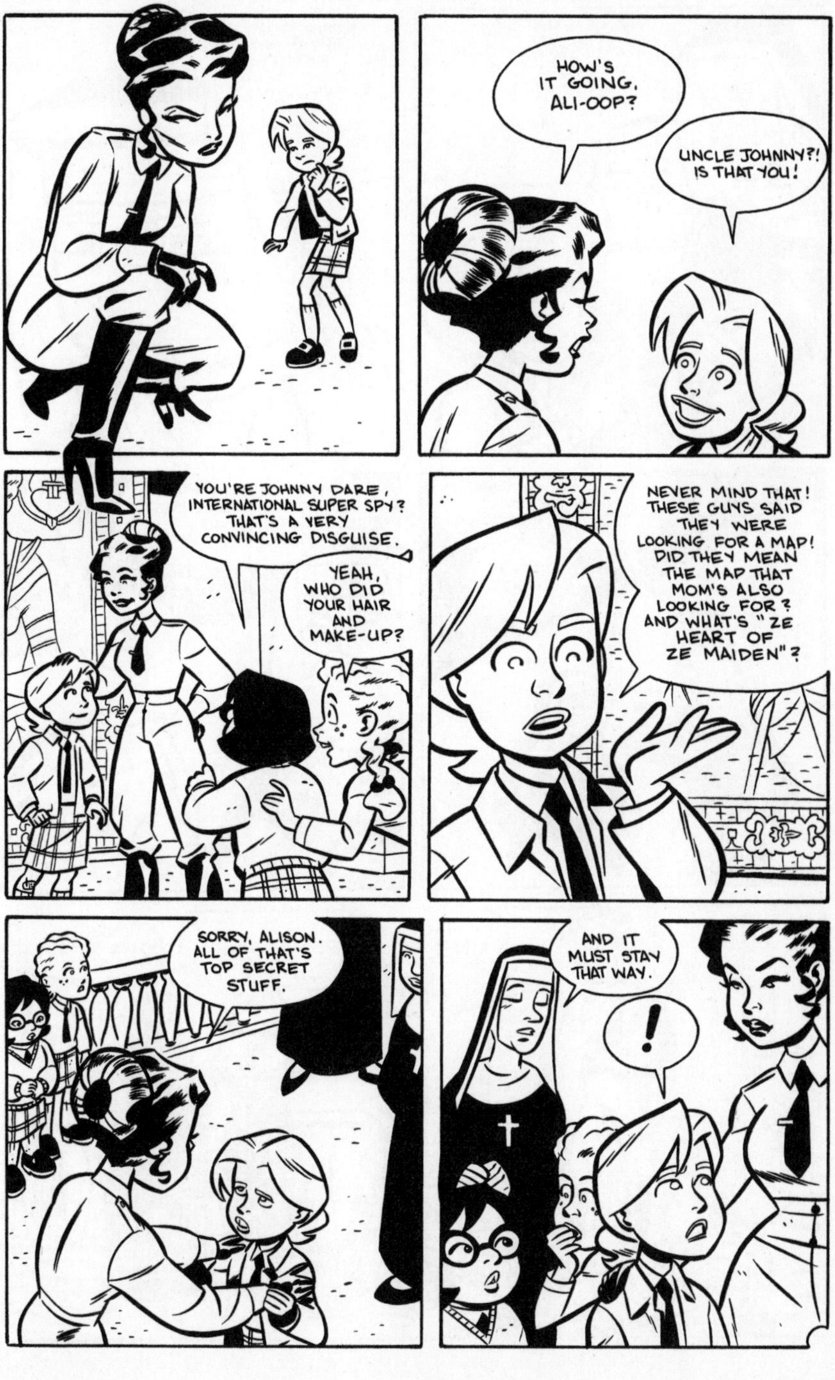
HOW'S IT GOING, ALI-OOP?
UNCLE JOHNNY?! IS THAT YOU!
YOU'RE JOHNNY DARE, INTERNATIONAL SUPER SPY? THAT'S A VERY CONVINCING DISGUISE.
YEAH, WHO DID YOUR HAIR AND MAKE-UP?
NEVER MIND THAT! THESE GUYS SAID THEY WERE LOOKING FOR A MAP! DID THEY MEAN THE MAP THAT MOM'S ALSO LOOKING FOR? AND WHAT'S "ZE HEART OF ZE MAIDEN"?
SORRY, ALISON. ALL OF THAT'S TOP SECRET STUFF.
AND IT MUST STAY THAT WAY.
!

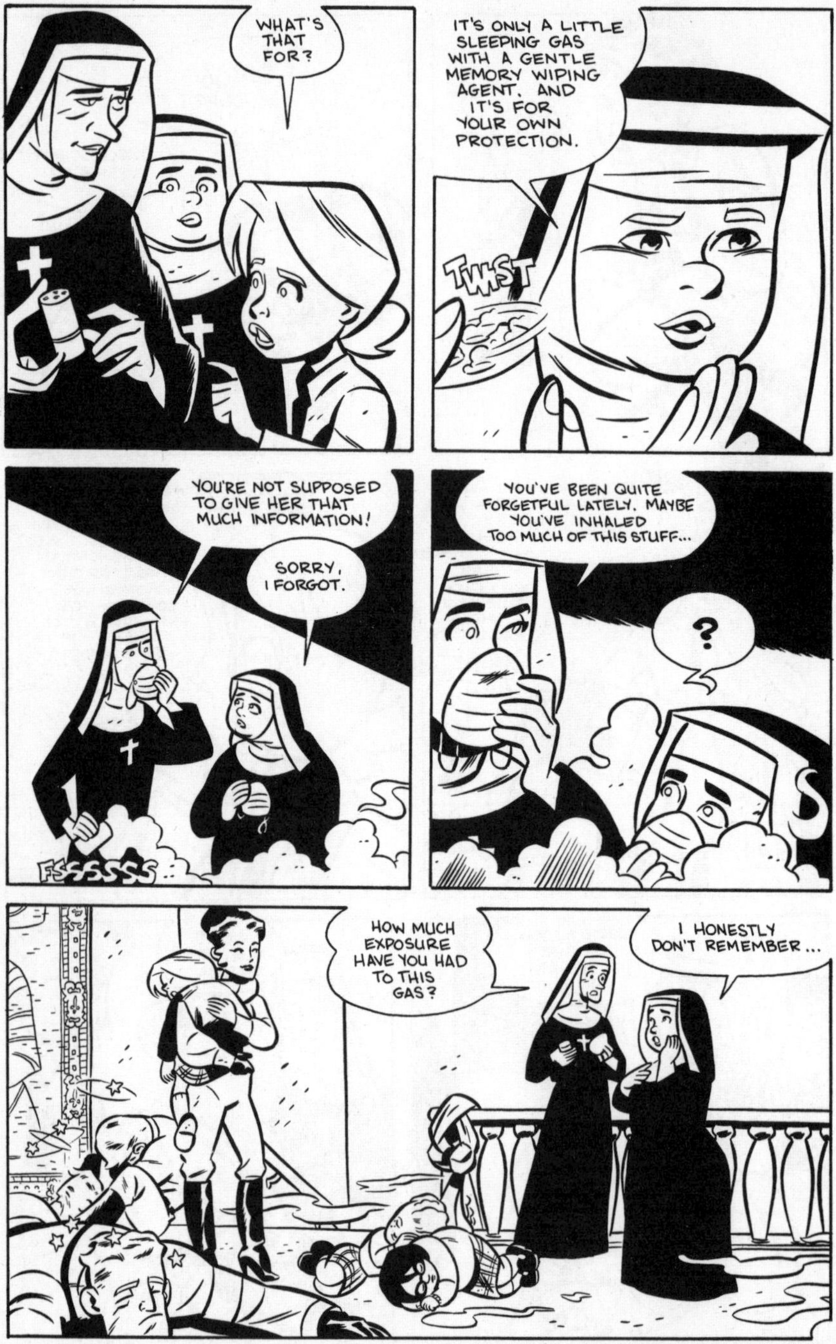
WHAT'S THAT FOR?
IT'S ONLY A LITTLE SLEEPING GAS WITH A GENTLE MEMORY WIPING AGENT. AND IT'S FOR YOUR OWN PROTECTION.
TWIST
YOU'RE NOT SUPPOSED TO GIVE HER THAT MUCH INFORMATION!
SORRY, I FORGOT.
FSSSSSS
YOU'VE BEEN QUITE FORGETFUL LATELY. MAYBE YOU'VE INHALED TOO MUCH OF THIS STUFF...
?
HOW MUCH EXPOSURE HAVE YOU HAD TO THIS GAS?
I HONESTLY DON'T REMEMBER...

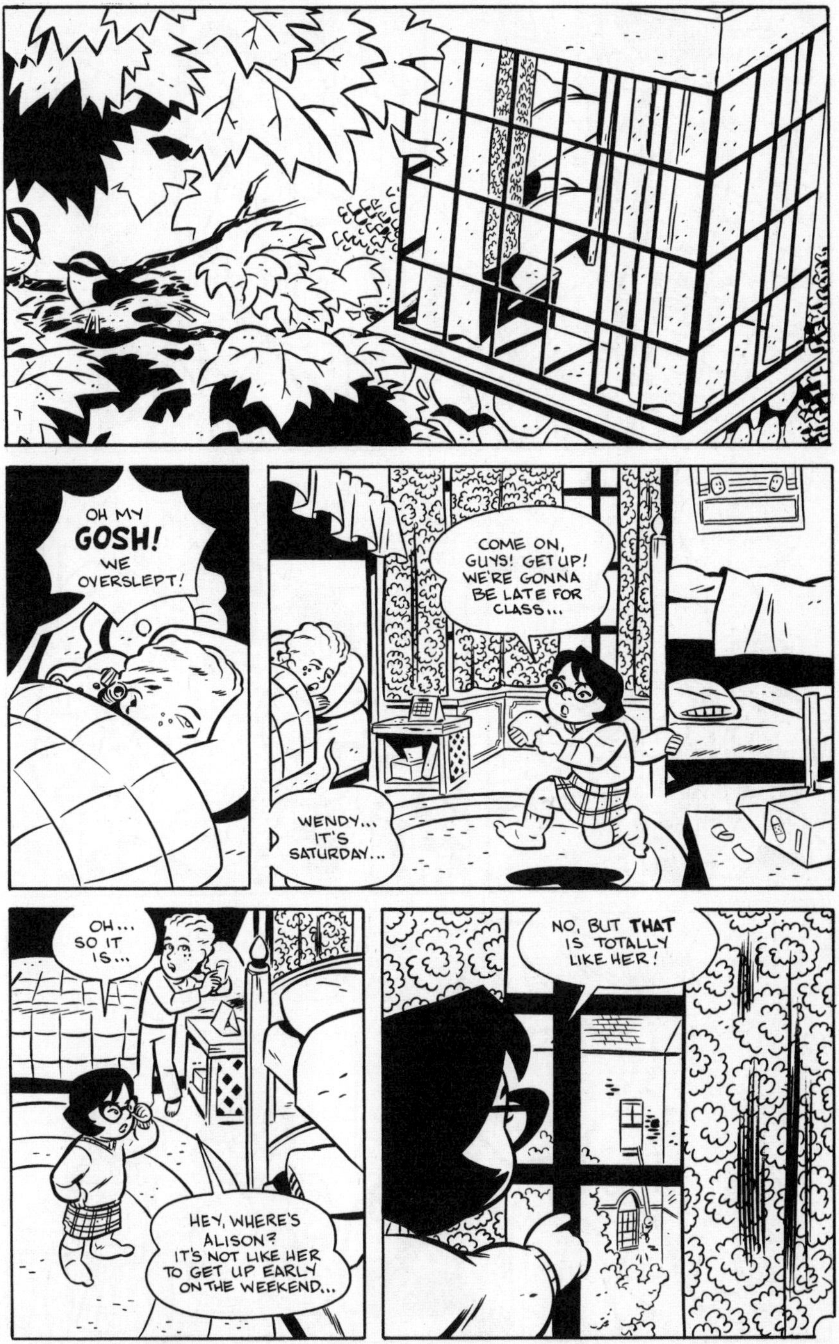
OH MY **GOSH!** WE OVERSLEPT!
COME ON, GUYS! GET UP! WE'RE GONNA BE LATE FOR CLASS...
WENDY... IT'S SATURDAY...
OH... SO IT IS...
HEY, WHERE'S ALISON? IT'S NOT LIKE HER TO GET UP EARLY ON THE WEEKEND...
NO, BUT **THAT** IS TOTALLY LIKE HER!

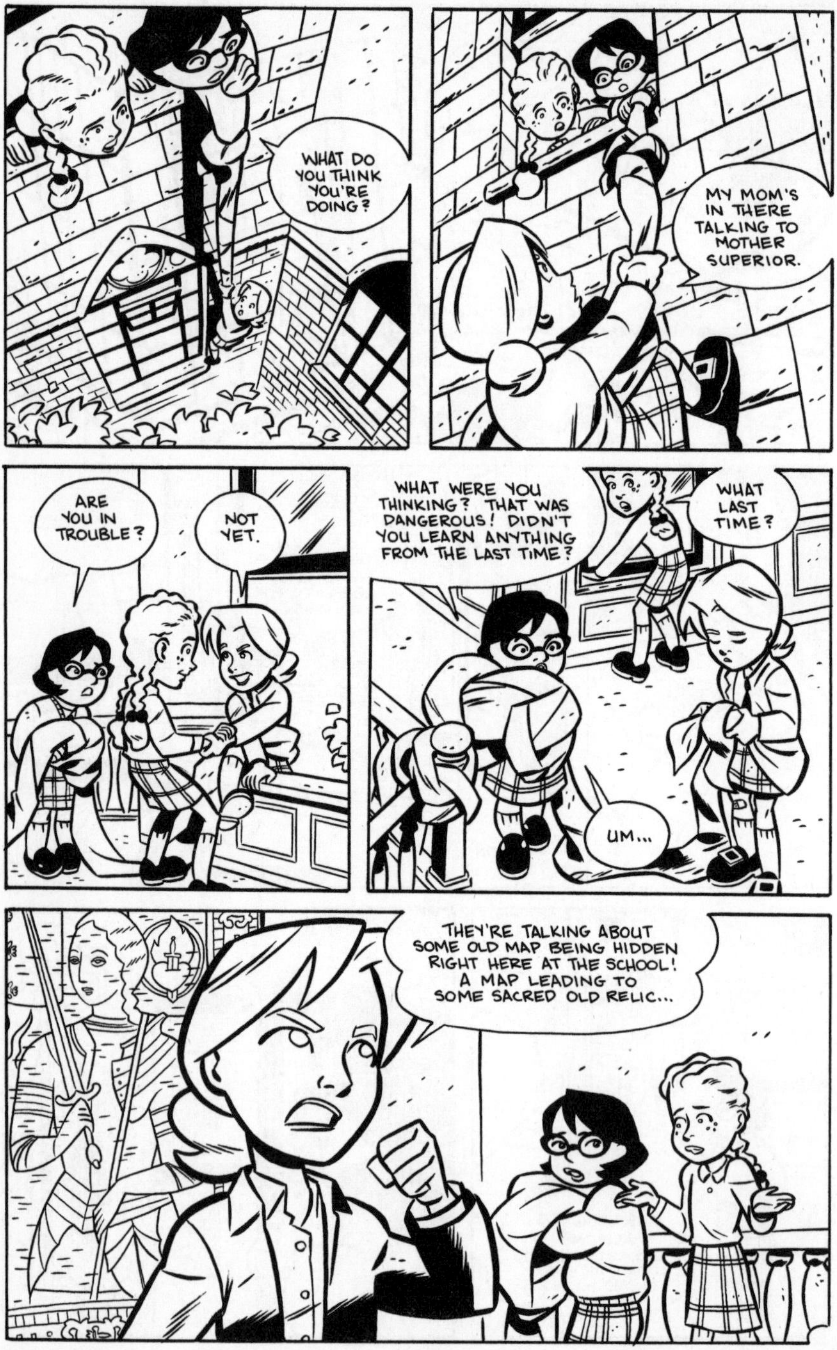
WHAT DO YOU THINK YOU'RE DOING?
MY MOM'S IN THERE TALKING TO MOTHER SUPERIOR.
ARE YOU IN TROUBLE?
NOT YET.
WHAT WERE YOU THINKING? THAT WAS DANGEROUS! DIDN'T YOU LEARN ANYTHING FROM THE LAST TIME?
WHAT LAST TIME?
UM...
THEY'RE TALKING ABOUT SOME OLD MAP BEING HIDDEN RIGHT HERE AT THE SCHOOL! A MAP LEADING TO SOME SACRED OLD RELIC...

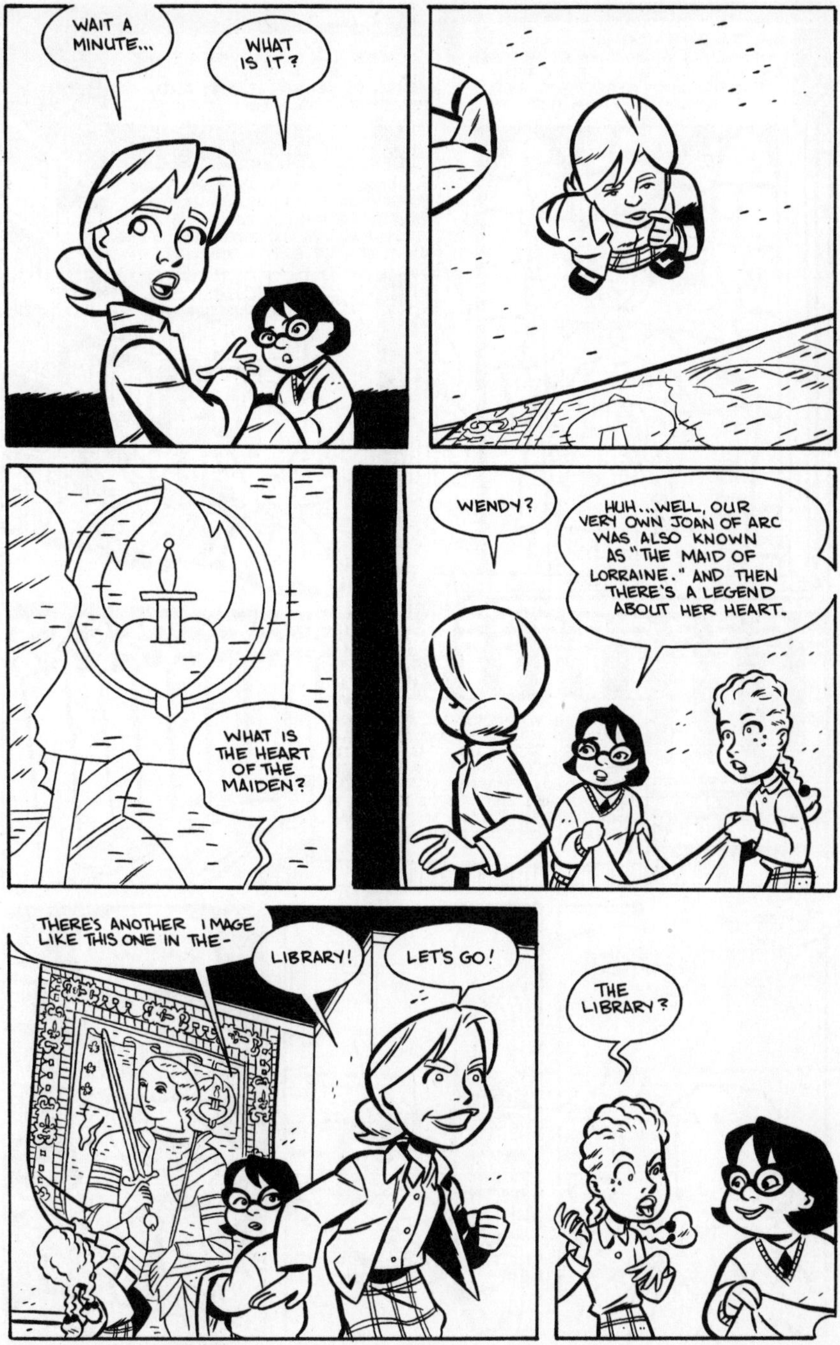

WAIT A MINUTE...
WHAT IS IT?
WENDY?
HUH...WELL, OUR VERY OWN JOAN OF ARC WAS ALSO KNOWN AS "THE MAID OF LORRAINE." AND THEN THERE'S A LEGEND ABOUT HER HEART.
WHAT IS THE HEART OF THE MAIDEN?
THERE'S ANOTHER IMAGE LIKE THIS ONE IN THE-
LIBRARY!
LET'S GO!
THE LIBRARY?

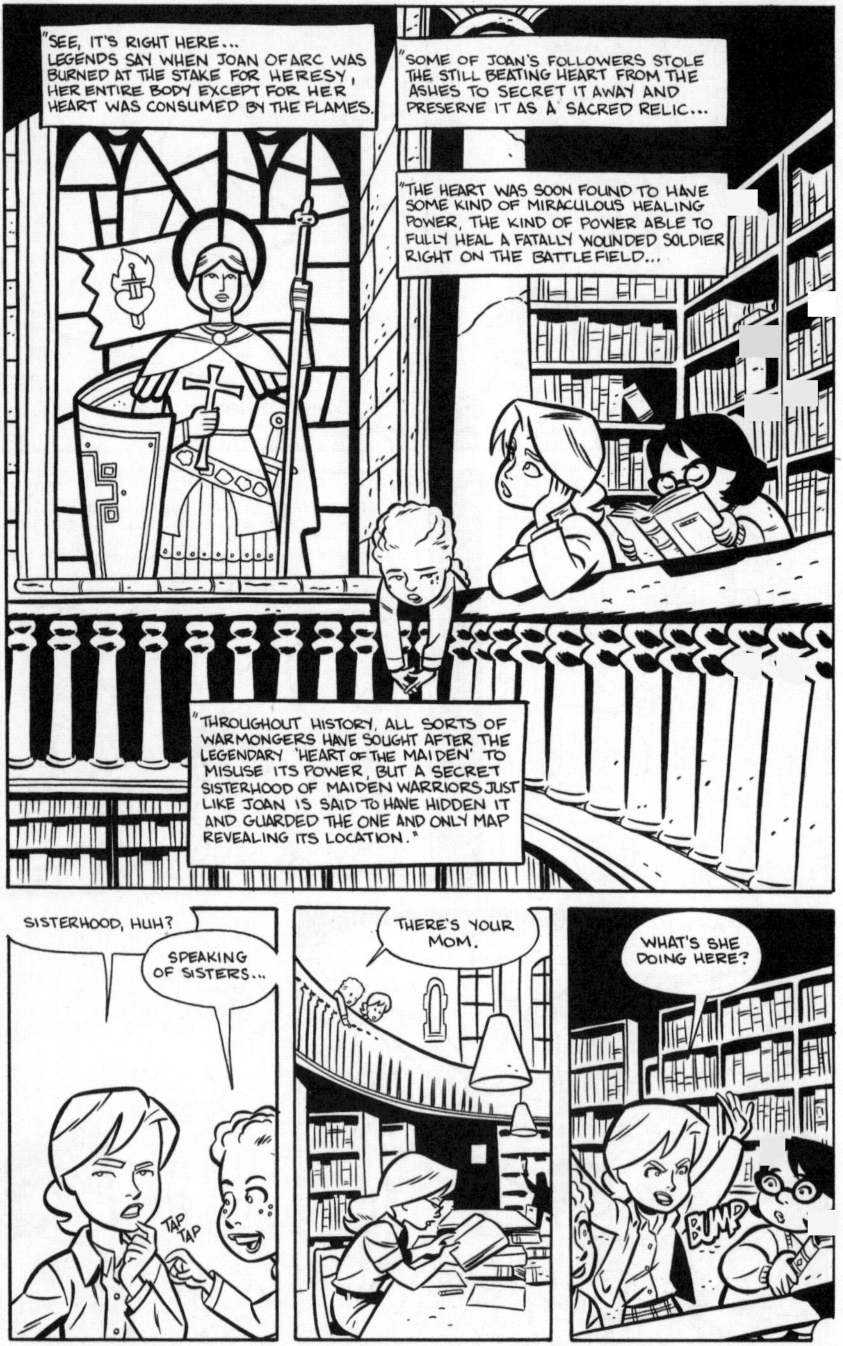
"SEE, IT'S RIGHT HERE... LEGENDS SAY WHEN JOAN OF ARC WAS BURNED AT THE STAKE FOR HERESY, HER ENTIRE BODY EXCEPT FOR HER HEART WAS CONSUMED BY THE FLAMES.
"SOME OF JOAN'S FOLLOWERS STOLE THE STILL BEATING HEART FROM THE ASHES TO SECRET IT AWAY AND PRESERVE IT AS A SACRED RELIC...
"THE HEART WAS SOON FOUND TO HAVE SOME KIND OF MIRACULOUS HEALING POWER, THE KIND OF POWER ABLE TO FULLY HEAL A FATALLY WOUNDED SOLDIER RIGHT ON THE BATTLEFIELD...
"THROUGHOUT HISTORY, ALL SORTS OF WARMONGERS HAVE SOUGHT AFTER THE LEGENDARY 'HEART OF THE MAIDEN' TO MISUSE ITS POWER, BUT A SECRET SISTERHOOD OF MAIDEN WARRIORS JUST LIKE JOAN IS SAID TO HAVE HIDDEN IT AND GUARDED THE ONE AND ONLY MAP REVEALING ITS LOCATION."
SISTERHOOD, HUH?
SPEAKING OF SISTERS...
TAP TAP
THERE'S YOUR MOM.
WHAT'S SHE DOING HERE?
BUMP

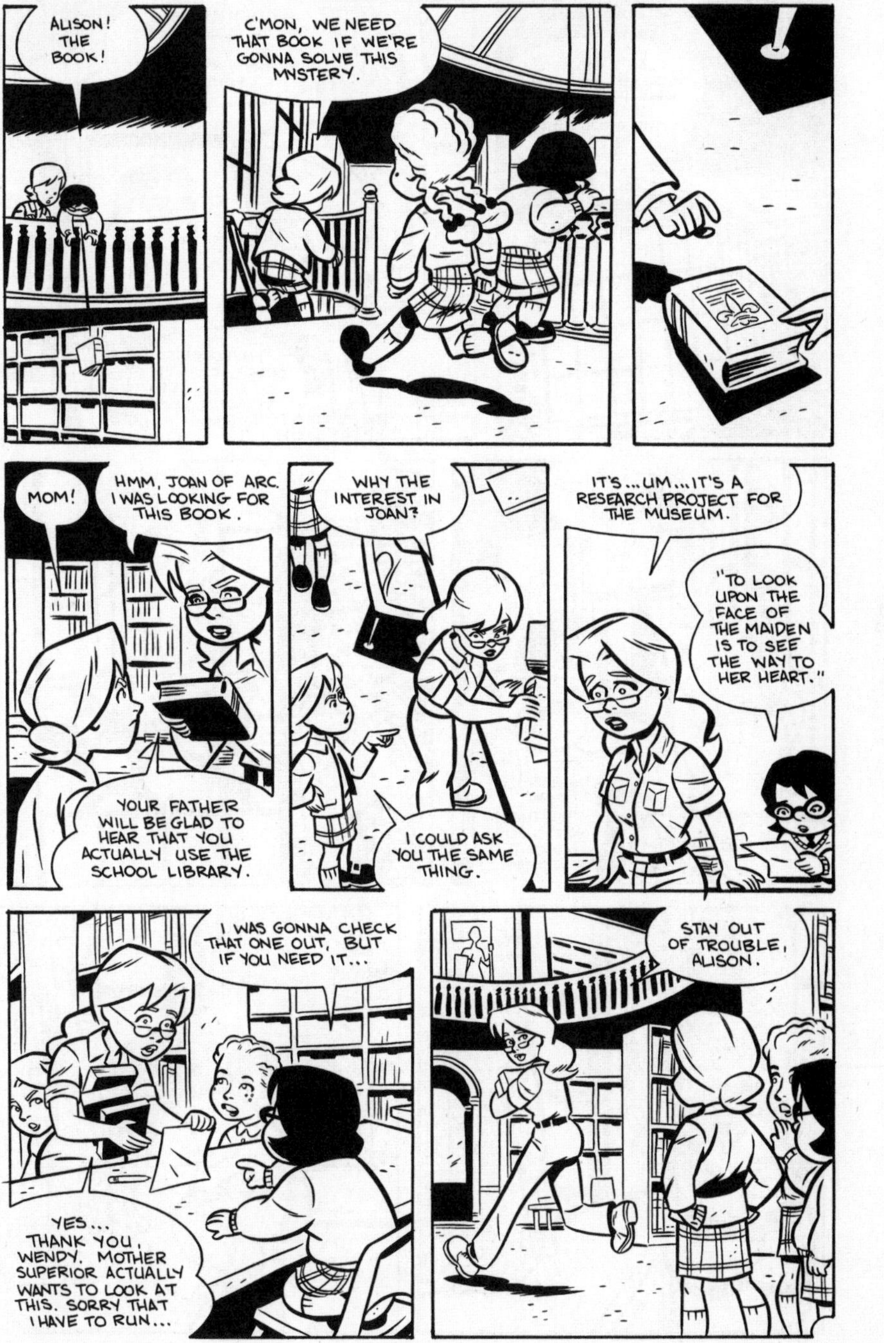
ALISON! THE BOOK!
C'MON, WE NEED THAT BOOK IF WE'RE GONNA SOLVE THIS MYSTERY.
MOM!
HMM, JOAN OF ARC. I WAS LOOKING FOR THIS BOOK.
YOUR FATHER WILL BE GLAD TO HEAR THAT YOU ACTUALLY USE THE SCHOOL LIBRARY.
WHY THE INTEREST IN JOAN?
I COULD ASK YOU THE SAME THING.
IT'S... UM... IT'S A RESEARCH PROJECT FOR THE MUSEUM.
"TO LOOK UPON THE FACE OF THE MAIDEN IS TO SEE THE WAY TO HER HEART."
I WAS GONNA CHECK THAT ONE OUT, BUT IF YOU NEED IT...
YES... THANK YOU, WENDY. MOTHER SUPERIOR ACTUALLY WANTS TO LOOK AT THIS. SORRY THAT I HAVE TO RUN...
STAY OUT OF TROUBLE, ALISON.

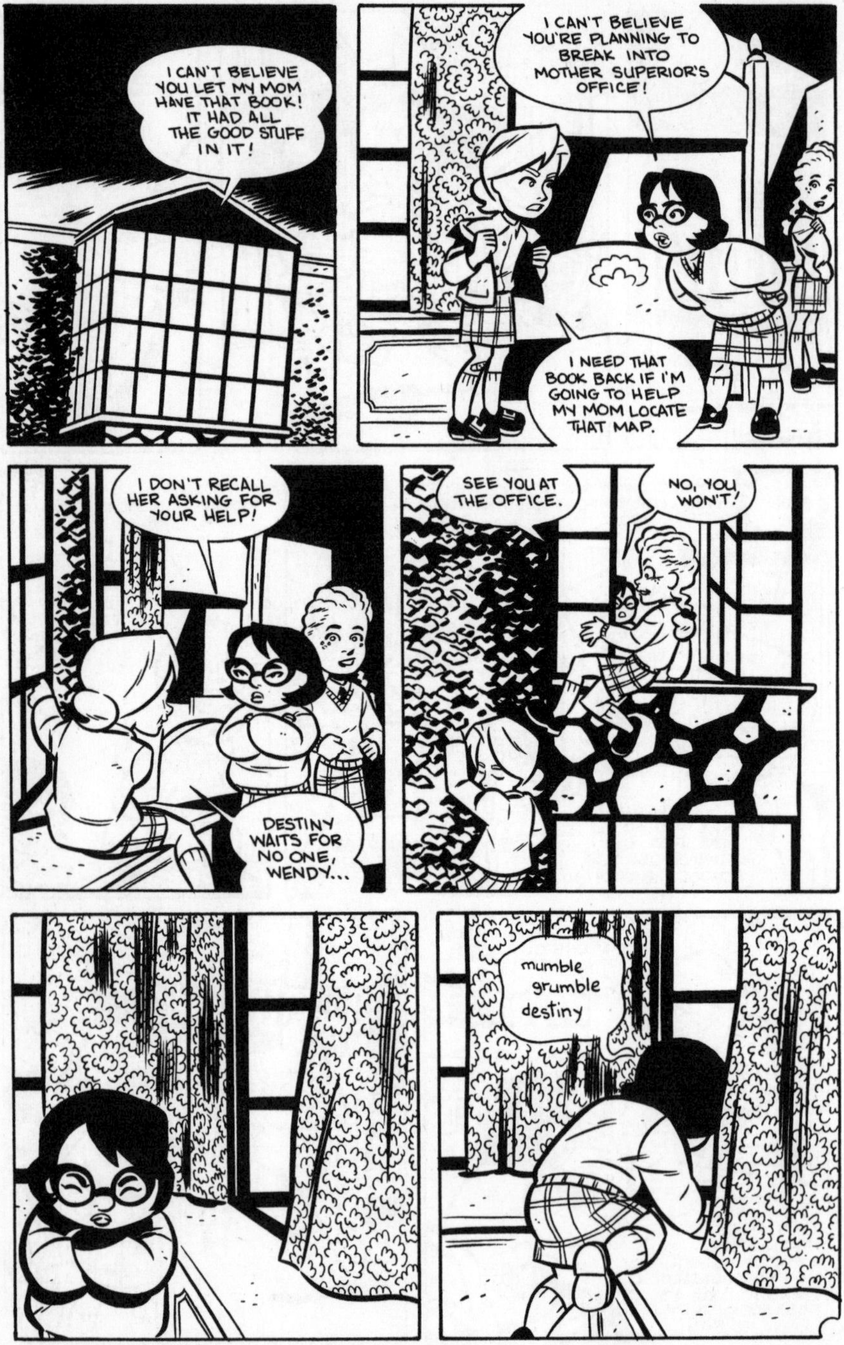
I CAN'T BELIEVE YOU LET MY MOM HAVE THAT BOOK! IT HAD ALL THE GOOD STUFF IN IT!
I CAN'T BELIEVE YOU'RE PLANNING TO BREAK INTO MOTHER SUPERIOR'S OFFICE!
I NEED THAT BOOK BACK IF I'M GOING TO HELP MY MOM LOCATE THAT MAP.
I DON'T RECALL HER ASKING FOR YOUR HELP!
DESTINY WAITS FOR NO ONE, WENDY...
SEE YOU AT THE OFFICE.
NO, YOU WON'T!
mumble
grumble
destiny

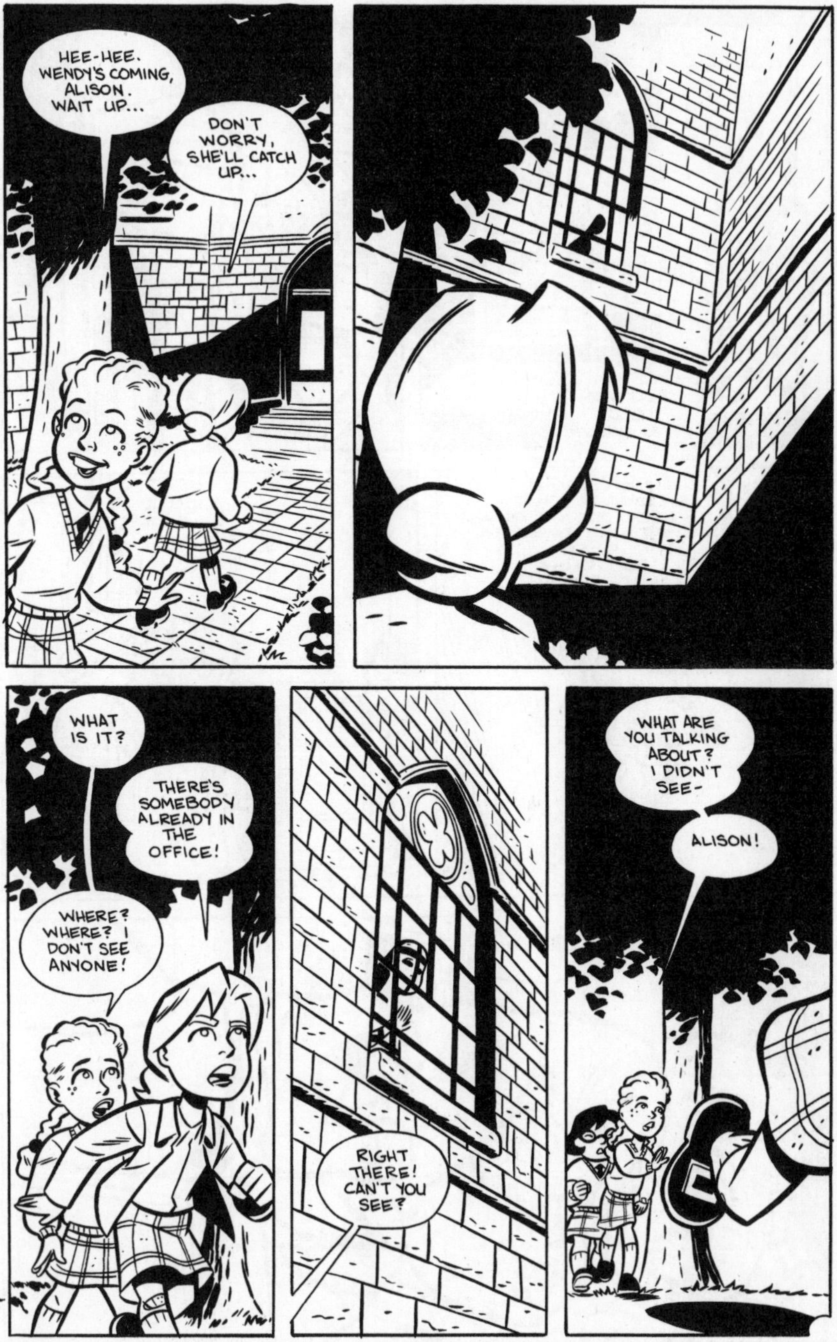
HEE-HEE. WENDY'S COMING, ALISON. WAIT UP...
DON'T WORRY, SHE'LL CATCH UP...
WHAT IS IT?
THERE'S SOMEBODY ALREADY IN THE OFFICE!
WHERE? WHERE? I DON'T SEE ANYONE!
RIGHT THERE! CAN'T YOU SEE?
WHAT ARE YOU TALKING ABOUT? I DIDN'T SEE-
ALISON!

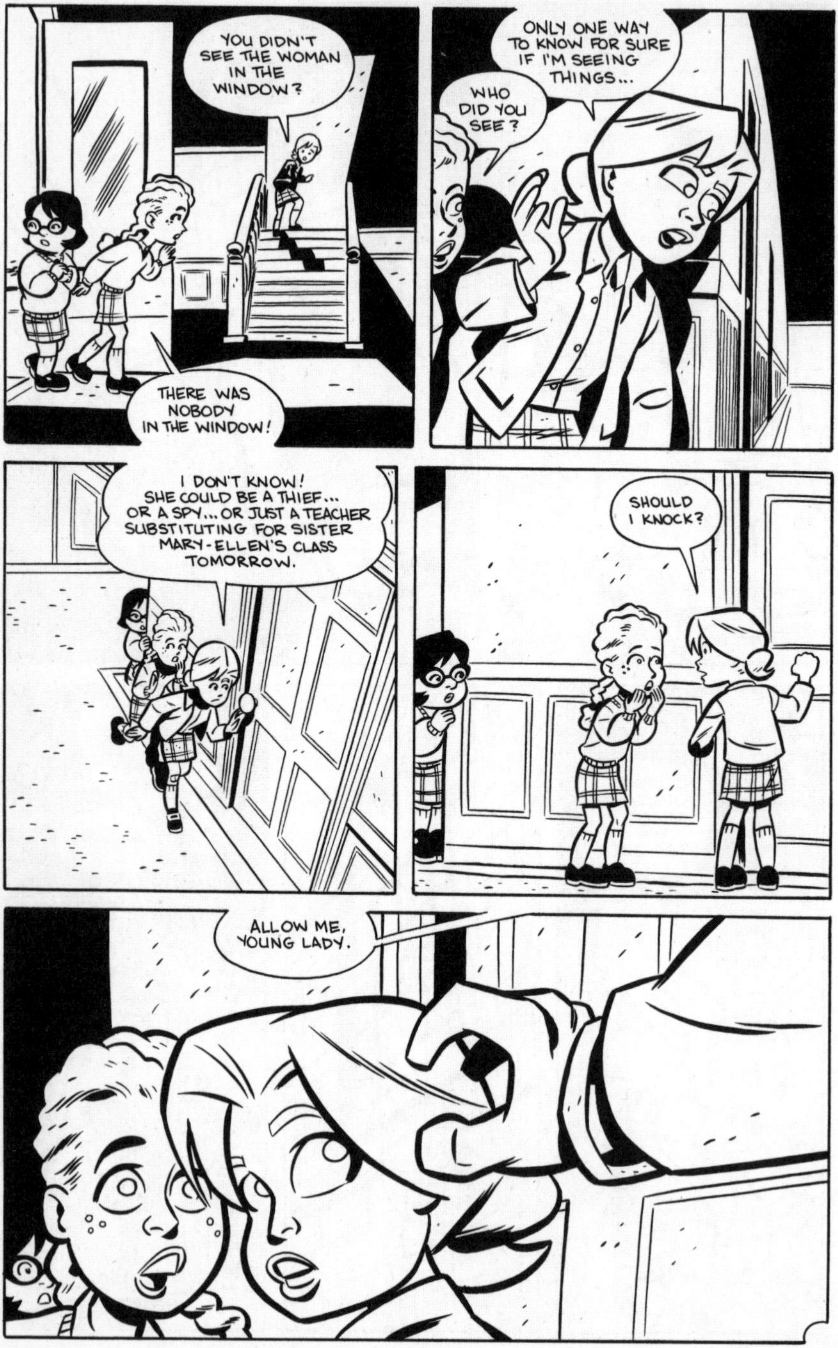
YOU DIDN'T SEE THE WOMAN IN THE WINDOW?
THERE WAS NOBODY IN THE WINDOW!
ONLY ONE WAY TO KNOW FOR SURE IF I'M SEEING THINGS...
WHO DID YOU SEE?
I DON'T KNOW! SHE COULD BE A THIEF... OR A SPY... OR JUST A TEACHER SUBSTITUTING FOR SISTER MARY-ELLEN'S CLASS TOMORROW.
SHOULD I KNOCK?
ALLOW ME, YOUNG LADY.

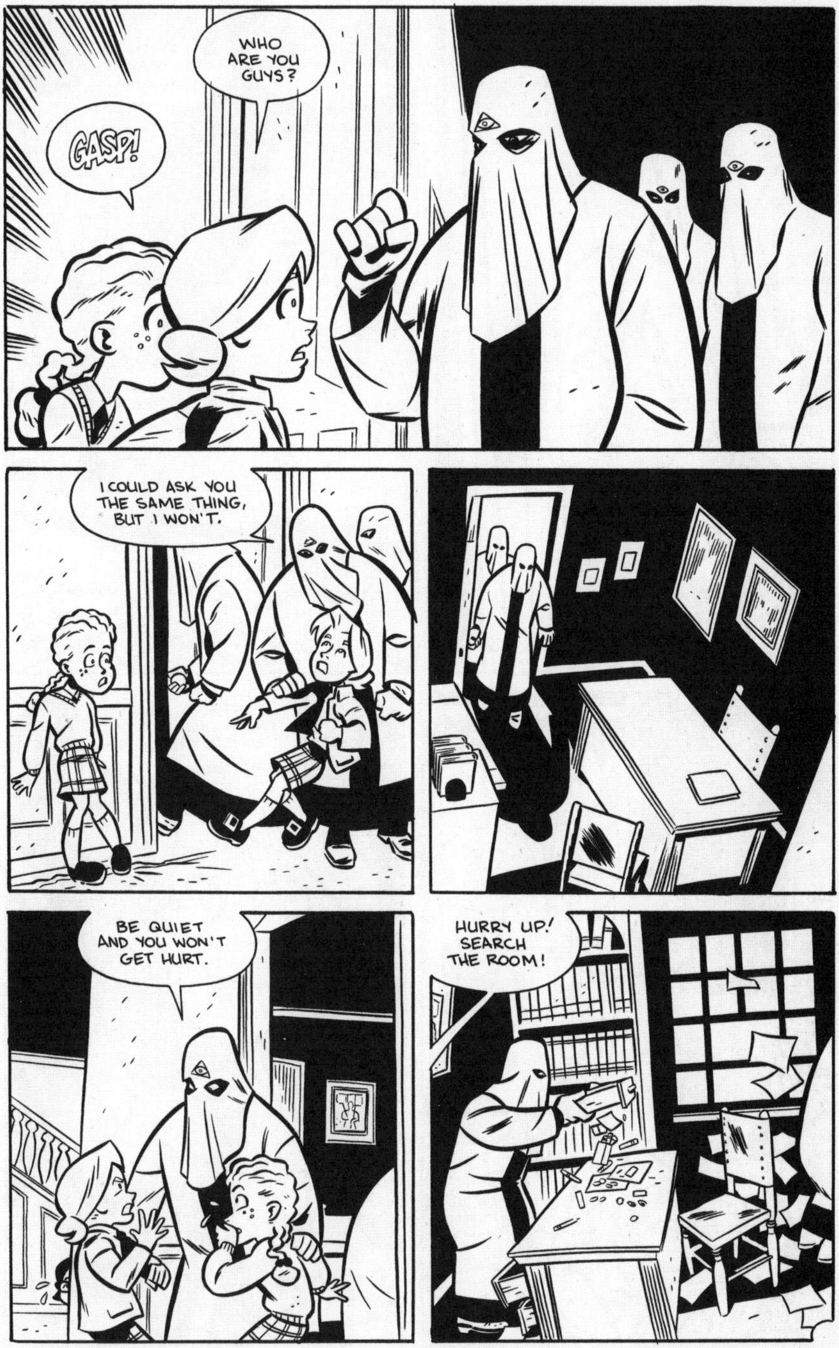
WHO ARE YOU GUYS?
GASP!
I COULD ASK YOU THE SAME THING, BUT I WON'T.
BE QUIET AND YOU WON'T GET HURT.
HURRY UP! SEARCH THE ROOM!

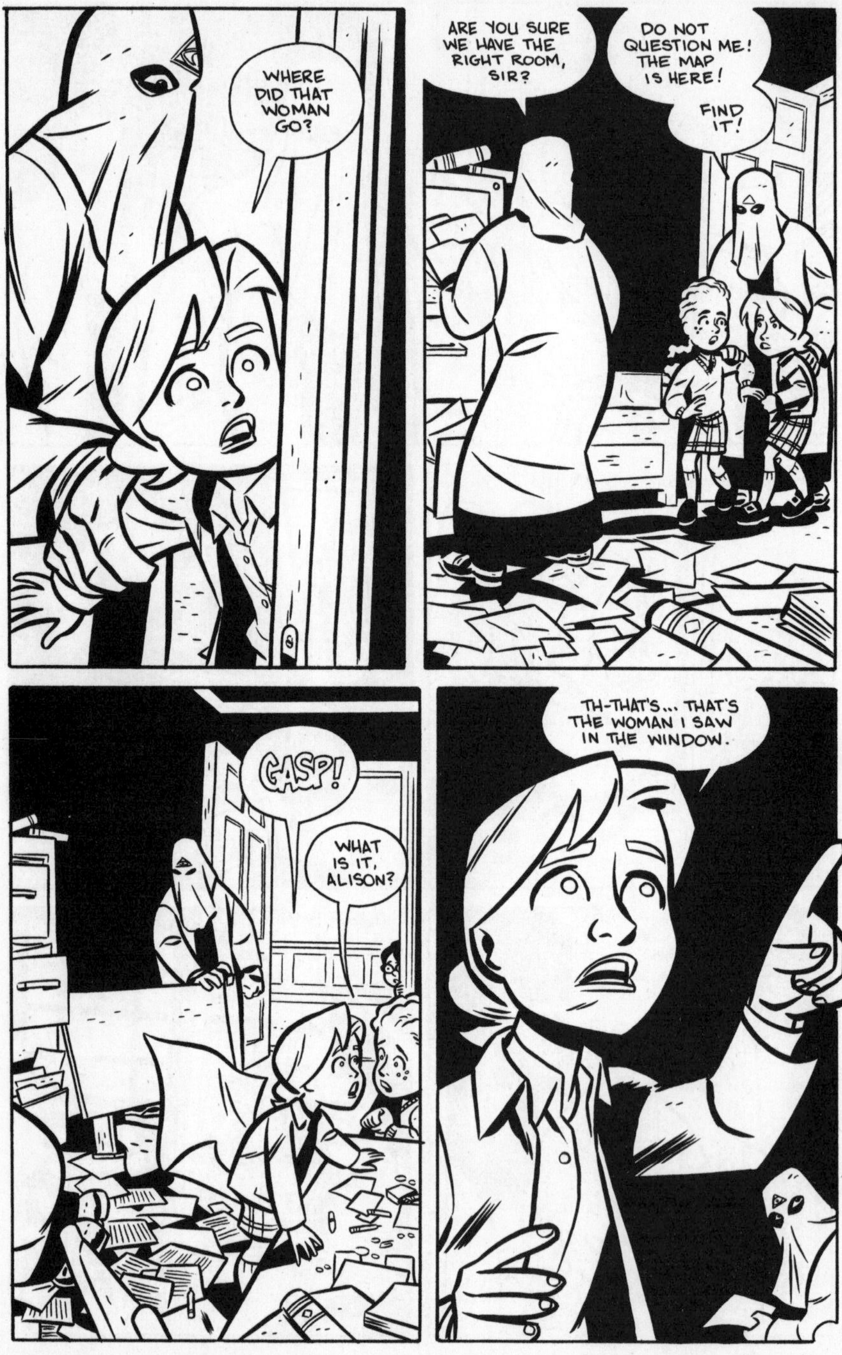
WHERE DID THAT WOMAN GO?
ARE YOU SURE WE HAVE THE RIGHT ROOM, SIR?
DO NOT QUESTION ME! THE MAP IS HERE!
FIND IT!
GASP!
WHAT IS IT, ALISON?
TH-THAT'S... THAT'S THE WOMAN I SAW IN THE WINDOW.

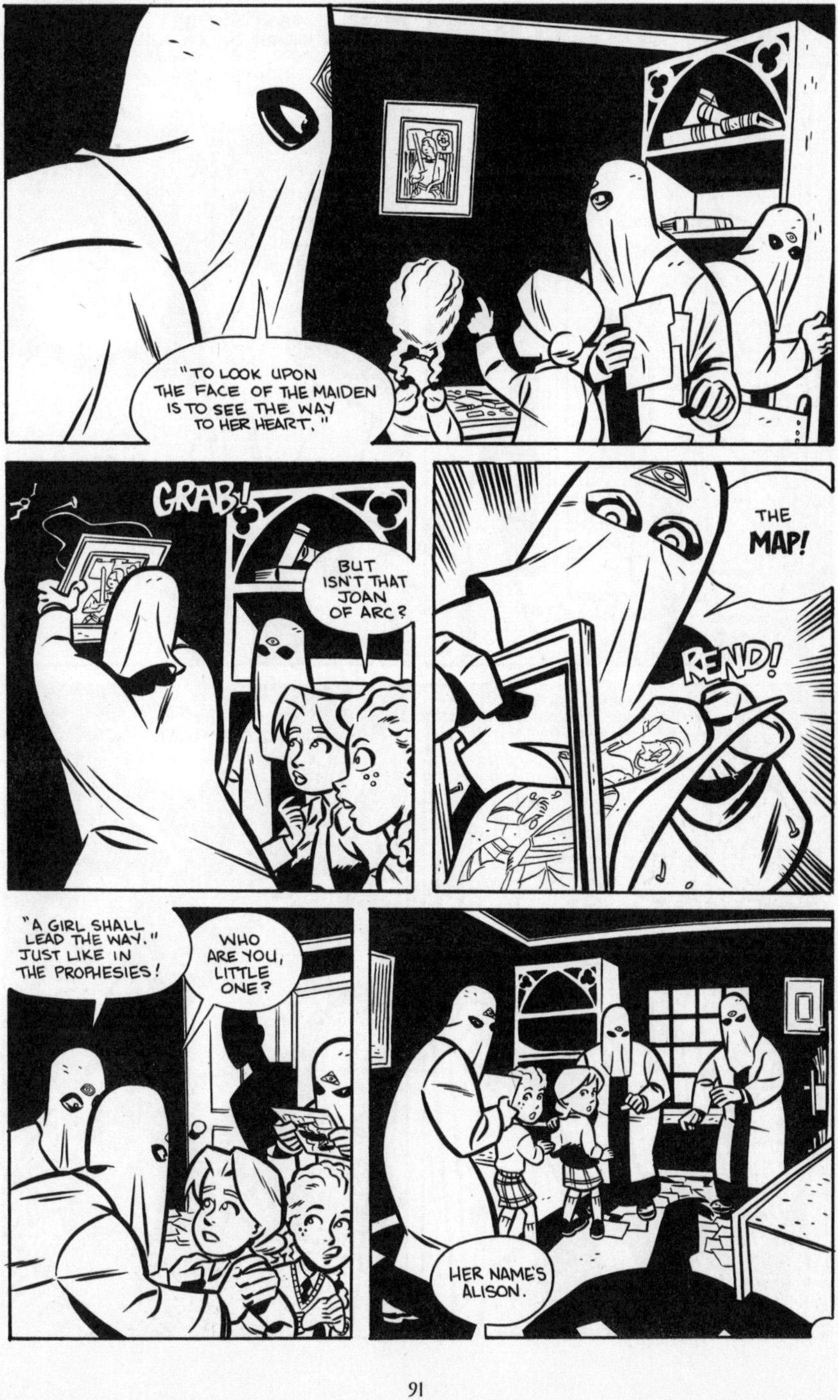
"TO LOOK UPON THE FACE OF THE MAIDEN IS TO SEE THE WAY TO HER HEART."
GRAB!
BUT ISN'T THAT JOAN OF ARC?
THE MAP!
REND!
"A GIRL SHALL LEAD THE WAY." JUST LIKE IN THE PROPHESIES!
WHO ARE YOU, LITTLE ONE?
HER NAME'S ALISON.

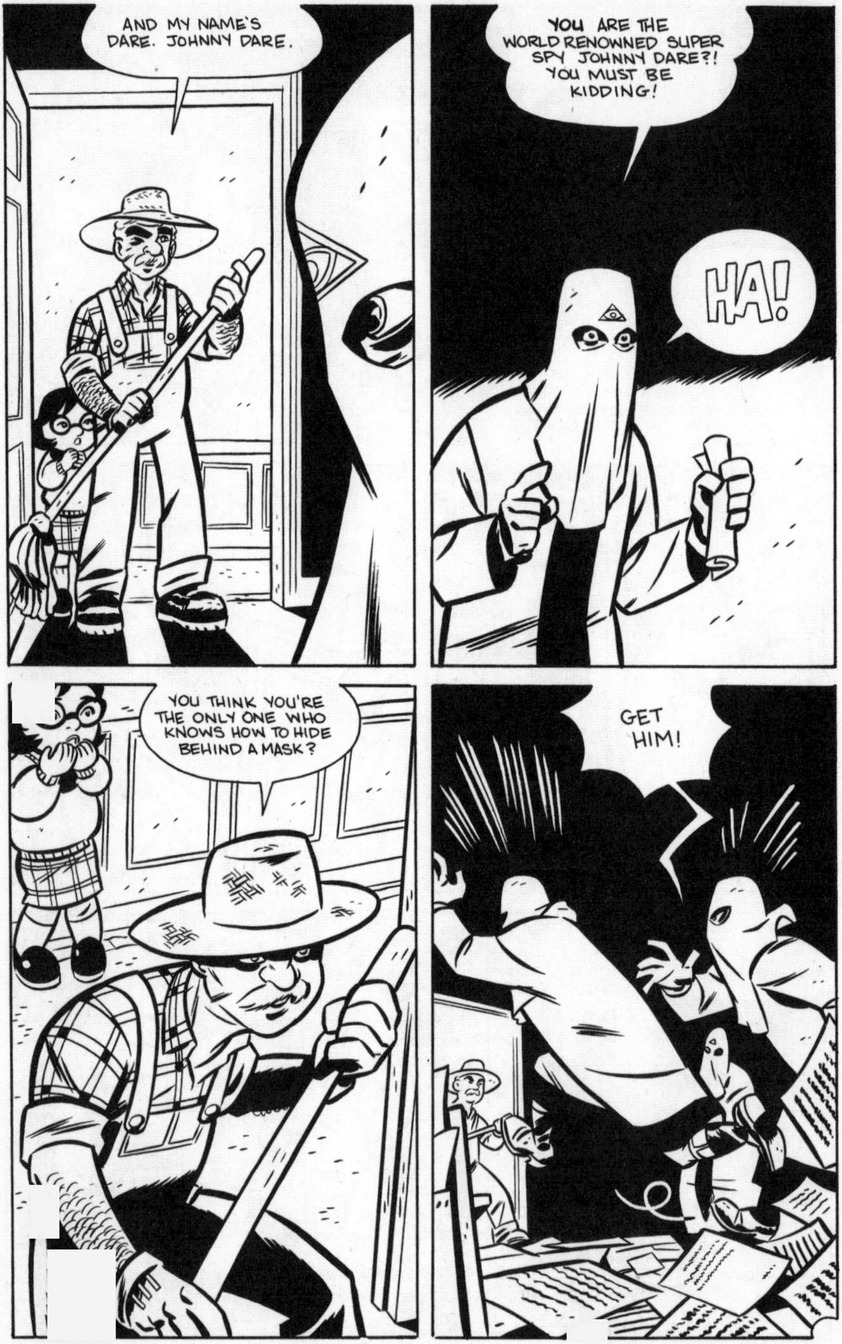
AND MY NAME'S DARE. JOHNNY DARE.
YOU ARE THE WORLD RENOWNED SUPER SPY JOHNNY DARE?! YOU MUST BE KIDDING!
HA!
YOU THINK YOU'RE THE ONLY ONE WHO KNOWS HOW TO HIDE BEHIND A MASK?
GET HIM!

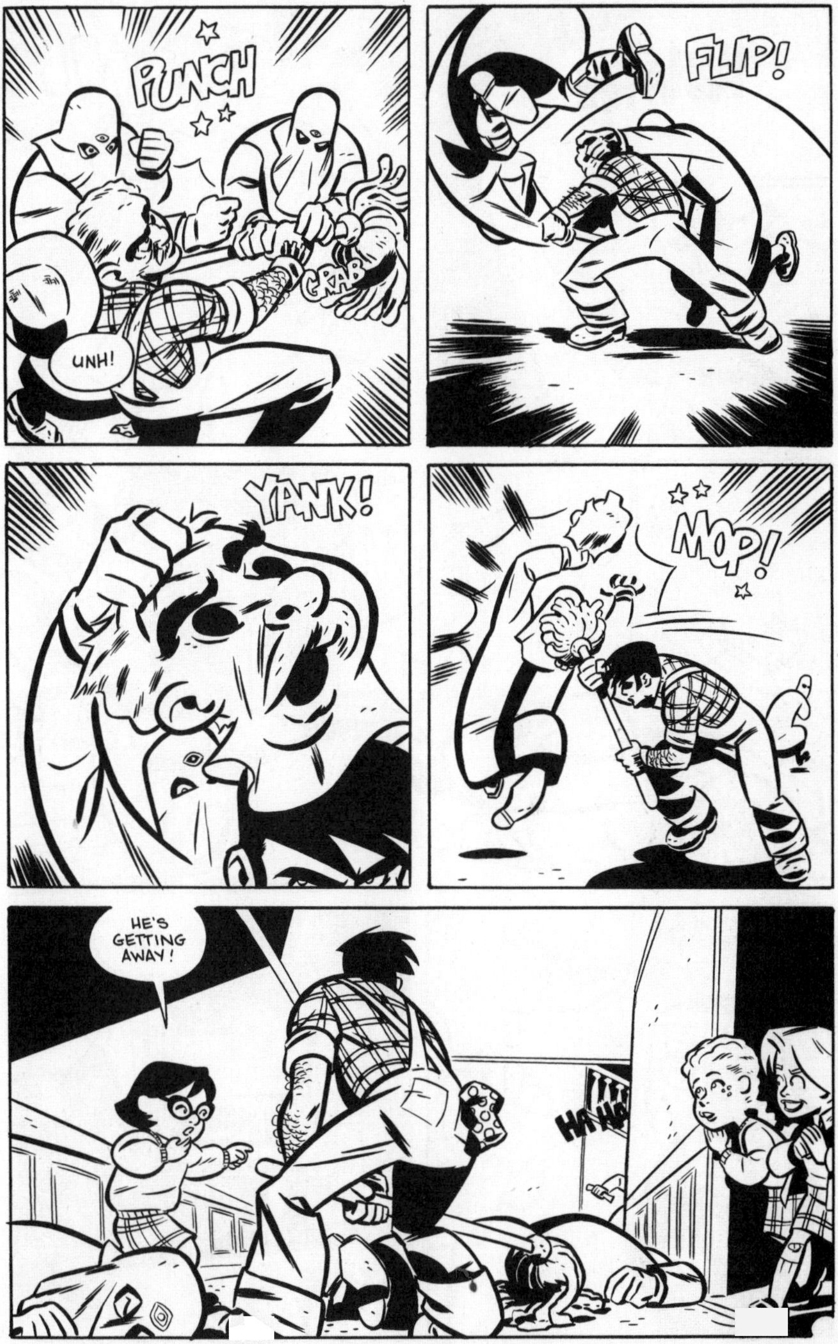
PUNCH
GRAB
UNH!
FLIP!
YANK!
MOP!
HE'S GETTING AWAY!
HA HA

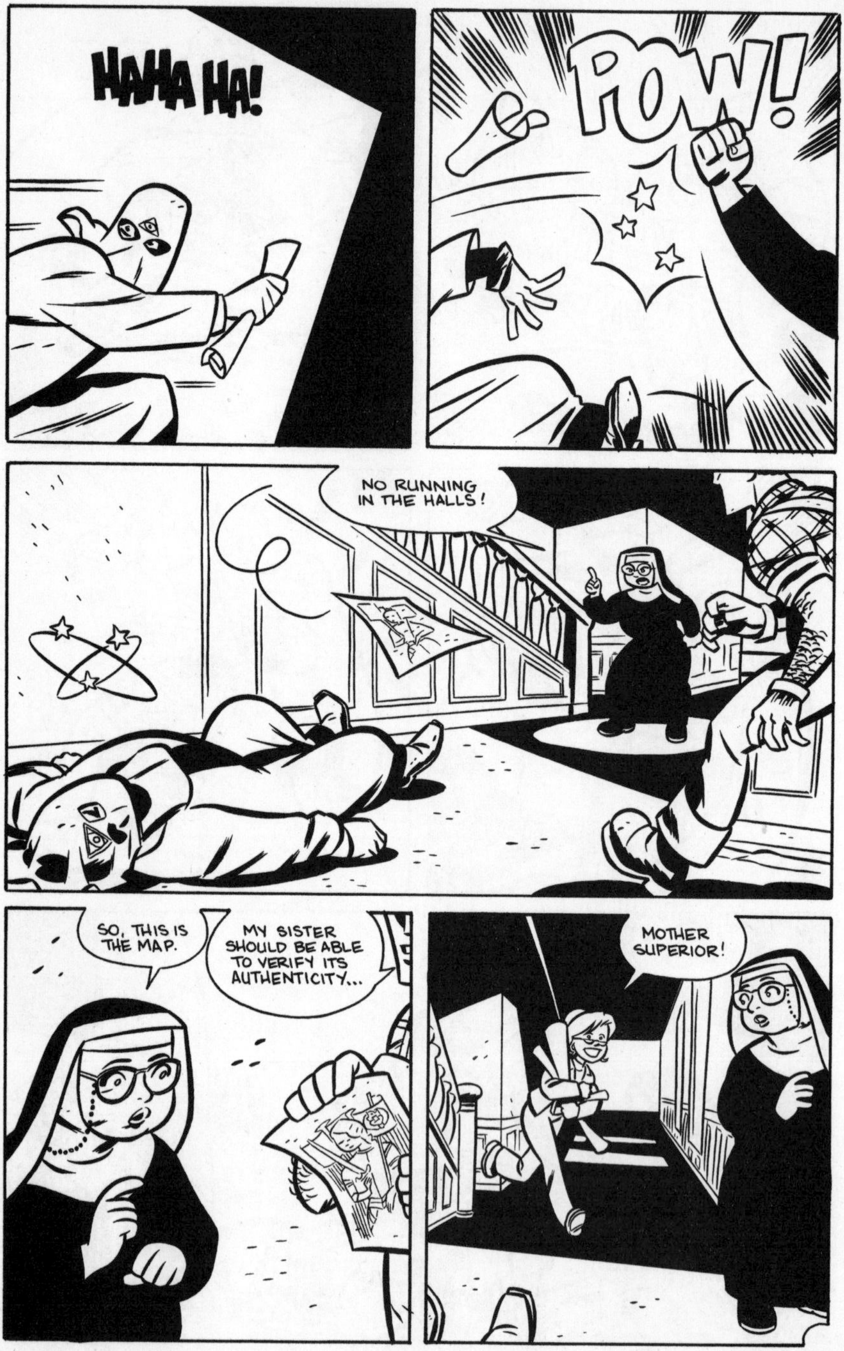
HAHA HA!
POW!
NO RUNNING IN THE HALLS!
SO, THIS IS THE MAP.
MY SISTER SHOULD BE ABLE TO VERIFY ITS AUTHENTICITY...
MOTHER SUPERIOR!

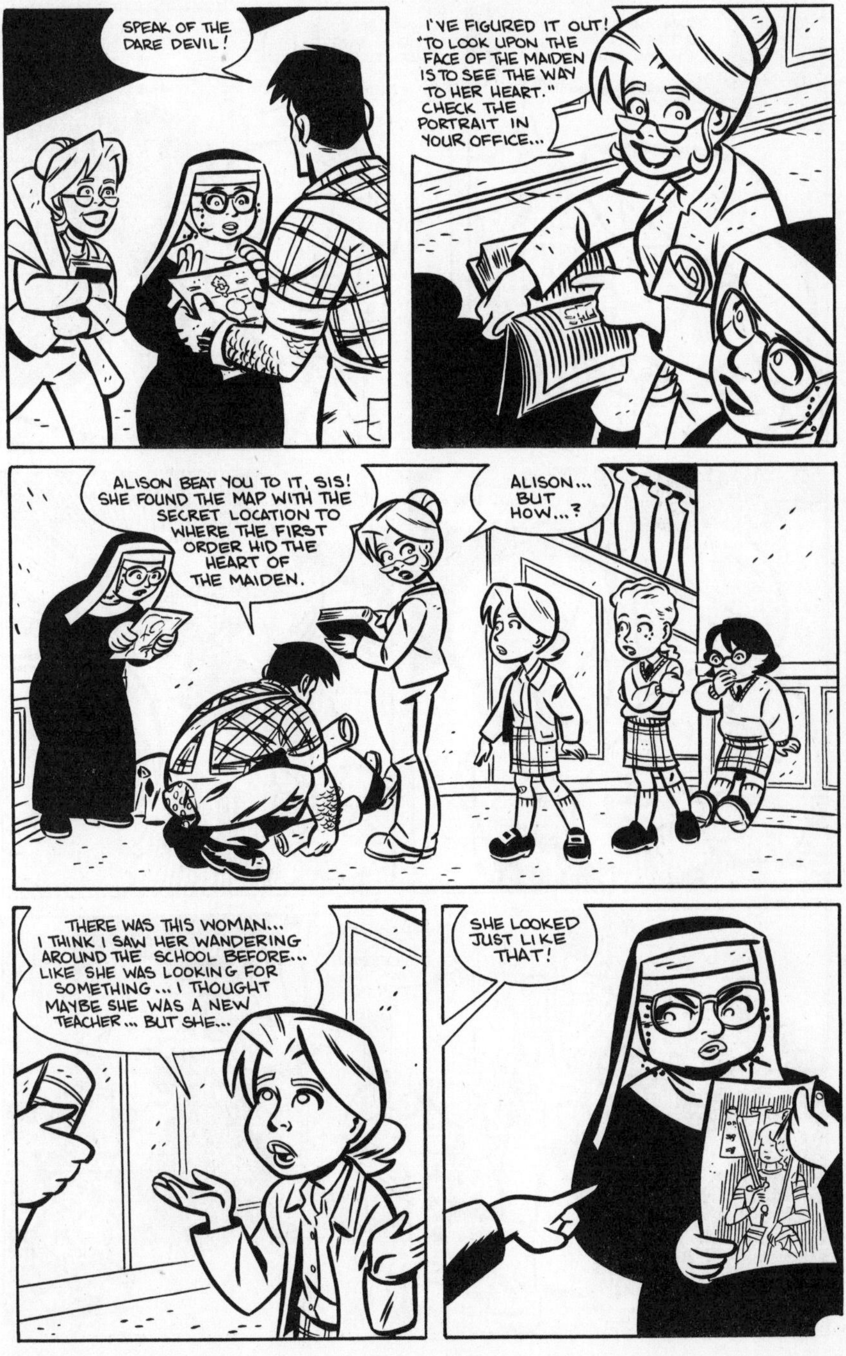
SPEAK OF THE DARE DEVIL!
I'VE FIGURED IT OUT! "TO LOOK UPON THE FACE OF THE MAIDEN IS TO SEE THE WAY TO HER HEART." CHECK THE PORTRAIT IN YOUR OFFICE...
ALISON BEAT YOU TO IT, SIS! SHE FOUND THE MAP WITH THE SECRET LOCATION TO WHERE THE FIRST ORDER HID THE HEART OF THE MAIDEN.
ALISON... BUT HOW...?
THERE WAS THIS WOMAN... I THINK I SAW HER WANDERING AROUND THE SCHOOL BEFORE... LIKE SHE WAS LOOKING FOR SOMETHING... I THOUGHT MAYBE SHE WAS A NEW TEACHER... BUT SHE...
SHE LOOKED JUST LIKE THAT!

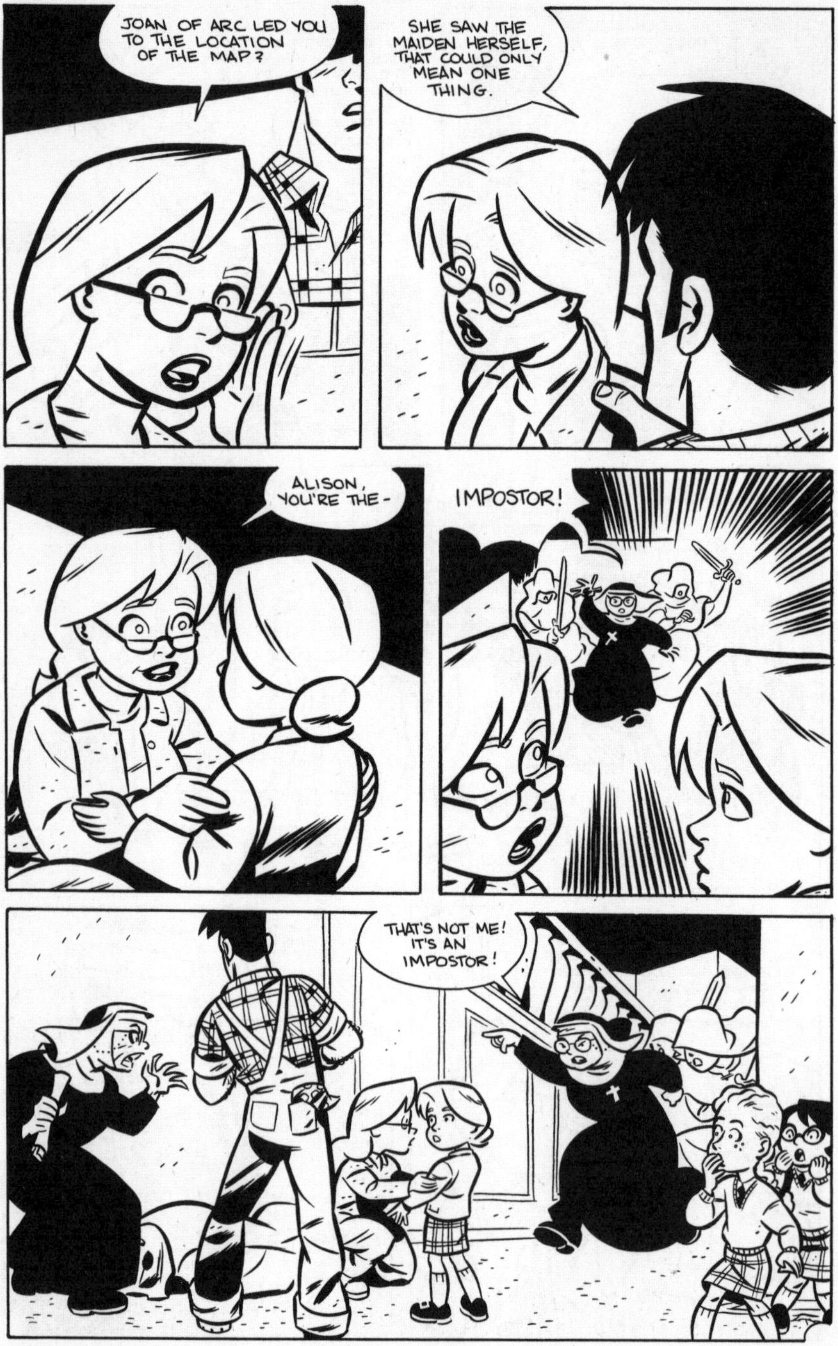
JOAN OF ARC LED YOU TO THE LOCATION OF THE MAP?
SHE SAW THE MAIDEN HERSELF, THAT COULD ONLY MEAN ONE THING.
ALISON, YOU'RE THE -
IMPOSTOR!
THAT'S NOT ME! IT'S AN IMPOSTOR!

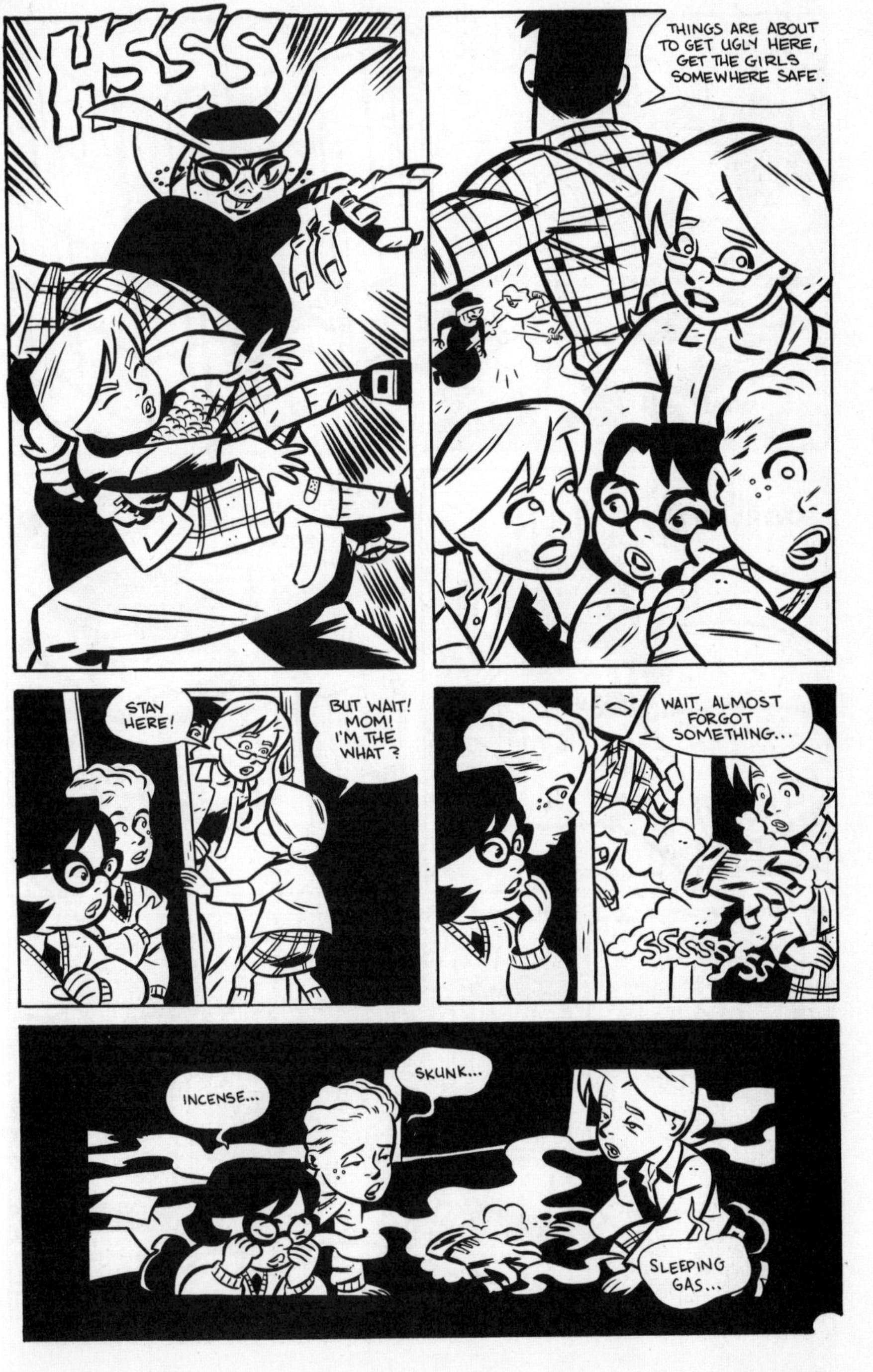
HSSS
THINGS ARE ABOUT TO GET UGLY HERE, GET THE GIRLS SOMEWHERE SAFE.
STAY HERE!
BUT WAIT! MOM! I'M THE WHAT?
WAIT, ALMOST FORGOT SOMETHING...
SSSSSSS
INCENSE...
SKUNK...
SLEEPING GAS...

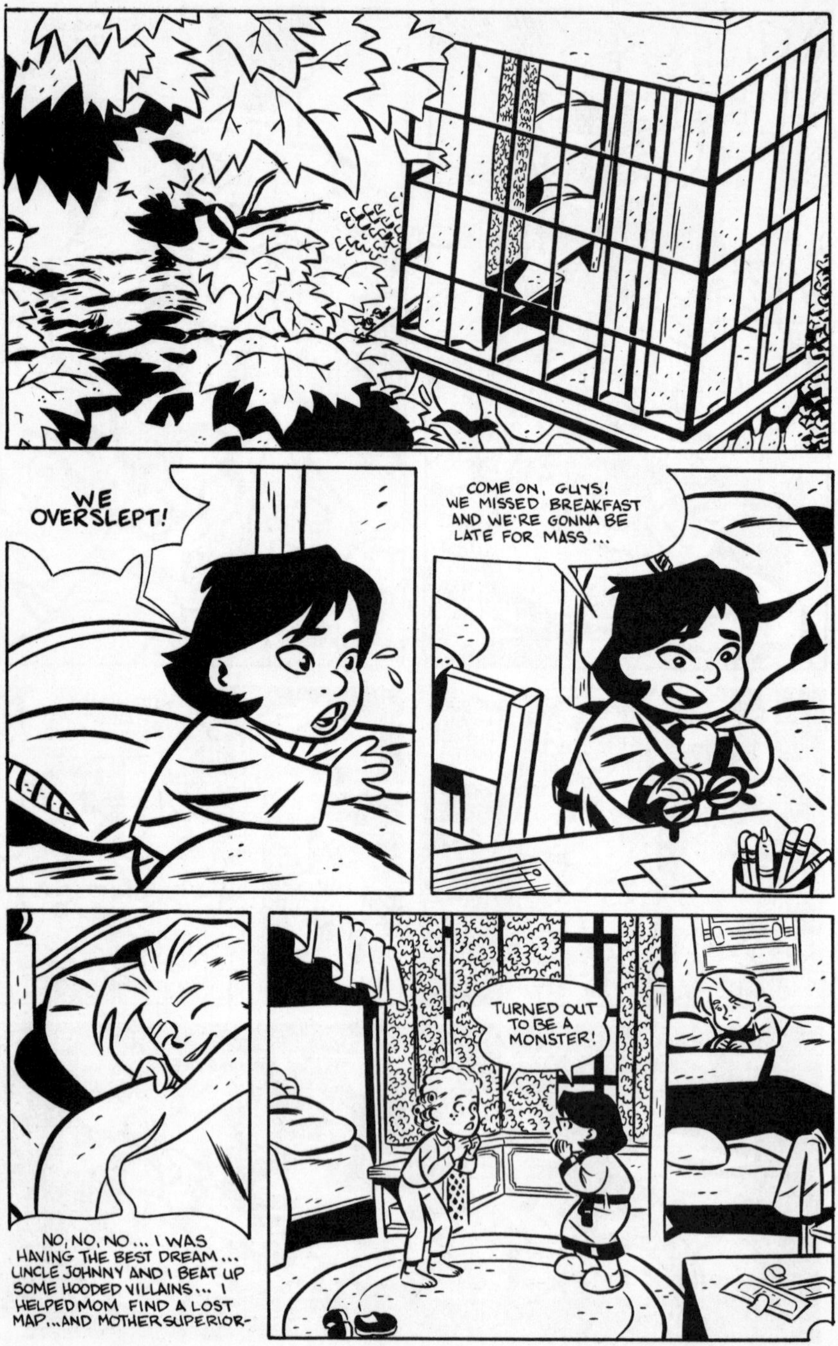
WE OVERSLEPT!
COME ON, GUYS! WE MISSED BREAKFAST AND WE'RE GONNA BE LATE FOR MASS...
NO, NO, NO... I WAS HAVING THE BEST DREAM... UNCLE JOHNNY AND I BEAT UP SOME HOODED VILLAINS... I HELPED MOM FIND A LOST MAP...AND MOTHER SUPERIOR-
TURNED OUT TO BE A MONSTER!

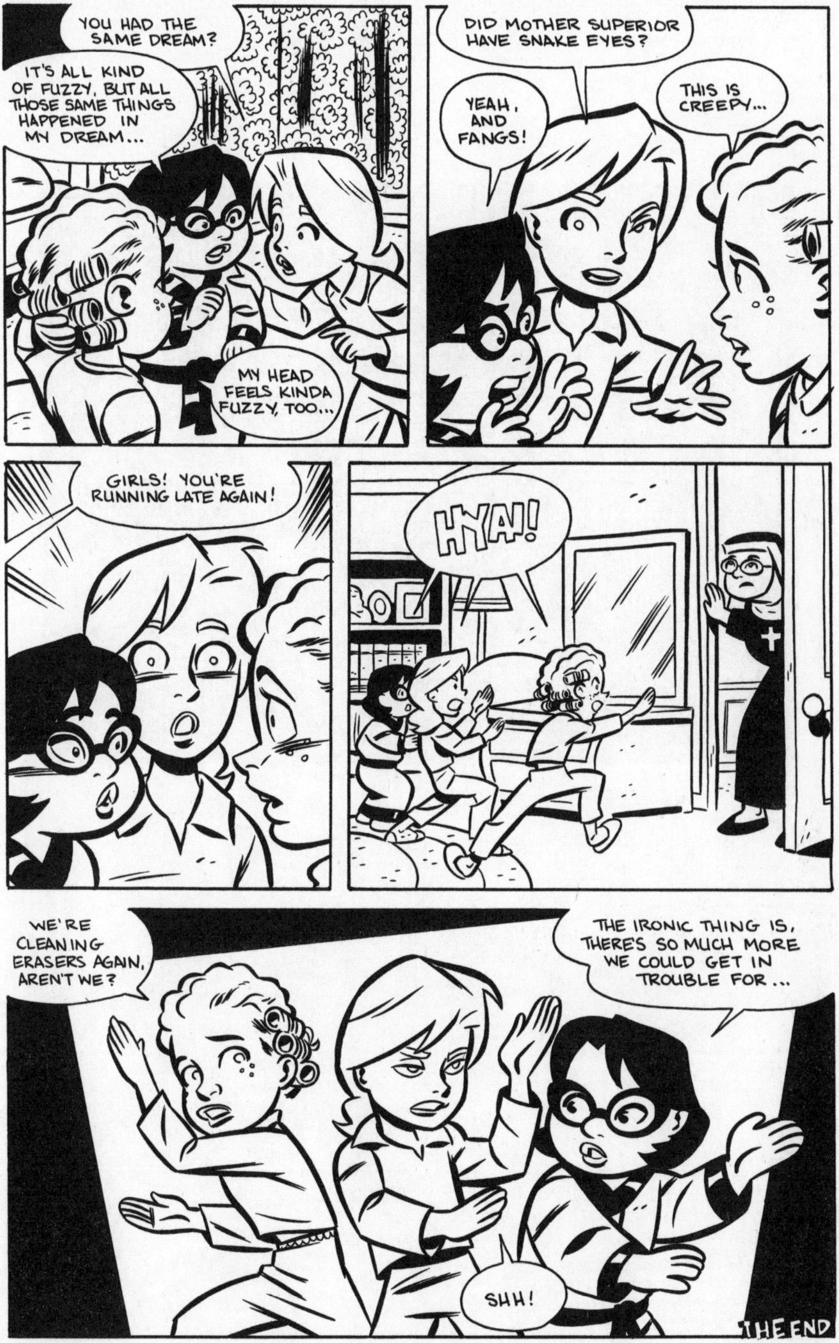
YOU HAD THE SAME DREAM?
IT'S ALL KIND OF FUZZY, BUT ALL THOSE SAME THINGS HAPPENED IN MY DREAM...
MY HEAD FEELS KINDA FUZZY, TOO...
DID MOTHER SUPERIOR HAVE SNAKE EYES?
YEAH, AND FANGS!
THIS IS CREEPY...
GIRLS! YOU'RE RUNNING LATE AGAIN!
HYA!
WE'RE CLEANING ERASERS AGAIN, AREN'T WE?
THE IRONIC THING IS, THERE'S SO MUCH MORE WE COULD GET IN TROUBLE FOR...
SHH!
THE END

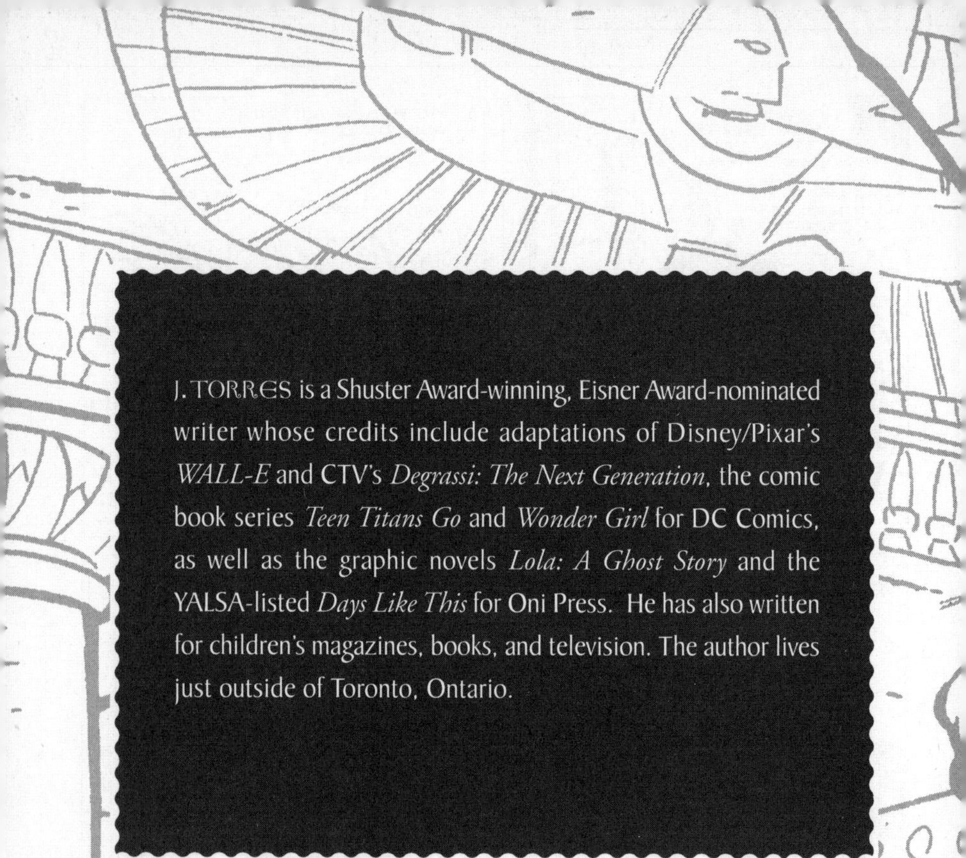

J. TORRES is a Shuster Award-winning, Eisner Award-nominated writer whose credits include adaptations of Disney/Pixar's *WALL-E* and CTV's *Degrassi: The Next Generation*, the comic book series *Teen Titans Go* and *Wonder Girl* for DC Comics, as well as the graphic novels *Lola: A Ghost Story* and the YALSA-listed *Days Like This* for Oni Press. He has also written for children's magazines, books, and television. The author lives just outside of Toronto, Ontario.

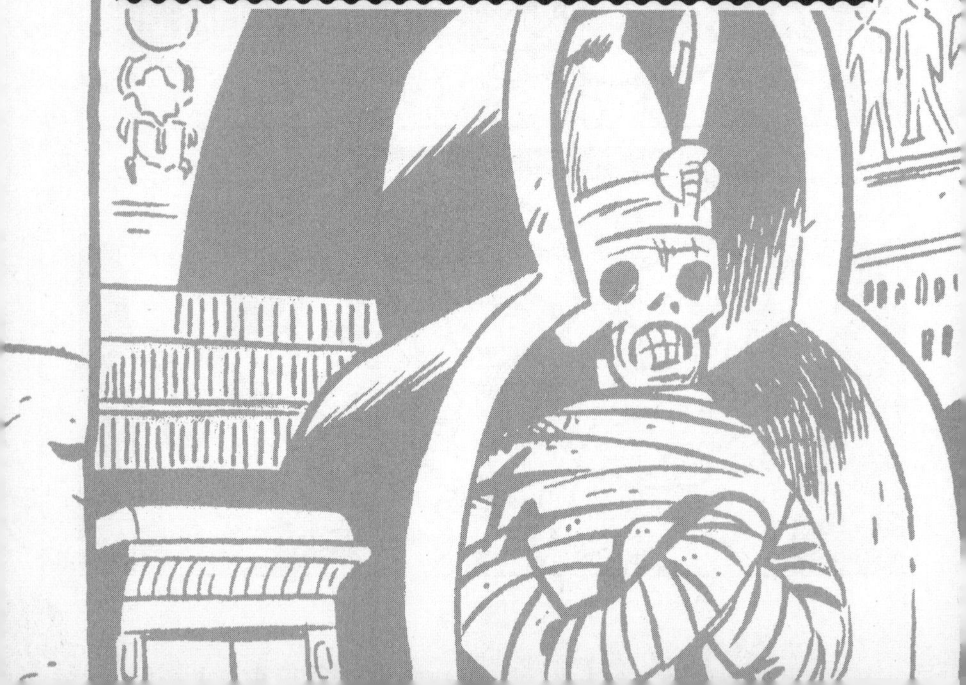